Start Somewhere

Start Somewhere

Frank Griffin, aged eighteen, goes to a day school in a northern town. Like his classmates Peter Mohan and Anthony Popkin he is intelligent, self-questioning and avid to learn. One night Griffin and Popkin are walking home with Mohan's girl-friend, Anne Cooper. Both boys are strongly attracted to Anne who is clever and captivating, and when she proposes that they climb into the locked park Popkin eagerly agrees. Griffin, reluctant but weak, follows. The spree ends in disaster with Popkin's arrest and subsequent public humiliation at school. Frazer, the school captain, and Mohan, the vice captain, both resign in protest at the headmaster's handling of the situation. Griffin, as guilty as Popkin, is promoted. Though at first he successfully buries his moral anguish under a pile of work, the shared guilt finally throws him and Anne together and results in a more serious crisis.

START SOMEWHERE

Michael Standen

Shoestring  Press

first published by William Heinemann Ltd, 1965
© *1965 by Michael Standen*

Printed by Parker and Collinson Ltd.
Nottingham NG7 2FH
(0115) 942 0140

Published by Shoestring Press
19 Devonshire Avenue, Beeston, Nottingham, NG9 1BS
(0115) 925 1827
www.shoestringpress.co.uk

Reprinted 2009
© Michael Standen
The moral right of the author has been asserted.

ISBN: 978 1 904886 93 8

CHAPTER 1

THE sky was smeared with orange. The lights were sodium—Frank Griffin knew that much of science—but the effect was sulphur and he liked it. Lately his mind ran on Hell and Time and Death. These abstract ideas appealed to his intellect because they were not too abstract. He was, besides, in love—or meant to be before the end of the evening.

There was something wrong with his brakes and the angry ticking noise under the saddle was mounting to a crescendo and spurring his mind into elation. A sort of metronome. His father had warned him about those brakes but the feeling flooding him now was beyond his father's wisdom. He stood on the pedals to take the downward sweep of the concrete road at full gallop. A warm onrush of air swept over his face. He shed tears. He shouted at two respectable pedestrians on the orange-splashed and cavernous pavements.

Frank Griffin was eighteen and still at school. His father had had something to say about that, but not a great deal when it came to it. Frank's mother believed in Education enough to fight her husband over it. Not that it wouldn't have been harder all round but for Graham. Graham had obliged by failing the eleven plus and Graham, a couple of years younger, was about to leave school and become available in the shop. Mr Griffin conceded that Graham would do; that he was more appropriate. At the Secondary Modern they did less to warp a boy's mind. When his wife said that it was the best solution: Graham would be settled and Frank, with education, would get on on his own, he agreed with her. But secretly he wanted to see Frank fail.

The wide estates ended at the ring road. Night made something of them, gave them a spaciousness they lacked in day-

1

time: 'From larger day to huger night.' Now there was a hill to tackle and cramped streets lit like stage sets. Here the texture was different and you felt different. Some of the houses were old, even pre-Victorian. They were divided by a fretwork of alleyways with here and there a tiny walled garden supporting perhaps one tree. A few tin advertisements, painted between the wars, still clung to their brickwork.

The road turned into juddering cobblestones. He swept down a short hill, through the imposing back gates of the girls' school, and came to a raucous halt. He was in a dark place of bicycle sheds and dustbins. Popkin materialised.

'Griffin, did you know you're in charge of a discussion group?'

'No,' said Frank. Nervousness touched him in the bowels.

'Straight up. You're on the list.'

'Has it started?'

'It's not seven yet.' Popkin stared at the lighted door. When there were girls about he took off his glasses and was blind.

'Let's go in anyway,' said Frank.

The school-hall-cum-gymnasium was transformed, visually. Tables at the side had overcome the wall-bars but not quite vanquished the school smell of gym-shoes, young bodies penned in, old hymns.

Griffin noticed settings first, people second.

The conference-goers were the usual mixture: members of other schools—familiar conference faces; others from his own Sixth of course; a few older clerical or educational persons; the girls. Popkin said, 'I say, Griffin.'

'What?'

'Is Anne coming?'

'Anne, I know not Anne.'

'You know. I can't remember her maiden name.'

'Is she married or something?'

'Surname, surname.' Popkin blushed.

Frank knew he meant Anne Cooper. Anne Cooper was the vice-captain of the girls' school. He could see her a few yards away talking to Peter Mohan. When Popkin saw her too he stood still and silent like a worshipper. Griffin moved away.

He had the discussion group to worry about. Chairmanship wouldn't be easy: he was unsure of himself and he liked argument better than compromise.

The conference, arranged by the Student Christian Movement, was called: 'Good & Evil: The Problem of Suffering'. Frank had decided beforehand that suffering was a fact not a problem; but he could see that for the religious it might be a problem. How could God be omnipotent *and* all-loving? They were here to crack that old nut. If you wanted it both ways, where did cancer come in and old age and the daily frictions at home?

He was thinking about it when Mohan grabbed his blazer.

'Introduce you to Anne. This one's Griff, Frank Griffin, always in a daze.'

Frank took Anne's hand in true middle-class fashion. She was wearing a simple grey dress and a sort of starched white blouse. Frank found it difficult to look her in the eye with any degree of social ease. In the Joint Sixth Form Society she was Bella Donna. The intellectuals who had christened her were pleased with their pun. Popkin had risen to verse. A fragment in his distinctive handwriting had come to light beginning:

> You are my poison and its antidote;
> You are my hope, you are my lack of hope.

Though they had ridiculed him, they were all affected by her. Mohan was wondered at: his self-confidence and good luck.

'Hullo,' said Anne. 'I hope you're not another bloody scientist.'

'English, History and French.'

'I'm glad.' She really did sound glad. It was flattering.

Mohan put in a good word. 'Frank's a good chap.' And Mohan, whom they regarded as socially adept and deeply intellectual, sounded unsure—of all things—of himself. It made Frank a bit more confident. 'You do the same?'

'Except for Latin instead of History. We wear our subjects like labels.'

'A flower show, that's all we are. Diverse cultivations,' said Peter, scanning the hall.

3

'And soon we'll be labelled by our salaries,' said Frank, suddenly oppressed by the future. His father's remarks about the fewness of idle studying years augured a coming blankness —some higher falutin equivalent of the shop. The puritan-commercial tradition of home taught him a fact not found in the liberal-cultural tradition of school: You paid for what you'd had. Even a sunny day was on credit; it would rain

'Would Sheila do for your Popkin?' Anne asked Mohan.

'Do your own match-making.'

Frank was shocked. It seemed the girls were as impure as they were. He'd heard it said they were worse. But he still saw them somehow as remote and above all the feverish unrest.

A bell went; there was a scuffle for chairs; headmasters and officials assembled on the platform. The Reverend Canon Someone started things off.

Slumped on steel and canvas, Frank studied the backs of rows of girls: their necks, shoulders, heads of hair. From this you had to guess at the beauties. But the turned head so often disproved him that he decided to listen.

'If you ask me why the innocent suffer when evil-doers so often seem to get away scot-free, I can only throw out two suggestions. One is to ask: Who are the innocent? God only knows—and I say that reverently.

'The other is to quote His word. "The wages of sin is death." Death, mark you, not cancer or stomach troubles. Our answer as Christians is that death, like evil, is unnatural; is, if you like, an enemy. You might tell me the innocent, too, die. I say no. This is that leap of faith which many to-day will not make. Make that leap and you have your logical position. Bunyan had it—generations of believers have had it. Once a man came and overcame these enemies. He killed Death. May I suggest'— stopping to polish his glasses, the speaker radiated myopic goodwill—'that you leave aside the old chestnuts and get down to considering what sin and evil really are?'

There was tea if you were quick enough, then division into discussion groups. Frank was pleased when Mohan asked him what he thought of the speech.

4

'He did his best. At least he didn't get on my nerves like most parsons.'

'Ah,' said Mohan, who was a Catholic, 'these modern nerves. Tell me—we don't know each other all that well—you're not mentally arrogant, are you? Allowing nothing but what you understand.'

'No more than usual, I suppose.'

Mohan took his arm with nervous energy. 'Let's nosh some tea.'

Griffin saw the intelligence and maturity in his face. On him the school blazer was out of place.

Tea was being dispensed by the girls. They did it charmingly and were aware of their charm. Young ladies in the Great War, mopping the brows of Tommies.

Although Mohan had not pushed himself, they got the first cups. It was one of the times when Frank's egoism broke down and he recognised superiority: a stage beyond him if not beyond his capabilities; a window on a further terrain.

'I must have a fag,' Mohan announced. 'Come on. The thing doesn't resume for another ten minutes.'

A french window had been left open, partly for ventilation but also perhaps to allow of philosophic withdrawal into an enclosed but large courtyard, a square of grass surrounded by a wide gravel walk. Most of the building—those dark, immoral rooms—had been soundly locked up by order of the headmistress. For Autumn the night was warm.

They sauntered to the far end. No one else had come outside. The flare of the match which Mohan struck on the rough wall momentarily lit up his thin face and straight, fair hair.

'Have one?'

'No. No thanks.' Griffin didn't smoke and, careless as he was of school rules, he was usually aware of them.

'Cigarette smoke and starlight,' observed Mohan, blowing a luminous cloud towards heaven.

'Perhaps I will have one.' Having a cigarette from Mohan was different. Cigarettes were part of that glimpsed extension of experience. It took about half a minute to get the thing to light.

'The true sinner sins deeply. Inhale.'

Griffin swallowed the smoke, was surprised not to be coughing his heart up. It dizzied his brain like a touch of drunkenness. He told Mohan.

'I can just remember that. Sinners blunder on in search of the first sweet pang. See, we really are finding out what sin is.'

'Evil and all that, I don't get it,' said Frank. 'I mean it doesn't mean anything to me personally, it doesn't to most people. And if you send missionaries to the South Sea Islands, innocent natives start creeping with guilt. It's wicked. A disease. People ought to keep it to themselves'.

'One in the eye for the Holy Catholic Church.'

'Oh, I'm sorry.'

'Don't be, for God's sake,' said Mohan. 'And I say that irreverently. I'm not offended. I promise not to convert you unless I'm drunk. I don't positively believe in any of it myself.'

When more figures came out into the courtyard, Frank trod on his cigarette. Mohan lit himself another.

'You'll be trying for a schol at Christmas?' Frank, in his second year of the Sixth was still hazy about university entrance. Unwilling to talk shop, Mohan merely grunted. Then he said: 'Anne's expecting an escort home. I think she took to you. I can't make it to-night. Would you mind?'

'Of course not.' Frank felt nervous again.

'Might do her good,' said Mohan privately. 'I'd rather you took her than any of my year. Thanks a lot.'

'Nothing,' Griffin mumbled.

'Going out with her's a bit of a strain. She's too attractive and the flesh suffers. It's like flying a kite in a high wind, I mean. They want us back.'

In the doorway a portly religious gentleman was calling them back from Limbo. They went, Frank remembering that he had left his programme and the notes he had taken on his chair.

He was in charge of half a dozen souls in one of the brightly lit downstairs classrooms. A large, angular lad, soon dominated the discussion. Practising humility, Frank could see something of himself in the cleverness and aphorisms pouring forth. Here was someone who collected his own and other people's sayings

6

as assiduously as small boys collect stamps. But in a way this voluble atheist was a godsend. Whenever Frank managed to shut him up, complete silence followed.

So the twenty minutes trailed past in a lame *pas de deux*. The bell sounded and they were nowhere near getting a question ready for the panel. Frank was tired of it. A discussion of the problem of suffering! A committee for the improvement of a sewage system. Mohan's certainties underlying his cynicism —the knowledge of Good and Evil—it all lost meaning. He looked at the talkative one who was leaning forward expounding, his great shadowed head like something on Easter Island. He was the same thing, his atheism was only the reverse of the same dud halfpenny. The conference got off to the final lap. Anne Cooper caught his eye and waved. She was beckoning for him to go and join her. This meant leaving the masculine part of the hall and going across to where the audience was mostly girls. The division had happened with no prompting from above. The headmistress had left no instructions about seating arrangements. Her action had been to ensure the fastening of all doors leading into rooms of sexually inviting darkness. The hesitancy of youth had acted much higher up the slope to baffle the lewd landslide which she feared. Precautionary against immorality, she was the evil-minded one.

'Anne wants us to join them,' said Popkin, removing his glasses.

'I've been asked to take her home.'

'What?'

'I'd rather not but I was landed with it. See you'. He moved at exactly the right moment. The reverential hush heralding Question Time kept Popkin in his seat and saved Frank making small-talk with Anne and her curious friends. Slumping beside her, he nodded briefly and became absorbed in studying his programme. He experienced a remote feeling as if he were outside his own body and getting sensations of self-consciousness at second hand. Now he was scarcely half listening to the well-meaning and intelligent speakers.

They were dealing with Easter Island's question. It admitted that pain could be useful (the burnt child, etc.) but queried the

7

justice of (innocent) children being born crippled. No real answer was given; perhaps because it wasn't a legitimate question, mixing the moral and actual like that. The speaker used it as a springboard into metaphysics proper. The Devil, he said, was a knotty problem: one Christians had squarely to face. Could we pick and choose? Keep God and send the other packing? He thought not. Men were always circuitous in questioning authority, witness the early phases of the French Revolution. At first they had blamed only the King's ministers but it had ended in the demise of the King himself.

Frank looked over his shoulder. Several comrades were politically offended. What argument was that? they wanted to say. And so the good man's words fell on stony ground among the flowering thorn.

They must be wondering about him. Poor Popkin might be out of his wits. Mohan had left and he had agreed to do him a favour. So what?

Anne touched his arm. He managed a better look at her.

'One more question,' she said.

'. . . Is it Reason which has made Man fear Death? Animals are not afraid of it. . . .'

'Neither am I,' Anne said. 'Put that in your pipe and smoke it.'

'I thought animals were,' said Frank in a whisper. The little shared superiority was pleasant.

But when the conference ended suddenly, Anne disappeared.

The cloakroom was a dimly-lit chaos of brown-, blue- and black-blazered partisans. The army surplus knapsacks which they preferred to childish satchels and spent hours initialling in ink were kicked all over. It was a stampede for buses, fish and chips, girls.

Frank's comrades were getting the best of it. More of their fathers were down the pit than in banks and they shoved opposition aside with a compensatory cheerfulness. Frank felt clan loyalty for all his dislike of blazers.

He did not escape notice.

'Hey up. What's come over you?'

'You play it cool.'

8

'I'm surprised at you.'

Thankful the light was dim, Griffin made large denials. Popkin asked him which way they were going.

'I don't know.'

'I'll come with you. She lives in the Park. It's on my way home so I might as well.'

'Christ!' Frank was going to say that he'd lost her, that she had probably gone home already, that anyway he was only doing Mohan a favour. He didn't though. Popkin came with him to the back gate.

There they stood under its pompous iron: 'thirties baroque if there is such a thing: municipal. A few lads were waiting for girls but the main rush had gone. Now it was colder and a thin mist had formed in the dark air—gauze festooning the streets of houses outside. Frank rested his bike against the gate-post.

'Taking each other home?' asked a lad in a crash-helmet and lined coat.

'I'll push your face in,' Griffin said, annoyed and foolish. He knew who it was under the motor-cyclist's clobber and hated him. A few years had passed since he had been bullied by him —three years, not very long.

'So now you're trying for Mohan's bird. My, she changes boyfriends more'n I change my underpants.'

'Shut up,' said Griffin, but not too loudly: Draper was strong and ready with his fists.

Popkin countered by starting a profound conversation. Several minutes passed. Draper asked if some girl had been at the conference. He had apparently rolled up on the off-chance of giving her a lift. Popkin again, rambling on about moral philosophy. Frank was caught between his alter ego and Draper's id. The school looked deserted. He was on a fool's errand. Already the caretaker was on his nightly ritual of locking up and switching off.

' 'Spose he's a eunuch,' said Draper cheerily.

Then came the last stragglers; Anne and a couple of others. A tang of scent in the night air explained their lateness.

'Where's Joan Morley?' Draper announced loudly.

9

'Went ages ago,' said Anne in measured tones. Her companions giggled.

'I'm waiting for her.'

'There's no law against that.'

'Bitch!' Draper flung himself across his motor-cycle which, luckily for him, started first kick.

As the noise died away, Anne said: 'Good riddance to bad rubbish.'

'Joan was playing with fire,' observed the taller of the other girls rather primly.

'Shall we be going?'

'Yes,' said Anne. 'I should have introduced Sheila, Sheila Ford. And this is Glenys Mathers. Actually we were all sitting together but I think you were too rapt to notice.'

The little party moved off; Frank encumbered with his bike. Wheeling a motor-bike would have been worse—until he realised that then he could have whisked Anne home on it. She walked beside him, Glenys and Sheila followed, intimately conversing. Popkin kept up, nowhere.

'You're very quiet,' Anne said.

'Am I?' Frank looked at her and his bike nudged sharply into the kerb.

'Here we all are: a party of young people. So much nicer than being picked up.'

Griffin's main urge was to mount his machine and escape to lonely communion with the stars or sodium lamps or whatever it was he had been doing. But Mohan had asked him to do the gentleman for him and, as well, he could not pretend to himself that Anne's near presence was boring. And he felt a sort of responsibility for Popkin.

Popkin, however, was going to manage on his own.

'Anne,' he said, 'are you going on to the university?'

'Oh, we all do, don't we?'

'I wonder how many girls are virgins when they finish the course?'

Frank winced; Anne laughed.

'I'll tell you in three years' time,' she said.

They were breasting a steep hill built over by wealthy lace

manufacturers in their grandparents' early days. Up here all was still 'select', though corrosion was taking place on the lower slopes where the Irish and West Indians were living out their rowdy, overcrowded lives. The moonlit mist unfixed the nineteenth-century classic, making it Venetian; turning solid pretensions into the backcloth of a dream. They had the wide road to themselves.

When the other girls reached the road where they turned off to get their bus, Anne detained them with unnecessary questions. Standing by, Griffin scented an ulterior motive, perhaps only because he was used to scenting them at home.

'Where do you live?' she asked Popkin.

'The other side of the Park.'

This was a lie. Frank was half aware that Popkin needed to turn off here to get his bus.

'Do you two know each other?' Anne bracketed Sheila and Popkin in her question.

'Well, not before you introduced us.' Sheila looked uncertainly at Popkin and he—allowing for the poor light—looked at her as if his main impression was that she washed with carbolic soap.

'Come on,' said Glenys. 'We'll miss it.'

'Good night, then.' Sheila's earnest, reticent figure followed Glenys. Anne and the two boys continued down the hill.

'What's she do?' Popkin asked.

'Languages, if by "she" you mean Sheila.'

'She's not in your set then.'

'She is for Latin.'

'*Amor vincit omnia*,' Popkin said darkly. Contemptuous silence. Frank was sick of the situation. They were passing the oldest of the corporation's parks and the only one to start life for the disportment of the commonalty. It was a museum without a roof: arboretum, aviary, shrubbery, home for crippled statues. It was closed for the night.

'Have you seen the new muscovies?'

'Never been in,' said Frank.

'Not seen the parrots?'

'No.'

'Why, they've a parrot dating back to William IV. He's falling to bits.'

'That's how I know history: parrot-fashion,' Popkin said.

'What are we waiting for? If you haven't seen the parrots.'

'The gates are locked. We can't,' said Frank.

She led them across to the fence. 'Anyone coming?'

'All clear,' said Popkin.

'Give me a leg up.' She stretched to place her hands on the spikes. Her handbag hung looped over her arm. Frank placed his hands under her shoe, stirrup-fashion.

'Hup!' He assisted the ascent, bracing himself from the closeness of her body and keeping his puritan eyes shut. Anne landed daintily. Popkin wanted to throw the bike over: it might give them away he said. Surprisingly agile, he then followed the girl. Now it was Frank's turn. With no desire to do so, he grappled with the fence. He had one foot on the saddle of his bicycle and the other between the spikes when he saw a policeman.

'Come on,' shouted Popkin from the other side. 'What are you doing?'

The constable, mounted on an ancient machine, was forcing himself uphill with dispirited solidity. On the opposite side of the road he might notice nothing. But Popkin was hopping about below, showing off.

'Griff, come on!' rang out at the critical moment.

The policeman looked up. Frank had the sensation of their eyes meeting somewhere in the shadow of that helmet. He jumped, running.

He was in a land of rhododendron bushes, gravel walks and shallow rockeries. It was much darker in the park. When he stopped, his heart was bursting. A low whistle nearly felled him, Anne in her tightly belted raincoat emerged, luminescent. She was laughing to herself; much amused apparently.

'They've got my bike,' he gasped.

'Oh dear, you do look funny.'

He was angry and suffering from shock. Where's that damned fool Popkin?'

'Melted into air, thin air.'

'You don't need an escort. Is this what you usually get up to? No wonder Mohan asked me to do it.'

'I'm sorry.'

But he was angry enough not to be taken in by the injured tone.

'It's probably an offence to enter the park when it's closed.'

'Here's your friend.'

Popkin rushed up. 'They're opening the gates! There's a police car.'

Anne was laughing again. The boys looked at each other, anxious blotches in the night.

'I must show you this parrot.'

'Where's she gone?'

'Stick together,' said Frank, going after Anne. But Popkin remained where he was. The path curved downwards behind a screen of thick bushes. On the other side Griffin heard the police, Popkin, silence.

Anne was standing by the lake motionless. He explained, more alarmed than angry, what had happened.

'I'm sorry I'm not taking this seriously,' she said.

'There'll be the devil to pay. He was in the school blazer.'

'But it's so stupid if there's trouble, so out of proportion. Don't you see it? What can it matter?'

'It looks bad I suppose. Reflection on the school.'

'Oh dear. I hadn't thought of you as a pillar of society.'

'I'm not!' he said hotly. To be called that after a career of rebellion and strenuous individuality!

'No, that's right. You're not.'

These subtle placings of emphasis and transpositions of tone with, behind them, miles of suggested superiority—it was infuriating. It was the work of the best novelists, what hours of earnest discussion had warned him of. In this way male integrity crashed headlong.

'I'm not the prefect-type if that's what you mean. But don't you see what could follow on from this escapade?'

'What could transpire surely; what could *transpire*.'

He stared at her. 'The point is this,' he went blindly on, 'people enough want to do dirt on the Grammar Schools, not to mention the local papers. There's teenage morality and all that'—he got it out. 'And there's my bike.'

Anne said, 'I'll let you off the parrot. We'll get along home.'

'What about Popkin?'

'We can't do a thing.'

They had the freedom of all that tended ground. No other citizen had risked legal proceedings to glimpse the romantic scene. The lake picked up scraps of silver and orange foil from moon and street lights and washed them, by rippling, away. Ducks slept comically at their feet and the trees brushing by their heads—the tattered fringe of a denser darkness—had been culled from every continent.

But Anne was silent and Griffin cross and humiliated.

CHAPTER 2

'Do you have to sit there, Frank? I know your studying's important but so's laying tea for your father as well.'

Tea at the Griffins' was an evening meal served at six-thirty. Mr Griffin liked it to be the demarcation line between shop and home life. Its timing gave his stomach three hours to digest, and his stomach, as they all knew, was bad. His homecoming was as ritualistic as any office gent's. During the day he remained in the shop, mashing his tea there, using the separate lavatory and, except at lunchtime, never coming into the house. Frank quite expected him to don coat and bowler one day to cross the dividing corridor. He moved his books and, as at a signal, his father came in carrying his rolled evening paper under his arm like an umbrella.

Charles Griffin was forty-eight, thin, tallish, with a tooth-brush moustache and bad teeth. He nodded to his son, patted his wife's shoulder and sat down to read.

Two minutes later, the inevitable. 'What's this I see?' Frank read on. . . . Here I disclaim all my paternal care,

Propinquity and property of blood,
And as a stranger to my heart and me. . . .

'What's that, dear?' Mrs Griffin asked her husband, intimating to Frank that he'd missed his cue. Frank rudely put his hands to his ears.

'Some lad questioned by the police. Popkin. Do you know him, son? A lad at your school.'

'In the paper?' Frank felt quite sick.

'In black and white. Here love, a lad at Frank's school.'

He rushed over the details. To-day was Saturday. He'd last seen Popkin yesterday in the darkness of the arboretum. What had he said at the police station? Simultaneously he saw Popkin covering up for Anne, inventing some dangerously complex pack of lies. And he heard Anne's ridicule.

'They got his bike as well. Seems they caught him red-handed trespassing in the park. He'd left it there as broad as day.'

'Do you know him?' his mother asked.

'There's a Popkin in the Sixth.'

'That's bad; in the Sixth,' said Mr Griffin with a good deal of satisfaction.

He was like a Nazi, thought Frank, reading about a Jew. But the police had his bike, that was a fact. He accepted a cup of tea from his mother. He needed to take his father's mind off the paper. To change the subject he asked what sort of a day it had been in the shop.

'Not bad, son. Usual Saturday rush. That sluttish Mrs Dawes is wanting credit now, because I let the Doctor have it.'

'Did that tinned fruit drink sell?'

'So-so,' said Mr Griffin. He was pleased. Secretly he had some awe of the layer above which in time might enclose his son; recognition of his work was obscurely reassuring. Mrs Griffin was more acute. When she heard Frank expressing interest in fruit drink, she was surprised.

'I think I'll go out,' Frank announced.

'Without your tea?'

'I'll do myself an egg when I get in.'

'Let the boy go,' said Mr Griffin in rare good humour. 'It's Saturday night. There's ten bob in the vase.'

Frank took it, kissed his mother and went out the back. He opened the shed door and switched on the light. The peeling whitewashed interior looked empty without his bicycle there. On an impulse he unfixed the lamp from his father's dusty and flat-tyred machine. It worked. Frank stared at the lamp. Opening the door into the kitchen, he called out that he had borrowed it. He caught permission being granted over the noise of the television. A light rain fell. At the bus-stop he had a soaking wait of five minutes.

The Coopers lived on the edge of a private estate. There were a few Regency buildings and many Victorian ones. Large villas stood in ample grounds along roads kept up at the expense of the inhabitants. It meant poor and pockmarked roads but also privacy. Black and white frontier poles guarded all exits and there were notices forbidding the passage of 'through-traffic & sight-seers'. The last, Frank took to mean crowds of Ruskinesque workmen coming to gape at their betters. The Park was seedy now and its purpose—to escape the money-making squalor outside—had been superseded by improved transport. To-day you cleared off to some dapper southern town where advertisement hoardings were banned.

Frank fingered the lamp in his pocket and gazed at the Coopers' house. Last night Anne had asked him in but with an hour's walk in front of him he had refused. It was less than twenty hours since he had stood in this road but it seemed longer. Something about the house made him comb his hair.

The door was opened by an old man in a smoking-jacket. Frank mistook it for livery. His father's parents had once been domestics in a country house so Frank was better acquainted than most with the idea of uniformed servants. At first there was confusion. The man seemed stone-deaf and unaware of it. He was talking about bedding plants when a lady—presumably Mrs Cooper—came to the rescue.

'Father's a little deaf,' she said. 'Do come in. A friend of Anne's is a friend of ours.'

The old man stood aside, laughing at his error. 'Young fellow wouldn't speak up,' he kept saying. 'I'm no one to be afraid of.'

'Anne went out earlier but you must stay for a cup of something, a glass of something if you like.'

Griffin tried to decline the offer but Mrs Cooper's old father was down on his knees sealing the exit with draught-excluder. He followed her into one of the front rooms. It was splendidly large and comfortable. Half the furniture was modern but the Coopers' had avoided the magazine stereotype of contemporary grace. Socially uneasy, Frank felt somehow at home. The books were more important than the shelves and not there, as he imagined of many middle-class rooms, merely as adjuncts to the latest bookcase. The room behind the shop would go three times into this.

'How stupid of me! Let me put your coat in the cloak-room.'

Frank divested himself of his shabby raincoat. As he did so, the heavy lamp in the pocket nudged him. Beneath he had on of all things his blazer and a knitted cardigan which tucked over the collar. He counted himself lucky to be wearing a tie. Mrs Cooper went out with the coat and came back with an opened bottle of beer.

'I like meeting Anne's friends,' she was saying. 'I like it because one's never more alive than at your age. I know how that sounds but it's true. Do you drink beer?'

'Thank you,' said Frank. Mrs Cooper was, he saw, a well-tended middle-aged woman. He did not like to see women of her age attractive.

'Anne is out rather too often. We don't lay down rules. What right have we?'

When he was seated, beer in hand, the old man came in.

'That's the ticket, join the family circle,' he said. 'Fetch my pipe, Mavis, there's a good girl.' Mrs Cooper left them alone. The old man stared hard at Frank out of his baby's blue eyes. Frank's head was busy: there was the strangeness of Mrs Cooper's being called Mavis; there was a momentary night-mare that the ancient man imagined him to be a suitor for Mavis's hand.

'I was a sailor,' the old man began. 'I was at sea in the last war on a coastal tramp. Like an old lavatory cistern she was but you get used to anything and you get to like your ship. Parker, that was my mate, could always lay hold of new flying-boots. And things were hard to get in the last war. We all wanted to know where he got them but he was as tight as a steel trap. "Off my land," was all he'd say. We played a lot of cards and when Parker won he'd grow talkative. But when we asked him what we were all dying to know, he'd say "Off my land," same as ever. One time he won a lot and I asked him where his land was. "Follow me," he said. "But promise not to say a thing." We went over miles of salt-marsh to where he had an osier patch. That's where he went for his new boots. Right in the middle of it there was a German aeroplane. He took them off the corpses.' The old man laughed quietly to himself and seemed to swallow his laughter like medicine.

Mrs Cooper opened the door and called, 'She's here!'

Griffin got to his feet standing foolishly.

'Well, well,' said Anne. 'Here's a surprise.'

'Excuse my coming,' said Frank. 'It's a matter of some importance.' Heavy, official-sounding syllables, he realised, rolling on the carpet like stones.

'Wow!' she said, livening up. 'Do you want to go into the conservatory?'

'I have got something to tell you.'

'And we do really have a conservatory.'

They went through a modern kitchen where Mrs Cooper was making cakes.

'Just another suitor, Mummy. I'll take him into the conservatory.'

'Now, what's it about?' she asked encouragingly when they were there among the great potted plants. 'We say anything here; there's a sort of immunity. A place of no consequences like the Rostovs' in *War and Peace.*'

'I don't know that book.'

'Stop being sullen. *Please.* You look ridiculous.'

'I'm not here for chit-chat.' If that was like his father, too bad. Since tea he had lost the faculty of making himself witty and intelligent in conversation. Anne was taking off her light-coloured raincoat—the same one as last night. He noticed how beautiful she was without reaction. Laboriously he explained: Popkin was in the papers and possibly on a charge; he could not have told the truth as the bicycle had been accepted as belonging to him.

Anne said nothing for some time. Then she laughed. Frank walked up and down whilst she rummaged through local papers in the house.

'You'll make me nervous. Is this it?'

A corner of the front page bore the news:

QUESTIONED BY CITY POLICE

Anthony Popkin (18), a pupil at John Campion Grammar School, was questioned by police last night about trespassing in the Arboretum park. He is understood to have declined to give any reasons for his whereabouts there. He had left his bicycle against the fence. *Note.* The July vandalism against rare fowl kept in the park remains a mystery.

'Good God,' said Anne. 'It's fantastic.'

'It could be serious. I said so at the time.'

'I like that sly hint about the ducks though. A peer of the realm was once charged with sodomy with a duck. The court found that the duck wasn't an animal within the meaning of the act.'

'So what are we going to do?' Frank hadn't heard her; only that even now she was being maddening.

'Be terrifically serious, I suppose. Lawyers.'

'It *might* blow over,' said Frank. 'Popkin's good at covering up and the head's got influence.'

'Why didn't the fool tell the truth?'

Conscientiously, Griffin tried to put himself in Popkin's skin to give an answer. 'He's in love with you.'

'Good God,' she said again. 'Now I really am worried.'

'He is, or thinks he is, I think. That's why, anyway.'

'Perhaps it is all my fault.' It was mournfully said but Frank couldn't tell whether as an ironical flourish or from a change of heart. 'I'll phone the police. This isn't my kind of thing,' she said and started crying.

Immediately Frank lost his head and found a handkerchief.

'I'm all right. Stop fussing. I'm not putting on a helpless woman act, if that's what you think.'

'It might make things worse if we said anything now.'

Anne, depressed in a way he had not seen before, listlessly agreed to leave well alone until Monday; Frank went back across the town to face Sunday with a wretched pretence of working.

'Schools are terrible,' Mohan was saying. 'They give you an illusion of thought when most of the time the thought's been done for you and all you have to do is to climb over it. They send us out to conquer a complicated gymnasium with prizes for them what gets to the top first. "Gymnasium", note, means "school" in several continental languages.'

'You just want to get out and start earning.'

'A pig like you thinks so. I'm not a materialist.'

'Well, I like school; I like rugger and I like schoolgirls. I can just see myself in twenty years' time joining the Old Boys and following little girls home.' Frazer finished his fifth bottle of milk and belched.

'You're more perceptive than we think,' said Mohan. Frazer, the school captain, was their best common-sense specimen. Massive, red-faced, black-haired, with a loose, smiling mouth he was a comforting presence.

'Your religion, Pete; it never lets you rest. It ties the intelligent ones up in spiritual knots and lets the others off with assured security.'

'You are getting bright; but lay off religion. Not because of offending me but because nothing you say about it will be true.'

'It's all bull.' Frazer got up. 'See you. I'm off up the wall-bars of dinner duty.'

The door Frazer went out of was choked with small boys. They gathered daily outside the prefects' room clamouring to give in their lines. Mohan surveyed his indolent colleagues. Some feigned sleep whilst others prolonged idle conversation about jazz and motor-bikes. To a man, they knew about the crowd outside. Mohan went to the door. He was swamped by first-formers all wanting to get away for their milk. The waiting was worse than the lines and the prefects knew it. 'Mohan! Mohan!' they clamoured. My name, he thought, cried out for pity.

'These first! Me and my mates've all got lines for Popkin.'

They were children with small faces; facial bones which hadn't set; sparrows' eyes. Mohan felt his size among them. He disciplined them into a line and they had to hand up their papers in some order. He knew his authority was unquestioned and that he was liked. Consequently the fact of power let him rest.

'Fifty each?'

'Yes, sir,' said one, smaller and more timid.

Freed from their impositions, the small boys ran off. Mohan, watching them, felt a slight nostalgia. Lately he had found himself in an elegiac mood; hence his often-expressed desire to have done with school.

'You should let the little bleeders wait.' Draper eyed him from the bench where he was sprawling in a detritus of bags and books.

Mohan thought again about power. Did it corrupt? Acton had said so so epigramatically that no one questioned it. No, corruption was there already and power only gave it room to show itself. This pleasing *pensée* lost its edge when he recalled how orthodox it was.

Indolent Draper took his silence personally.

'I had a bugger of a time last week in junior detention. Know why?'

'No. Why was that?'

'You'd had them the previous night. You let them out early.'

'I apologise.'

'Apologise yourself out of hanging, you could.'

'You shouldn't be personal, Draper,' somebody put in. Everyone was listening: Draper versus Mohan symbolised something.

'I can be much bloody personaller than that.'

'Personally bloody,' said a precise wit.

'Keep it cool,' Mohan said.

'O.K., Vice-Captain. I'll bide my time,' said Draper. Then, with an uncontrived laugh, 'I'm in luck.'

Peter sat down by the window. Personal feuds annoyed him; nor did he like the role of elder statesman. But he did like it; he liked this school world too much. On top of the pile of impositions he read, 'I must leave the ducks alone'. There it was, fifty times repeated in a large hand boldly and uncertainly written on scrappy, lined paper. He screwed it up. The remainder all said the same thing: 'I must be orderly in the bus queue.' The spelling of 'queue' varied widely. Draper, he reflected, would have made them do the lines over again, that is if Draper could spell the word himself. Mohan resisted a craving to smoke. It was done in the prefects' room but never when Draper was around. 'Half his power is our cowardice,' he thought. He lit a cigarette.

'What does this bloody *Weltschmerz* word mean?' somebody said. 'It says "world-sorrow" here. What's that when it's at home?'

Mohan was more pleased than usual to see Frazer come in.

'Hi,' said Frazer. 'I'll swear I'll kill that meal-woman one day. Perfectly simple problems are last-ditch stands with her. Some crazy kids wanted more spuds. Compared to her, Thermopylae was nothing. What's that you've got there, mate?'

'Lines,' said Mohan, clearing a chair for Frazer to sit down.

'You started giving lines?'

'These are Popkin's.'

'Jugg wants us in about that soon after two.' They found the headmaster's confidences the heaviest burden of office. The name—Erasmus Hare, M.A.—was a joke; the man was not.

At ten past two—Hare's 'soon after' represented ten minutes, his 'some time after' half an hour—they knocked on the study door. By accident or design the architect, who was rumoured to be the headmaster's brother-in-law, had sited this door in full public view. You could scrutinize it through the library's plate windows; you could see it from the playground and the bus-stop; you seemed to pass it on the shortest of journeys. Even on sunless days, light flooded its threshold. The airy hall in which you waited was known as the fish-tank. The headmaster would allow about a minute to elapse before he illuminated a sign above the door saying 'Enter'. It was inadvisable to knock twice.

'Does it take him longer to hear than most people?'

'No, I don't think so,' said Mohan. 'There are two probable explanations.' Frazer appreciated the Haresque phrase. 'It's either that he wants everyone to know who's on the mat. Or else he indulges in evil practices.'

'A minute to get his trousers on, you mean.'

'If you must be so bloody crude, yes. Lights, lights, lights.'

Adjusting their ties and faces, they marched in.

Hare was carefully arranged among papers and telephones. The three coloured 'phones, red, green and black—rich as a source of myth—had never been satisfactorily explained.

'Frazer, Mohan,' said the headmaster, scrupulously fair to each syllable, 'sit down.'

'Thank you, sir,' Mohan said. In these interviews the talking was mainly up to him. Bill Frazer had never quite mastered a childish streak of hysteria.

'Something rather serious has come my way from the Chief Constable. I think you must know to what I am referring. It was emanated by the local Press on Saturday.'

'Popkin, sir,' said Peter. Could 'emanate' be used like that? One hardly questioned such self-confident English usage as Hare's but after all his field was Economics, 'that bewitching science', as he had once startled them by calling it.

'Popkin. I wonder why it is that the very things we don't want to get about find their way into the only rags which in our age of universal literacy are universally read?'

Instead of saying 'Supply and demand', Mohan contented himself with marvelling at the man's gifted management of syntax.

'As the highest officers of the school, I need not remind you of the gravity of this sort of thing's happening. I made him a prefect which adds a worse dimension. We had a discussion about that. I asked your advice, I remember. Do you still regard him as the right material?'

The highest officers swopped glances which was not difficult as Hare was examining the lampshade. Mohan was afraid that Bill would go off into disastrous laughter. But he had underestimated him.

'You didn't, sir, If you remember, you said there was no one better available. All we were asked to do was to give him a hand.'

'Precisely. And did you?'

'Certainly,' said Frazer. 'I regard him as quite a good bloke.'

'Bloke? What is that?'

'Fellow then, chap, person.' Frazer was excited and his sincerity put sophistication in its place. 'I don't believe this duck-stuffing nonsense. Popkin's quite intelligent. He's not a hooligan. If you want me to resign from school-captain, sir, I will.'

'Steady, Frazer. We must, as sane beings, remain calm.'

'I'm sorry.'

'There's no call for apology. We of all people must deal trustfully with one another. I can tell you now in confidence that this thing may yet be kept out of the courts. The journalist ought never to have printed the story; his editor admitted that much to me over the telephone. I called this meeting to put you two in the picture. I like to keep in touch with my best boys. Thank you.'

His eyelids fluttered dismissal and he bowed his long head.

In the fish-tank they looked at each other, sucking in great mouthfuls of breath.

'The old bugger,' said Bill.

'Furtive and incapable.'

'The brick-chewing old basket!' Frazer suddenly went off into posthumous hysterics. Peter guided him along the corridor, laughing with him out of affection.

CHAPTER 3

FRANK sat on his bed trying to read. The boys had a room each; Frank's was much larger and better than Graham's: he took priority in theory because of his age but really because Mrs Griffin insisted that he have a room to study in. Outside the bow window green trolley-buses toiled uphill, their top decks glimmering in the fog. In the room, artificially immune, he had a shelf of books, a second-hand gramophone and a writing-table—all the requisites of Culture. But to-night he was disenchanted. Looking at his bastion, he saw it in terms of a girl's dressing-table, identical to hundreds in this range of red brick. Beauty in bottles; Culture in paper covers. Tipping *King Lear* on the floor, he lay back on the bed and studied the yellowed ceiling with its deltas of ancient damp.

The Friday night business had changed everything; had swiped him clean off his perch. 'I'm spiritually winded,' he said aloud between his teeth. Then, 'Spiritually winded! But I am, I am.' Sometimes he enjoyed depression. Sensitivity is a form of masochism. But he wasn't enjoying it now. Monday night, an essay to do. King Lear in the foggy suburbs. Once he could have purged himself by shouting the storm bits out of the window. But that was before Friday.

He made himself get up from the bed and retrieved *King Lear*. Books were to be respected; even his father had learned that. What respect his father had for Education had a touch of cringing in it though, the stamp of the shopkeeper. If only he had been bolder, a more real person, Frank would have respected him. He had been born true working class but he had sold out for halfpence. They were neither one thing nor the other, but suspended somewhere in between—the limbo of the pettiest petty bourgeoisie. Frank felt 'class' acutely since his visit to the Coopers. He was caught in a destructive vortex:

26

anything was bad enough to curse and when the wardrobe mirror showed him his face he cursed that.

Frank examined himself at close range. His face was heavy, squarish. Round the edges his hair and ears with the light behind them looked unnaturally ragged, like stuffing coming out of a medicine ball. His nose, mouth and eyes were redeeming. His mother had been good-looking in her youth. His expression was peevish, so he tried another one, then several more, as a woman tries on new hats. Since Friday he had fallen from his own state of grace; in the privacy of his room he spent minutes mirror-gazing. Before Friday he had never become involved with girls, on Friday he had. Last week he had been free of them—some walking through the night, some brief agonies but Intellect had been his guide; he had been secure. It was Anne Cooper who had devalued all his previous effort. She deserved punishment. Perhaps he should have kissed her in the conservatory; but, though that sort of thing was easy to imagine, it was impossible to do.

The door was pushed open. A knock and a question, 'Are you studying, Frank?'

Graham came in. Fresh from the glass, Frank looked for likeness. There was hardly any. His younger brother was smaller in build with darker more regular hair. He wore steel-framed spectacles, looked up to Frank and was interested in prehistoric animals. They didn't know each other.

'There's a friend come to see you.'

'Who?'

'He said you'd know.'

'Tell him to come up, our Graham.'

'He can't stay he said.'

'I'll come down then.'

Popkin was in the yard. Griffin went out into the dripping murk and closed the door.

'I've brought your bike back.'

'Thanks. No one noticed it wasn't around.'

'Didn't they? Good.' Popkin tried to sound pleased but his voice was that of a man wounded in the war admiring his wife's new curtains.

'You weren't in class to-day.'

'I stayed at home.'

'What was it like?'

'Just the police station. Ordinary. I've not been in a cell, you know.'

'Oh, I thought they'd locked you up!' Frank was ashamed of himself, that jovial voice.

'They phoned Jugg so the police dropped it.'

'I should hope so too.'

'You can't understand what it's like, being questioned. It's awful, not like human beings.'

'Yes,' said Frank.

'I'm coming back the day after tomorrow. That's Wednesday.'

'You'll miss French set-texts. I'll lend you my notes.'

'Thanks,' said Popkin listlessly.

Frank shivered. It was cold without a coat and the fog stank in his nostrils. They stood in silence. Popkin freed his trouser turn-ups from his socks. The only possible thing was to invite him in but Frank was unwilling to introduce Popkin to his father who was sometimes servile to the friends he brought home and who was a great one for introductions.

Finally Popkin made a move towards the yard gate. 'Good night,' he said.

'Good night.' Frank opened the plank door into the back alley.

'Oh, thanks for bringing the bike, Tony,' he called into the fog.

The school hall was the best of a bad job. It had been the first of the loosely linked school buildings to go up and the builders had followed the original scheme. Then there had been a change of Government. Building programmes had been cut back. Elsewhere in the school this saving was apparent: the library windows had cracked across three times and there was a crack in the wall of the physics lab where, it was rumoured, birds flew in to build their nests in the sinks.

But the hall was bright and overlooked the playing fields. Here the pupils daily assembled and the headmaster, who enjoyed Assembly, had spent many happy hours perfecting its form. Perfection, however, can never be conceived on the drawing board and about once a week he thought of improvements. It was a strained affair, especially for the prefects who were in the position of choreographers receiving contradictory instruction from the director, or of N.C.O.s ordered to do the impossible by High Command. For the junior boys it was a daily laugh, an invitation to anarchy.

Peter Mohan was checking hymn-books. Boys streamed by, holding up battered bundles of paper, the passport needed for entry into the hall. The duty prefect was issued with a duplicated form divided for the names into two columns: 'Missing' and 'Beyond Repair'. Each day a new sheet was clipped over the old. Yesterday's was crawling with names: Draper had been on. Mohan always excused the blank Wednesday sheet by the thorough density of Tuesday's. As the Lower School squeezed past, he toyed with the pencil which, anchored on a string, was one of Hare's masterly details. It was an occasion for wishing he'd pleaded his Faith to jump the column.

Pressure grew, forcing him to use physical controls. The stream had taken on a blind pushing haste like a military retreat. Looking up, he saw the coming of Hare. The gowned figure approached steadily through the parting ranks. Sometimes Peter saw him as the medieval symbol of Death; but when he had explained the fancy to Frazer, Frazer had blamed his religion again.

'Mohan, a word.'

The headmaster beckoned him to an alcove behind the piled chairs.

'Popkin is in to-day, is he not?'

'I haven't seen him.'

'I want you to locate him, Mohan. Seat him at the end of row "A".'

'I'm on hymn-book duty, sir.' Peter showed him the official proof.

'That is of absolutely no account. Now do as I say.'

'Yes, sir.'

This was ominous. When Hare was that screwed-up, something was sure to burst, and it wasn't one of his blue blood-vessels.

Popkin was not in the hall. He would be hiding in the locker room until the last moment. Bill was standing by the door in an attitude of thought. Assemblies were worse for him than for the others. As chief choreographer, he had daily to please director and audience, both of whom were Hare. Peter explained. Bill said:

'Nasty. Could be anything. Morally, Jugg's a threadbare sock.' Frazer liked metaphor. 'Still, there's sod-all we can do, Pete.'

Popkin was reading at the far end of the locker room. He was masked from the door by coats.

'Has assembly started, Mohan?'

'Jugg sent me to find you.'

'What's it for?' Popkin's sallow face lost colour.

'He wants you in the front row. Your guess is as good as mine.'

'This is some scheme of the prefects, isn't it? I'm not playing.'

Mohan traced his finger round one of the cast iron peg numbers: 59.

'You've no grounds, Tony, for saying that.' But he suddenly clearly knew that his grounds were fear.

'I can take a bit of ragging.' It was said pathetically.

Mohan was moved. Those who wanted mortification should stay in the world!

'It's an order from Hare. Get up!'

'You're a creeping Jesus,' said Popkin. 'I'm coming. I can take a joke.'

He carefully marked the page of his book and found his hymn-book.

Peter felt dizzy and sick and unlike himself. The word 'lies' hammered in his brain.

The school was assembled when they reached the door. Popkin had made things harder for himself. The school was silent. Seven hundred people; not one sound. They walked the interminable distance side by side. Popkin's shoes squeaked and every ear heard them squeaking. The first row was occupied half by small boys and half by the prefects who had not been involved in marshalling duties. Popkin slumped into the chair at the end. His knees seemed to give way but he landed squarely and perhaps it was only a clumsy sitting-down. Rather than find his appointed place, Peter stood at attention against the wall. No head had moved but the silence was unnatural.

Mr Hare uncrossed his legs and walked to the lectern.

'We will begin this morning as on other Wednesdays with some episode from the life of Our Lord. I hinted last week at the connotations, the wide everyday bearing of the events of His life. That one life was a specimen of our lives. It was all a long time ago, but have things changed? It is "ancient history" but ancient history which is going on all the time.' Smiling, he swept his eye over hundreds of obedient faces.

They had, it seemed, on previous Wednesdays covered prominent points in the Ministry and now—though far in the year from Easter—they were to consider the momentous fact of the Crucifixion. A brief outline of the betrayal was given. This was something the most worldly could grasp: they had all experienced loyalty.

Mr Hare thus neatly led his school on to the reading from Saint John. Departing from normal practice he read from the gospel himself. Seventeenth-century prose suited his voice which dealt correctly and impressively with cadences so often gabbled and smeared. When the priests had come into the garden and had been asked by Jesus whom they sought, Hare's voice took on vehemence and power: ' "They answered him, Jesus of Nazareth. Jesus saith unto them, I am *he*. And Judas also, which betrayed him, stood with them." '

The headmaster signalled for the hymn. McCormack, the music master, felt in his fingers the unusual hurry in the singing.

Bull, the second master, gave details of games fixtures in his normal, pleasant—but it seemed abnormally drawn-out—baritone. Then Headmaster's Announcements.

It had been brought to his notice that the writing on the lavatory walls which he had remarked on at the end of the previous term, though less frequent, was still being perpetrated. 'I cannot put the lavatories out of bounds,' he said. The faint ripple of laughter from the young and silly who did not understand the seasonableness of a joke may have been foreseen by the head. It gave colour and point to his, 'But I can take other action.' Mohan's eyes never left Popkin; he had seen the close application and attempt to sing; he saw now a hunching of the shoulders and he thought he could see a curling of toes in Popkin's suede shoes.

'I had rather not end on this note, but I must. Anthony Popkin, will you stand up?'

Popkin sat still, rabbit-still.

'Did the boy hear me?' No vehemence now—a polite enquiry merely—genuine bafflement. The prefect sitting next to Popkin touched his arm. Popkin looked round with slow, bewildered eyes.

'Be a man!' snapped Hare. Again there was a not unfriendly note in his voice. This was the bluffness of a firing-squad commander who can admire spirit in the man he is commissioned to turn into a bleeding sack.

'Mohan, get the boy up.'

Peter gulped. Then Bill Frazer came forward from two rows back, said something, and guided Popkin to his feet. Frazer returned to his seat.

'I think you all know that one of our number has come within a hair's breadth of bringing down disgrace on all of us. We can collectively be thankful that what transpired was not worse. I do not wish to hear it said that we are unable to discipline ourselves. We have our own justice here, as stringent a justice as in the world outside our walls. Popkin, get your mother to remove the prefect's braid from your coat. Have it off by tomorrow morning.'

CHAPTER 4

THAT evening for the first time in his life Frank Griffin went to a public house. In the Griffin family public houses were the desperate man's recourse. They were hemlock and ratsbane. The skyline of existence stretched from the chapel at one end to the pub at the other. Those were the extremes. Frank in an extremity of feeling had taken this hemlock. But he found that, like death, the public house swallowed your loneliness whole without diminishing it—if it was loneliness. It could equally well have been guilt, frustration, despair.

Frank sat among these abstract nouns looking at half a pint of beer. In any ordinary state of mind he would have felt acute embarrassment, fright almost, at being here. He had on his only suit and a clean shirt. Suicides, one imagines, often take leave of life in their best attire.

The Public Bar, long and old-fashioned, resembled a railway station. Plain oak had been used for the furnishing which comprised tables for snacks and beer, benches round the walls and the bar itself, massively long and high. A fire burned beneath a mantelpiece bearing the city's coat of arms. It was a city pub which so far had not sold out to suburban tastes. They made excellent pork rolls; it was a free house. But to Frank it was no more than the pub nearest the bus-stop.

As it was early yet, the place was catering for birds of passage and was two-thirds empty. Frank was reassured that the other drinkers were the sort he had fulminated against—respectable, middle-class men in blazers who had dropped in for a quiet noggin. An unreasoning uneasiness of men without ties was part of his buried inheritance from home. At school he loudly supported those of the weatherbeaten neck; and he

33

did feel a Ruskinesque admiration for the working man. Unfortunately he didn't know any.

Beer was unpleasant to his taste: it looked like rusty water and was sour in the mouth. Still, he went through with his half pint and then ordered another. The lady who was waiting on was cheerful and motherly.

'Awaitin' friends, duck?' she asked.

Frank nodded.

'Soon be fillin' up. Thank the Lord it's not Sat'dy.'

Further up the bench an old man was sitting, taking even longer over his beer than Frank was. Emerging from a dirty overcoat, the head was held erect at an angle other than that suggested by the shoulders. Facial flesh had fallen and the space between mouth and nose had shortened; eyes were liquid and pale but without the spark that was in those of Anne's grandfather. There was a resemblance between the two old men which Griffin had noticed when he came in, before he had settled down to gloom. Tired of his own worries, his questions with no answers to them, Frank wondered who this old man was and what he had been. He pictured him young and strong, imagined him felling trees in a wood.

As if in acknowledgement of the new train of thought, the old man turned. He had a grubby tie and collar; had been a clerk perhaps and not a woodcutter.

'Beer's good.'

'Yes,' said Frank, 'very.'

'They say beer's not like it was, but I say it's better.'

Griffin nodded. 'You must remember when it was cheap.'

''Salways been the same.' The old man thought about it. His mouth was forever working round in search of a position to rest in. Whereas Mrs Cooper's father had deafly ignored the world and asserted himself from his lair of silence, this man was apologetic.

'Don't let me keep you talkin',' he said. He owed the floor an apology for walking on it.

'No. I'm interested . . .' Frank was going to say 'in History'. 'I mean, things have changed.'

'Some 'ev, some not. They says there wor more life in them

34

old days. Most folk are better off now.' Here he was apologising to the present for his existence. 'What's yer trade, youth?'

'Me? I'm at school.'

'Ah.'

'What trade did you have?' Frank was more nervous keeping this conversation going than ever he was giving papers to the History Society or speaking in school debates.

'I wor set on at pit as a lad. Apprenticed to the blacksmith. I mind all the pits round Nottingham had proper blacksmiths up to 1914. That put an end to a lot of things one way and another.'

'You mean the war stopped you qualifying?'

'Things worn't the same after.'

'The Slump,' said Frank, who was doing twentieth-century history. The old man took colour from Bull's dictated notes. They covered the same period. Frank wished he could get more out of his companion. Did he remember the effects of the 1911 Insurance Act? Munich? It was odd that this man could tell no more of these things than the bricks of his father's shop.

'As to yer question a while back, I wor in the Coldstreams for nigh on four year in France. And I never did reckon out that war.' He shook his head.

Frank did some revision. They had taken three weeks over the causes of the Great War: Political, Naval and Economic. In spite of the aid of sub-headings, the outbreak *was* hard to understand; three weeks had been needed to comb out the strands.

'I hope you nivver see it. I'm a veteran, they tell me. One summer morning we crossed a great flat marshland place.' The old man furtively rolled himself a cigarette. 'And there like'— pointing towards the bar—'there was Germans only you couldn't tell there wor. Let us come right up, stepping over the shell 'oles. Then all on 'em opened up. Flat on yer face shamming dead. You can't catch old buds wi' chaff and I'd been in France three year at the time I'm telling you of. Do you know, lad, all me mates wor dead men when I opened me eyes?' He sipped at his beer. 'Best wor a wound to git yerself a pension when the peace came. Didn't get a powder-stain on this bit of

35

skin. A touch of shrapnel would 'ev tided me ovver nicely. But 'ere I am drawin' me o'd age pension.'

'Can I buy you another drink?'

'I'll mek it last, youth, thank yer kindly.'

Frank didn't press him. An old man, the century's veteran and he made nothing of it. Mrs Cooper's father had asserted his long life; his own father was full of opinions. Yet neither of them as far as he knew was the sole survivor of a platoon. There was no reason for thinking the old man stupid. Frank was puzzled. He would have expected opinions, personal experience put to account. Instead, nothing. He had accepted war, slump and pensioning-off dumbly. Frank was still worrying at it when Anne tapped him on the head.

'Alone and palely loitering?'

He looked up at her. 'Hullo.'

'Hullo. What are you doing here?'

'Getting drunk,' he said with some bravado.

'On half pints?'

'I don't like beer and I'm getting used to it.'

'Do I detect hostile undertones? And may I sit down?'

'I suppose so.' He shifted himself towards the pensioner.

'I didn't see you as a drinker.' To-night she was wearing a red coat in what was probably the latest fashion. She was made up in a skilful and 'evening' way. Frank was gratified to have her next to him. Once again she had swung his feelings round. The sporty young men at the bar now looked his way. He had lost the anonymity of a few moments ago—the anonymity of the old man. He felt someone and was no longer afraid of his surroundings.

'I'm meeting Peter,' said Anne.

'Is this your meeting-place?'

'Oh, I'm not meeting him here.'

'What are you doing here then?'

'Telepathy?' She smiled with a kind of sincere irony. 'I braved this den to partake of a fortifying gin. Isn't it terrible? What's Peter done to drive me to drink?'

The woman being within call, Griffin called for a gin and a pint.

'With lime,' Anne added. The order came without friendly comments.

'Of course,' said Anne, 'you must have been a witness of yesterday's assembly. Cigarette?'

He took one without inventing a philosophical justification. 'It was sickening.'

'So Peter says. He was right next to Popkin. Why didn't we 'phone the police, Frank?'

'I thought we'd have time to see what was going to happen.'

'Don't think I'm blaming you. I'm not. I was to blame.'

'No one's to blame. It was like you said. Fuss over nothing.'

'I know—but the fuss wasn't nothing, was it? Pete and Bill Frazer are in a hell of a turmoil. But I suppose you know about that.'

'We all want to kick Jugg's teeth in,' said Frank. It was a suitable remark: sufficiently violent to excuse its impossibility.

'How's Popkin taking it? I mean, has he gone to pieces or anything?'

'He doesn't talk to anyone.'

Anne sighed. 'It's the sort of bloody thing that's got no end to it.'

Frank made a noise intended to reassure.

'I told Sheila and Glenys that . . .' she faltered, 'well, that we had left him soon after they left us. What made me say that, Frank? And I've not told Peter nor anybody.'

For a few seconds Frank felt morally superior; until he remembered his father's bike lamp. But he didn't tell her about that.

'Perhaps we would have done the same in Popkin's place.'

'Would we? He's been heroic almost. That's what makes it so bad. I mean I don't feel grateful, I can't. He's such a fool. But did he do it for a schoolboy code of honour, or what?'

'I told you why he did it,' said Frank, returning to Truth.

'At least he wasn't in court, and he wasn't expelled. I'll be saying he's lucky next. Oh dear.'

'When are you meeting Mohan?'

'Good God! Now. It's the City Strings. They're doing the Archduke.'

'And not before time,' he said foolishly. Anne made a Philistine out of him, that among other things.

'Probably they'll hash it up, but still.'

'I won't keep you then.'

'Oh, why not come along?' she said. 'Better than getting drunk.'

As they got up, Frank looked at the old man and nodded. He had been the partner of the pre-Anne part of the evening. But if it was an oracle he wanted, he was wasting his time. His veteran was as unmoved by the advent of Anne as he had been by the slump and world war.

A long passage led them out to the street. It was tiled and smelly—beer with a hint of long-departed sawdust, straw, horses, leather. The City Square was alight with neon and the pavements were crowded. In the autumn air Griffin felt his two pints. Sociably light-headed, he kept up with Anne's quick, precise walking. Two acquaintances from school passed them and greetings were exchanged on the march. The coincidence was pleasing. They crossed the centre of the city. In spite of business alterations and one or two outstandingly hideous municipal erection schemes, the city remained compact enough for there to be a feeling of town. The jostlers-by were fellow citizens even if you didn't know them and didn't want to.

They entered the Mechanic's Institution, whose buildings—vast, obsolete and mysterious—echoed its title. A number of meetings were advertised at the door: Health Inspectors, The Living God and the City Strings. The *Archduke*, Frank noted, was Trio No. 6 in B Flat by Beethoven. It was to be played among dark green radiators in a basement room. The light was so poor that Griffin did not recognise the spare figure of Mohan until he came up to them.

The ease with which Mohan took the girl's arm was a surprise. He had forgotten how it was between them; the beer had washed away all the realities.

'I ran into this repository of culture,' she said, pointing at Frank.

'Hullo,' said Mohan. 'I didn't know you were musical.'

'I'm not really.'

38

'Come along to our record jam sessions: dinner-time, Tuesday and Thursday, in E.4.'

'I will. I hadn't heard about them.'

'He's a bit of a noble savage,' said Anne.

'Just a savage,' said Frank modestly.

The music might or might not have been well played. Anne and Peter seemed to think it was. Mostly it was lost on him, though the odd bar or juxtaposition of sound affected him. A slight shivering down his back was the sign, but mentally he found it difficult to follow any pattern for long. Mohan approved without apparent emotional disturbance. This, he supposed, was the mark of true appreciation. Part of Mohan's superior world was music and it would take, Frank thought, a long time for him to catch up. Perhaps it was not in him to arrive at serenity and self-assurance; perhaps he was capable only of receiving Life in jolts and flashes.

The trio, with a non-professionalism that must have been cultivated, packed their instruments and shrouded the piano to the applause of their well-satisfied audience. Anne and the two boys left without trying the good lady's tea and biscuits.

The ridiculous notion of their being a trio without instruments occurred to Griffin. To perfect yourself on an instrument which could be put away when you were tired must be soothing. They were condemned to practise only on themselves.

He asked who the musicians were, what they did when they weren't playing.

'They're all schoolmasters,' said Mohan. 'If I had to do that job, I'd sink into a decline and all me talent would soak into the sand.'

'Peter secretly wants to teach,' said Anne.

'Or be a Jesuit priest. Think of that—Peter Mohan S.J. I'd be another Hopkins if only I could find a Bridges. What about you, Frank? Will you ever make Poet Laureate?'

'Frank, why are Catholics so cynical?'

'We grow old very young and never really grow up.'

'Strewth,' said Frank appropriately.

'Where are we going?' asked Anne.

Mohan threw his arms wide. 'Miss Cooper's a narrow realist.

Here we are, all racing to damnation with a show of working out our own and all she asks is whether we're going to a coffee-bar or the bus-stop.'

'He's impossible.' Frank couldn't decide how flippantly she meant that. The way she looked in his direction was ambiguous. Was it gross self-flattery that he thought Mohan was the outsider despite the placing of his hand on the girl's arm?

'The bus-station it had better be,' said Mohan. 'It's ten-fifteen.'

The bus-station was a let-down. Their fellow citizens stood about like parcels; the kaleidoscope had come to settle in the form of a mere queue. Children up too late were protesting about it. Parents were nasty to each other. Along the wall the parting couples welded themselves together as if they would never part.

Mohan's philosophy of damnation seemed remote, here where cynicism might have applied it. And Frank—minus music, minus beer, minus the motion of the street—felt himself out of place. The others were silent, standing about. His ideas of courtship were vague; he wondered whether they wanted to join the others by the wall. He was on the verge of excusing himself when his bus pulled in. In the noisy scramble he turned with relief to say good-bye.

'There's something coming off at school tomorrow,' Mohan said, giving him a cheerful salute.

'Keep off the beer,' said Anne in what he was coming to think of as 'her most coquettish vein.' After their silence their cheerfulness at seeing him go was apparent.

He bundled himself upstairs behind the drunken boots of a swearing Irishman. He couldn't doubt now who was the outsider: he was. He sat behind two lads of his own age who were conducting a discussion about 'bleddy Maggy' and how free she was with it. He listened and found their talk distasteful. But when he looked down from the window and saw Mohan and Anne kissing each other he suffered a sharp and devastating pain.

40

CHAPTER 5

'GRAHAM'S leaving at Christmas,' announced Mrs Griffin at the breakfast table. 'It's his fifteenth next month. It doesn't seem fifteen years, does it, Charles?'

Her husband paid no attention. Eating toast and reading the *Daily Express* was all he could manage with a stomach like his. His stomach chilled the sunlight in summer and the fire on a winter's morning. Toast was all he could get down; after minutes of dogged mastication.

'Is that so, our Graham?' Frank asked.

'You don't have to stay when you're fifteen.'

'Don't look as if you've got bellyache,' said the father. 'It's not the end of the world. I was at work nearly two year when I was your age. They're work-shy, the youngsters of to-day.'

'Depends on what you call work.'

'Frank, don't contradict your father.'

'Who is?' said Frank. 'What's the point of using words if you won't define your terms?'

'Time was when work was work. There was no Welfare State then. When you were old enough, you went to work.'

Mrs Griffin foresaw a disastrous day. She thought her eldest had more sense: her husband was only to be hauled over the ridge of breakfast by patient teamwork; breakfast was an emergency—surely Frank knew that. Mr Griffin was staring at his sons across the *Daily Express*.

'And when I was *your* age I'd been at work near on *five* year.'

'Pass the marmalade, our Graham.'

Mrs Griffin fussed with the teapot. Sometimes, in spite of her peacemaking, the three males in her household collided head on. She was Gertrude to three Hamlets, only a better housekeeper.

41

'Did you hear me?'

'Yes. You went to work when you were thirteen.'

'You have got ears then?'

'That's right.'

Mr Griffin snorted. He'd advanced too far and couldn't follow up his advantage.

'Do you mind leaving?'

'It's best to get started soon after you're fifteen. I can learn the trade in the shop.'

Frank heard the echo there of their father's worldly wisdom. Had he failed the eleven plus, he would be in the shop now. Probably Graham was giving way for want of any alternative. He felt sorry for him, but had his own problems.

'It's nearly half eight, Charles.' It was worse than she had feared if he needed reminding. His routine must be badly upset for him to sit so long. And he wasn't reading the paper either; Frank had made him morose.

'While we're at it, what kept you out last night? After a bit of skirt, are you?'

'I went to a concert.' Frank coloured. Mr Griffin was pleased at this sign of success.

'I thought we were paying for you to better yourself studying. Now when Graham's your age and pulling his weight in the shop, well that's a different matter. Not that I think girls'll bother Graham.'

'Don't tease the boy; he works hard enough,' said Mrs Griffin.

'So concerting with girls is work now.'

'I don't suppose you were all work and no play at their age. Be reasonable, dear.'

'Oh, yes he was,' said Frank. 'Grovelling and counting pennies from morning to night.'

'What do you know about it, eh?' Griffin smashed his fist on the table, jutting forward the bad teeth and the wire moustache. 'You who don't know the back of a wench from the front!'

Mrs Griffin screamed. When all her efforts failed, she had her battle-order ready. 'I never thought to hear such language!'

she shouted. 'In front of our sons. I never, never thought to hear it!'

The three males watched her. She was strident, hysterical, going at it three times too loud. Her husband tried to calm her but she was howling among the debris of the upset teapot. Helplessly they fidgetted and looked at each other until it subsided.

'He shouldn't make me say such things,' Griffin was saying.

'Get out all of you. Go along to school, ducky,' she added, speaking to Graham who had started snuffling.

They left the table feeling guilty. As Frank righted the teapot, he could have cried himself—though he could not have said why.

Beyond the plate-glass of the Private Study Room it was raining. The straight, regular fall produced a low, steady noise and grained the landscape, making it resemble some Impressionist's skilful and painstaking reproduction. Frazer and Mohan had retreated here. Their final arrangements were better made away from the crowded waiting-room atmosphere of the Prefect's Study.

'Pissing down,' said Frazer. 'It'll be a mud bath to-morrow if we play at all.'

Mohan staring out through the rain said nothing. His reflection stared back into the room and he felt an almost soothing melancholy. What they were about to do would, for him at any rate, be beneficial. It would help to make the break with school and set him free. He wondered how it would be for Frazer— harder probably: he was the captain and his approach to things was less devious, more honest, Peter thought.

'Jugg'll be free in ten minutes. We'll do it then. Should spoil his tea with any luck.'

'Seen Popkin?' Peter asked.

'He's in the library, quiet as ever.'

'Don't you wish he were more—I don't know—noble, likeable?'

'Don't see it makes any difference, cock. This is our own

screwball idea. You work out the philosophy of it, Pete. It's not my line. Jugg asked for a kick in the groin and I'm quite happy to oblige.'

'I suppose you're right. Fancy making history on a day like this.'

'Five minutes,' said Frazer.

'How are you getting on with Lucy?'

'Seem to have packed it in. Said all we've got to say to each other. We were talking about the weather last night. When you get to that routine it's time to say good-bye. I wonder if its a parabolic curve or something. You know, "This is where we came in". It was the weather when we started. Intimacy deepens—religion, childhood, what it's like to have periods. Then, lo and behold, the weather again. But we never reckoned to be passionately in love. You and Anne, that's a different thing. I'd hang on to her, though I bet she can be pretty trying.'

'Who can tell?' said Mohan.

They had judged their arrival in Hare's room nicely. His tea was brought in and Frazer winked. Had the Head ordered two extra cups, Peter thought, they might have called the whole thing off. On such thin threads does Principle hang. But then if Hare had had it in him to do that the situation might never have developed. In spite of his theory that you should dislike a person's bad qualities while at the same time contriving to like the person who had them, Mohan simply disliked the headmaster and was quite happy to. Hare was in no hurry. It was seldom his pupils came unbidden; such visits were inimical to efficiency. They had a few minutes to wait his pleasure.

Mohan noticed that an electric fire had been brought in to supplement the good electric heating. It was a copper one and looked early Victorian. It was possibly the oldest electric fire in the world. He imagined Faraday or someone knocking it up in the hut on Battersea marshes where they were getting chilblains discovering Electricity. It made Hare less hateful because it was the first of his personal possessions that Mohan had ever seen.

The Head finished what had probably been an imaginary spell of paper-work carried out solely for their benefit—that is,

44

their discomfort; addressed himself to his tea and smiled thinly at them across the telephones.

'I am informed of your intention,' he said.

'I don't think you can be, sir,' said Peter. For all his thinking Hare an insignificant man, his first words had been effectively shocking.

'Economists watch the market. It is our second nature and I am not so out of touch as to leave myself unacquainted with conspiracy.'

'Mohan and myself—we want to resign, sir.'

'Is that so, Frazer? And why all of a sudden this extra-ordinary decision?'

'We'd rather not say, sir.'

'And you, Mohan, do you concur in that?'

'It's complicated.'

'On the contrary, it is apparently simple, is it not?'

'We want to resign, sir. Frazer and I would rather not carry on as heads of the school.'

'You are both excessively silly,' said Hare. 'It's not good enough, Mohan. This is not an attitude I had expected.'

'We didn't either, sir,' said Bill. 'It was Popkin. The way you crucified him in Assembly wasn't right.'

'Since when have you been the source of morality in my school?'

'Since Wednesday,' Frazer said rather finely. 'I got Popkin to stand up. That was it.'

'Mohan?'

'Frazer's said what I'd have said, only better.'

'You must be in quite a glow,' said the headmaster. 'Moralists *and* orators.' Then he recollected his position. 'You both know what this means? Of course you don't. What if it meant Pop-kin's expulsion?'

Frazer said, 'I don't see how it can.'

'Are you accusing me of blackmail?'

Frazer and Hare stared each other out. The Head seemed to recant.

'This is most unpleasant. There can be no question of black-mail on either side. Let us go back, shall we? I did not enjoy

45

demoting Popkin. There are many duties which one does not enjoy. You, Mohan, are not fond of hymn-book duty. As you go through life you will be giving orders, ruling people; and inevitably you will be forced into doing unpleasant things. This is the law of life. At your age you do not see it. I was your age once. There have been many years of experience since that time. Do you see something of the truth of what I say?'

They nodded.

'Think of the school, Frazer. Is a change of captain *in medias res* beneficial? Think again of your own positions. Universities are not impervious to school honours. These are tough times for getting a place. Worse, think how it would be if they asked you why you resigned. Picture explaining to some august stranger in a year's time these imagined wrongs. Have I said enough to convince you?'

He had said too much.

For some moments he surveyed them, his fingers drumming among the telephones. He smiled like a victor offering unlimited mercy. He first asked Frazer if he had reconsidered the matter.

'No, sir. I can't speak for Mohan.'

'I'd like to resign,' said Peter.

'Very well. I warn you that life brings problems where resignation is no answer. Remove your insignia of office by Monday morning.'

'Thank you, sir.'

CHAPTER 6

'THUS the poem has no easily followed direction; everything mingles giving an apparent lack of organisation. But as a work of art *The Waste Land* does possess a unity. This is obtained by "musical organisation", the broad sweep of its subject and the fact that it has many literary allusions and echoes.' Anne's pen lingered on the last full-stop. It had been a long and trying essay; like T. S. Eliot's poem, she thought. Now she'd finished it, she had a pang of conscience. Did she believe a single word she had written? Mrs Copley would award an Alpha it was true; and the quotes were in order, not to mention the references to F. R. Leavis. It was a good poem: clever, complex and with some fine lines. Modern life was corrupt and dreary and we were, she supposed, all waiting for metaphysical rain and physical sunshine. She laughed irreverently, signed her name and pinned the pages together.

There was a tap on her door and her grandfather shuffled in.

'It's all right, Anne. Only your grandad. They won't let me rest to-day. Your mother's cleaning the whole damned place. I can't find my pipe and they won't let me look. So I've come to you for a chat.'

Anne groaned. Her grandfather was wily enough to come armed with his hard-luck stories.

'I've got to get ready,' she shouted.

'It's not as if I make a mess. Seamen know how to look after themselves. Just because I'm old doesn't mean to say I'm dirty, does it?'

'Do mind out of the way, grandpa.' Anne guided him aside to get at the wardrobe.

'I'd help if she'd let me. I've got my uses like everything else.

47

Take tadpoles, you couldn't think of anything less useful than them.'

'Where are my shoes?'

'Well, the women in China use them for contraceptives. Trouble is I'm not wanted.'

'Of course you're wanted.' She patted the old man's shoulder. 'But I want to change!' she shouted.

'Oh, yes. Want to change. Go ahead, girl. I won't look; not at my own granddaughter. I'm past all that; I thank God every day what I am. I'll look out of the window and tell you what's going on.'

Anne stripped off her jeans and sweater and picked out the first dress to come to hand. It was her red one, old but she liked it; she got rid of those she didn't care for. Not having worn it for some time, she was annoyed to find it tight round the waist. Slimming she hated the thought of, along with the idea of motherhood and the women's pages in the Sunday papers.

'There's nothing going on,' said the old man, 'so I can't tell you about it. I suppose it'll be like Sunday when I'm dead. Church or nothing. I don't call that a choice. Now the house will be full of your friends and I'll have to go to bed.'

'You can join us.'

'No. I'll go to bed. . . . Lord! there's two dogs going at it right in the middle of the road. That was a terrible embarrassment in my young day. I'm surprised sex didn't die out. But they say the parks are full of people doing it in broad daylight. Raining again.'

Anne looked at the old head, birdlike at the window with the white hair lit—fragile and thin over the crown, minute and bristly on the edges of the ears. She liked his presence in the house in spite of the troubles he caused, the scenes with her father. He was a candle and the wavering life in him was simple and translucent.

'You can turn round now and button these up.'

He fastened the hooks and eyes with great care. 'Some young man will only be undoing them, I expect. They don't realise their good fortune. In my day we joined the scouts just to learn how to get through some of those knots.'

'Anne! People are arriving,' Mrs Cooper called from the hall.

Bill Frazer was standing on the doormat steadily wiping his feet and listening to an explanation of the sogginess of Mrs Cooper's sausage rolls.

'Hullo, Bill.'

'Am I early? Has Pete told you we lost yesterday? Twelve-three. Like playing on flypaper. Perhaps that was why our fly-half hardly moved.'

'I didn't see him yesterday.'

'That's right. He said he was going away somewhere.'

The bell rang. Frazer stopped wiping his feet and opened the door again. A bevy of guests had arrived together.

The old man hovered on the stairs between life and death. He enjoyed a bit of commotion from a distance, but an evening of being entirely unwanted was too good to miss, so he went up to his room.

'We all here?' Anne asked.

'All except Lucy I think.'

'Is *she* coming?'

'Of course she is, Bill. And don't you be nasty to her.'

The visitors, who had come for an informal drink, ran into an 'at home' organised by the mother. Seated, they watched a number of trays of food coming in. Everything was there from a fresh fruit-salad to the delinquent sausage rolls. Mrs Cooper, by upbringing Bohemian, had occasional outbreaks of conventionality. Anne was sorry that they coincided with these gatherings. With her own generation her mother behaved differently; but with younger people she was middle-aged and respectable.

'You know where the pâté is, Anne dear, should anyone fancy some. Excuse me running off like this but my husband and I are attending a function this evening.' Mrs Cooper gracefully withdrew.

'She's not always like that,' said Anne. 'She has this theory that our generation is terrifically class-conscious. I don't know —are we?'

'Probably,' said Mohan. 'We just don't admit it.'

49

'I'm not,' said Sheila. 'Education should iron that sort of thing out, surely.'

'Or in,' said Mohan. 'I'm sorry. That doesn't mean anything.'

'Pete's always saying things that don't mean anything, aren't you, cock?'

'As long as I say them well.'

'Someone's got to supply the scintillation,' said Anne. 'I've done my bit. There'll be four females when Lucy shows up and only two of you bright sparks.'

'No one else good enough to grace your salon.'

'I was looking round yesterday. My mates are only good enough for the rugger field.'

'Well, they might have added a touch of Lawrentian interest,' said Glenys darkly. Glenys rarely said anything.

'Made the numbers more even anyway, yes.' Sheila's voice came rather too shrill.

'You talk as if it's going to be a battle or a game, which perhaps it is,' said Mohan.

'I didn't mean to.'

'Don't listen to him, Sheila. What's it going to be? Music or sausage rolls?'

'Sausage rolls,' said Frazer. 'You can't eat music.'

'You'll get fat,' observed Glenys.

'Sometimes you're glad of a bit of weight on the rugger field.'

'For Pete's sake,' said Pete, 'this is an intellectual soirée, not a changing-room.'

'Go on then: you're the intellectual.'

'Given a hat, I would produce a learned paper from it. Or a rabbit.'

'A rabbit,' said Frazer. 'You can't eat a learned paper.'

The bell rang. 'I think I have produced Lucy.'

'Oh Christ,' said Bill, 'you haven't.'

Anne went to the door and Lucy, scented and breathless, came before them. She was tall, good-looking after the old, ample style, and enthusiastic.

'Hi! Had a spot of bother waiting for the bus. Some of you thank your lucky stars you aren't females. What a vee scrumptious spread! How is everyone?'

'Bill's full of sausage and I'm full of ideas.'

'That sounds a wee bit wicked, Peter. Can I dump myself?'

'Come here, honey.' Anne beckoned Mohan and, as soon as he had left the settee, she directed Lucy next to Frazer.

'Pass round the food while I see to the drink.'

'But surely I'm not the last to arrive,' Lucy was saying. 'We need more males.'

'It seems,' said Glenys, 'they are rationed.'

'But the war's been over ages. Anne, I thought there was a choice on the menu. Bill's a dear, etc. But we all know each other. Haven't you something new in stock?'

'I could bring grandad down if he was to be trusted.'

'We must know someone,' said practical Sheila, 'someone we could get on the telephone.'

'Well, there's always Fred of course. Old, rich and Polish, you know. One of my shadier amours.'

'Let's have Fred then,' said Bill. 'Several cheers for Fred.'

'Fred's in Italy,' said Lucy.

'Then why bring Fred up?'

'A lovers' tiff,' Anne said to Peter, smiling up at him.

'There's always those fellows who were taking us home that Friday,' said Sheila. They were the only fellows her bout of thinking had or could have produced.

'Not Popkin!' exclaimed Lucy, who had heard of that Friday's homegoing from Glenys. 'Popikin, Popikin, where have you been?

Befriending the ducks on Bethnal Green.'

'Shut up,' said Frazer, quite unplayful.

Sheila hurried it over, appealing to Anne: 'Who was it, the other one?'

'Frank Griffin.'

Mohan was looking down at her, intent and baffled. 'Griffin?'

'That's what I said.' Anne inspected her manicure. 'If you remember, you had something more important on that night than taking me home. So you asked Frank.'

'Yes, I know I did. Be fair.'

'What's "fair"?'

51

'Well, don't bristle then.'

'I'm not bristling, whatever that means.'

'Where does Popkin come in? I didn't know he was with you.'

'Why don't you fetch the police or something?'

'Is Frank Griffin on the telephone?' asked Sheila. The previous conversation had gone on too quietly for them to catch it.

'It's a shop,' said Bill.

'If it's a shop, it's sure to be on the telephone.'

'Sheila is quite a detective,' said Glenys.

Anne got up. 'A better idea,' she said brightly, 'is for me to look up the address and fetch him in mummy's car. He won't be able to refuse.'

'I'll go,' said Bill.

'What, and leave Lucy stranded? Anyway, there's something about the insurance. Peter, would you take over for a few minutes? You know where everything is.'

The way that Mohan agreed started four trains of speculation. Anne drove fast but lost time locating the street. Driving alone made her feel both freer and more anonymous. Even on short journeys she could imagine she was the sort of girl in American films who speeds across whole states, whose only background is limitless prairie, and who looks at life through the cool screen of sunglasses.

The darkness of the shop when she found it was forbidding. Above the window, she read: CHAS. GRIFFIN & SON. The '& SON' was a recent addition. She didn't know that Frank had brothers. She switched off the engine and was surprised to feel nervous. The shop was so dead-looking. There was a side-door with glass panels through which she could see a blur of dim light somewhere in that great brick box.

She had knocked twice before she heard someone coming. The door was opened a few inches and a man's face peered out suspiciously.

'Mr Griffin?'

'That's right.'

'I've brought the car round to collect Frank. Is it all right?

It's a small party.' Without meaning to Anne was using a cordial but rather condescending tone.

Mr Griffin opened the door. 'You can't be too careful in this district. Do come in, Miss.'

'Cooper, Anne Cooper. Thank you.'

'The car should be all right. This street's not busy in the late hours.'

'Oh, the car doesn't matter,' said Anne casually, forgetting herself that it was irregular to take it out without asking permission beforehand.

'Jane, switch that thing off.'

'You know it's my serial . . . Oh, how do you do?'

'Good evening, Mrs Griffin. Please don't disturb yourself.'

But Mrs Griffin had, in one deft movement, obliterated the commercials, removed her apron and dusted an armchair.

'This is Miss Cooper, my wife. We've introduced ourselves,' said the husband.

'Sit down and have a bit of a warm.'

Anne reacted to this invitation with a more natural smile.

'Sherry's a good warmer. Where are the best glasses, Jane?'

'Right under your nose. Men are awful in the house, don't you think?'

'My grandfather's very handy when Mummy lets him,' said Anne, trying to make their behaviour more easy. 'He was at sea for years. But please, don't bother about the sherry.'

'It's not mother's cooking sherry. I'm in the trade you know and you pick up a few wrinkles about sherries.'

A glass was put into her hand.

'This one's Graham, our youngest. He wasn't clever enough for your sort of school but I might make something of him in the shop.'

Anne smiled at the slight, bespectacled boy; she was trying to make up for his father's tactlessness. Mrs Griffin said: 'He's obsessed with those prehistoric animals. Frank was the same about dogs. We have quite a laugh about it.'

'It's an interesting subject for research.'

'There you are, son. They call him the Professor at school.'

Graham was sent up to fetch Frank and Anne sipped sherry in the small crowded room. She was rather enjoying the stir she'd caused. How Frank would take her visit was of some interest.

'Young lady to see you,' Mr Griffin announced.

'Thanks,' said Frank.

'There's some sherry,' said Mrs Griffin.

'Is it Christmas?'

'Miss Cooper had some.'

'Look after her, son; she's your guest.'

'Hullo. To what do we owe the pleasure?'

It was Anne's turn to be put out. He seemed to have taken up her secret game of being a lady of quality.

'We're having a party. I called round to fetch you.'

'I never received your gilt-edged card.'

'I never sent your gilt-edged card.'

'Frank, you know you're only moping up there in your room. Don't be so ungrateful.'

'Miss Cooper's driven over specially,' said Mr Griffin.

'That's different, if Miss Cooper's *driven* over.'

'This is only an invitation; not a Royal Command Performance,' Anne said, forced into more young-ladyness than she had ever wanted privately to enjoy.

'Isn't it? What if I happen to be busy on an essay? I'm tugging on my bootstraps, remember.'

'You know you're just moping because you won't be sociable of a Sunday night and watch television.'

'All right. I'll fetch my jacket.'

'Frank's very edgy,' Mrs Griffin explained. 'Studying affects him, I think.'

Her husband shamelessly added: 'Our class of people are better off doing real work. Between you and me, it'd be a clinking good thing if he got down to some.'

In the car Anne lit a cigarette. 'I'm sorry I came. I thought you'd be glad.'

'I might have had other arrangements.'

'As you obviously hadn't, why are you so cross?'

'I don't know.'

'Let's go. You can get drunk in real earnest tonight.'

If Frank had anything else to say, he swallowed it for they had accelerated to fifty miles an hour before the shop was out of sight.

Anne came back to an altered scene. Considerable inroads had been made into the trays of food; modern jazz was playing loud and Sheila was jiving with Glenys.

'Hi!' called Lucy from, of all places, Frazer's lap. 'Isn't this Bacchanalian!'

'What's been happening?'

'Peter's gone absolutely mad, hasn't he, darling?'

'He always was.'

'What has happened? Where is he?'

'Here,' said Mohan quietly in her ear. She started. He was unrecognisable when she turned round. The figure in the doorway was all in black. A long old-fashioned waisted coat falling to within inches of the floor, and a thick veil kept on by a velvet skull-cap blacking out the face. Lucy screamed with delight.

Anne was terrified, flooded with a child's fear of the dark, night-terrors compressed into a moment; it was worse though. The black figure was known, was Peter. She recovered into anger.

'What are you doing like that?' Her voice, directed into the impenetrable veil, was unnaturally forced and venomous.

'What are you looking at? What is it, under the veil?'

'Stop it; you're making me frightened.'

'I shall uncover then, like this.' His hand, in a black leather glove was lifted to the corner of the veil. There it paused; then slowly with a delicate, even movement began the unveiling.

Anne saw a nightmare face without features. She screamed and crashed down. The subdued desperation of the musicians continued to fill the room. Lucy was more or less thrown to the floor as Bill darted across. He lifted the girl and put her on the settee. In the doorway the black figure was standing unveiled. Griffin was looking over its shoulder. The others hardly realised what had happened.

'Pete, you silly, bloody fool.'

Sheila, the first to master herself, poured out some brandy. Competently, she chafed back Anne's consciousness. Mohan removed his head-dress. They saw his thin, intelligent face and his fair hair. The black coat set off his head to advantage. His expression was not that of a silly, bloody fool; in the circumstances his expression was puzzling. He seemed to be thinking about something else.

Anne came to quickly and was soon in possession of where she was and why she had fainted.

'Stop fussing, Sheila. I don't want any more brandy. Pete, where did you get that coat?'

'I found it under the stairs. I'm sorry, but you always said you weren't afraid of death.'

'Look, old cock,' said Bill, 'it's not my business but you ought to be bloody well ashamed of yourself. You're not, are you?'

'Would it help if I were? I'll try.'

'Don't be so sodding clever.'

'I'll try not to be.'

'I've a good mind to bash you; and I mean it.'

'Now we're sliding into the medieval—young rugger player threatens to bash up Death.'

'Sod you then,' said Bill, giving the words equal emphasis and going off to find a drink.

Frank came into the room. He was at a loss. Enough of the incident had registered to make his compass veer wildly. His contrived sullenness at home on Anne's arrival now looked childish; he had been acutely anxious when Anne fainted; he could find no explanation for Mohan's behaviour. Now Peter was dispensing the drinks and changing records as if nothing had happened. In his eyes, it seemed, nothing had: his behaviour was neither sheepish nor overtly propitiatory. This perhaps—dressing up and fainting—was a normal part of the relationship Frank had stumbled into. Anne was chatting with Sheila about school-work. She, too, seemed unconcerned. He went up to Frazer who was applying himself to the well-stocked drink table.

'Hullo, Griff,' said Frazer. 'Have some whisky. It corrodes the brain.'

Needing something, Frank took whisky. He did not know Frazer very well and was pleased to find him, the school captain, there.

'The room looks quite gay,' he remarked.

'It's the dim lighting. They might make you a prefect on Monday. Jugg should have ages ago.'

'Make *me* a prefect?' He found the news unexpectedly pleasing. Frank—obviously passed over—had spoken of lack of office as a distinction. It had bolstered his reputation of being a rebel, the man detached, the bird of passage not caught in any official net.

'If Jugg had passed over Draper, I'd have had some faith in the old basket. But a chap like you—Debating Society and so on—that's what the place needs. It's got plenty of roughnecks like me.'

The record stopped and Lucy said to the group in general: 'This is absolutely depraved. Positively pre-war, darlings. Look at William on the bottle. Brussels before Waterloo hardly enters the field.'

'Brussels,' said Frazer, 'was lucky. It didn't have to.'

'There, it's what I've been telling him for weeks. He's brilliant. And now he's turning into a verbal rapier.'

More drink was going down them than any of them wanted or were aware of. Mohan's butler-like stealth had been very effective.

'Don't you feel madly pre-war?' Lucy asked Sheila across the room.

'I don't think so. We don't want another war.'

'But that's what I mean. That's why we're all so absolutely desperate.'

'*You* are,' said Frazer.

'That was rude, darling.'

'For Christ's sake, you seem to think this is Hampstead or bloody Mayfair.'

'And it's only the provinces, isn't it, Frank?' Anne's voice brought a silence. They had all been watching her, noticing how much she was drinking.

'To me it's 'ome,' said Frank.

'We've been sold a substitute for life,' Mohan said, 'and we've come to prefer it to the real thing. As for what Lucy so lucidly said'—a general groan—'I don't think we can be desperate. If death means nothing to you, you can't be desperate; and all over the place people are opting for death. If you tell me that's all balls, I probably agree with you.'

'Anne didn't seem to like Death,' said Glenys.

'That was sly,' from Lucy.

'I play rugger,' said Bill. 'That's why I keep sane.'

'Who's for strip-tease,' said Lucy jumping onto a chair. 'Or party games at least. Postman's Knock sounds obscene I know, but there must be others.'

'Blind Man's Buff,' Sheila suggested.

'That sounds worse,' said Peter.

'What else is there? Come on, you people, think.'

'Scraping the barrel?'

'Thank you, Bill darling. You and your rugger. These party games are ancient fertility rituals. When we were tiny, we simply loved them. Let's be tiny again.'

'Hide-and-Seek then,' said Glenys in the husky voice which she liked to think, with some justification, was seductive.

'Hide-and-Seek. All right,' said Anne. 'Who'll be the seeker?'

'It would be just perfect if Peter dressed up again. How exquisite! We'd be hiding from Death.'

'She's barmy,' said Bill.

'Someone else,' advised Sheila. 'Anne has been quite frightened enough already.'

'Frank then.'

'That's a good idea, Glenys.'

Frank it was to be. After warning them not to stray into the old man's room, Anne led the hiders into the hall. 'We can go anywhere else,' she said. 'Only for God's sake don't break anything or get locked in a cupboard. Frank, stay there until twenty past, that gives us three minutes. No, make it five. There's a clock on the mantelpiece.'

When the door had closed, Frank started on the whisky. This was his chance to kiss a girl. Judging by her tone of voice and the glances she had given him, Glenys would make things easy in one of those upstairs rooms. She had suggested the game and she had suggested the seeker. It was twenty past. With one hand on the mantelpiece, he watched the ormulu clock for the passing of the final minutes.

In the hall he paused, listening. There was no sound. The six must be safely in hiding, holding their breath. All that held breath was almost palpable. He had never walked so softly. The ample, shallow stairs soon turned at a landing. There, framed on the wall, was the Lord's Prayer worked on a sampler with the name Moira Cooper beneath and the date 1832. In a search like this anything might be found—people he had never seen before, people who were dead. He shivered.

The lights went off suddenly with a click. Frank thought it was a fuse: at home the fuses were forever going. But he realised it could also have been the master switch. It would be like Anne to go down to the cellar to do that. She might want to get even with Peter. If anything, he was angry—his anger revived. Recently she had governed his behaviour and made him her fool to be tricked into trespassing, lying and misery; to be picked up like a parcel, just to make up numbers. On the point of shouting out, he remembered Glenys. On top of the drink, the darkness assured him of the exploit. He carefully felt his way to the first floor. Anne's thoughtlessness nearly cost the Cooper family what was perhaps a valuable vase. He wrestled with the thing before balancing it again on its flimsy perch. Still there was no sound or breath.

Frank leaned against the wall, trying to develop a sixth sense. The landing window materialised as a moon-washed square, silhouetting the statuette of a naked goddess which he'd noticed from the hall on his first visit. Could Anne be waiting for him in the conservatory? He was a fool; she had given him no sign. It was for Mohan she had staged this black-out; for him she had agreed to Lucy's wild proposal. They were together now, at this minute, in some hiding-place he would never find. Brutally, he imagined finding Glenys, kissing her until it hurt. The statue in the window was Glenys now, not Anne—the nakedness, not the moonlight. He went on his way and into a room with an open door.

His body was tense, he felt the blood in it. Death he could have effortlessly struck down. A cough swung him round. His quick hand brushed coats. He sensed the presence of a girl there, among the coats hanging behind the door. When he darted forward, the coats came down, one for a moment enveloping his head. He flicked it off and in the flurry he discovered the body of the hider and gripped her waist. The moist palms of his hands felt every strand of the rough dress material. His body and all his actions were unaccustomed to him, precise and quick. The girl's mouth on his tasted of the spirits he'd been drinking. She had no opportunity to struggle and the movements of her mouth were as appropriate for passion as for protest.

As soon as he'd released his hold, Frank was left stranded. Social situation had returned, the need for words. Phrases ran through his head which had momentarily had no consciousness, no thoughts, no phrases. Glenys, I love you. Even in the dark I love you. I found you in the dark. The tiny, impossible phrases skeltered through his brain. With a soft explosion it was light. His eyes were filled with the colours of coats.

Frank and Anne looked at each other.

CHAPTER 7

THOSE who had avoided rugger swam. The public bath was small and old-fashioned but convenient to the school. Priority went where it should, to the top. And in the season rugby football was the top. For every official thought given to the swimmers, twenty went to the state of the pitch. The masters in charge of swimming had battled for status with their ladder of proficiency certificates and their talk of life-saving. But on any Monday afternoon you had only to look about you to gauge the degree of their failure: the figures in the bath's close and overloaded air were all too obviously Refugees from Sport.

'Come on, you fellows! We don't *give* these certificates away. You have to work for 'em. I've not seen *you* in the water yet.'

The young master, safe himself in flannels, was rumoured to have been a Guards officer.

'It's cold,' someone complained. The master sighed. Before him on the brink Levis was standing, pelican-like, clasping his white body with great, gaunt arms and poking the blind hatchet of his face hopelessly over the waters. Impossible! They were poor material; and he thought of his days in the Royal Corps of Signals—not the Guards—of mess nights, his swagger-stick. And now this pustular contraption, and he couldn't even push him in.

'Griffin, for heaven's sake ask Levis to join you in there.'

'Come on! It's warm.'

'Can't swim,' said Levis.

'You can dog-paddle,' Frank shouted, demonstrating. The trim white master was coaxing from behind. Then Levis came in, suddenly in a cascade of angles. He made rapidly across the bath with a blind animal stroke. The master sighed again. What a ludicrous ending to a military career.

Frank was swimming hard; fighting for breath down on the

cold alien tiles of the deep end; flinging himself from the board —furious to be tired, to lose himself in action. Here at least he was the same, half naked. His blazer was away, out of sight with the braid folded and awaiting his mother's needle in the top pocket. A whistle went. They took themselves off to the showers.

Now it was over they all felt the benefit. Levis himself was discussing the breast-stroke. The chlorine in the air was replaced by relief. Unlikely people sang. Soap was plentiful and your nakedness relaxing. Puritans and Catholics could forget that flesh is unclean: there was too much soap and hot water about.

'Hullo, Frank. I tried to have a word with you. But you athletes!'

In the steam it was Mohan.

'Oh, hullo. I didn't see you.'

'I'm afraid I wasn't much in evidence.'

'I saw Hare first thing and he told me about making me a prefect. I didn't know that you and Bill had resigned.'

'Jugg's animal cunning.'

'I feel terrible. I would never have accepted.'

'Of course not. Anyway, what does it matter? It's not a question of the eternal verities.'

Frank took Mohan's hand, surprising them both. They were naked. What was good for the Spartans was embarrassing in the system emulating Sparta.

'And now Draper's been made captain.'

'Trust our Hare's banal sense of theatre.'

'All the same,' said Frank. He had nearly mentioned the mistake of kissing Anne but, for one thing, the moment had passed.

'Let it ride,' Peter said. 'No one's going to hold it against you.' He smiled. Mohan was one of the few whose body was beautiful. It was impossible to connect him with the black shape of Death. Griffin turned away and started dressing.

Frank went back to his studies. Before the conference he had worked hard but now in school and after he didn't give himself a minute. Even at meals there was a book. Mrs Griffin could not get him to let up, no matter how much trouble she took with boiled egg and fresh-mashed tea. The father, noting his son's studious obsession, told his wife that the scene at breakfast had had the desired result. But all she said was that she was anxious for his eyes. Graham volunteered for all the small household duties which the brothers usually shared.

At school Frank got the name of a hermit and a swot. There was some connection between this change and his being made a prefect but nobody could say what. It had taken time for the resignations to become universally wondered-at but now a web of hidden scandal was being discerned. The protagonists were callously uncommunicative, infuriatingly tactful. Draper himself was richer in wisdom than had been hoped. He filled his new position colourlessly, like some gas with just an unpleasant tang of presence. There was no organised protest at so unpopular a captain.

When a moment was spared to discuss Griffin, all that was arrived at was that promotion had made a swot of him. But he was only a fringe figure. Draper, Frazer and Mohan held the stage. Popkin of course had been re-assessed. The subtler observers thought that he might be the keystone, if the crazy arch of these happenings had a keystone.

After half-term the talk died down. Life in the prefects' room got back it's old quality of piecemeal administration and scholarship. Those going up for Oxford and Cambridge scholarships stayed only for one bottle of milk; and when a rugger player talked of Frazer as captain no one momentarily detected mutiny against Draper.

Early in November Draper called a meeting. Everyone was there on time, the headmaster having released prefects from dinner-duty. Frank found a seat near the door. He was sorry to be at the meeting and did not share the busy, idle curiosity of his colleagues. Grant, the new vice-captain—a tall red-haired scientist—stood in the focal position by the window. Draper had not yet appeared.

'Where's Draper?'

'He's coming,' said Grant.

'So's Christmas.' And, 'Licking Hare's a.o.'

'When he gets here, give him a hearing.' Grant, who sounded perpetually tired, spoke with no intonation. 'Being captain's not an easy job.'

'Bill Frazer would agree with you.'

'Sod Draper. I'm going.'

Grant wanted them to be patient.

Draper made his entry. There was some clapping. 'I'm not going to keep you. There's just one major thing.'

'Get it out then.'

'That'll do, Williams.'

' "That'll do," he says!'

'Don't make things difficult, Williams,' Grant wearily pleaded.

'It's about discipline,' said Draper. 'The Head wants a general tightening up. I happen to agree with him. As from now, senior prefects can give detentions like the masters.' He pulled a piece of paper from his top pocket. 'Looking through, I've got the names of the prefects who don't—who are not pulling their weight.'

Williams was on his feet, heel-clicking. 'Pliss excuse,' he said. 'Is dat ze same for to frow ze veight about, Herr Kapitan?'

'You're on my list. So's Griffin. It's bloody silly for some of us to give out lines when other people let them get away with it.'

'Am I on your black list?'

'You're efficient, Westbrook, we all know that. This is Hare's idea.'

'Pity him, pity him. There he stands.' Williams, excited, was on his feet again. 'And what manner of thing is he, comrades? He is but a poor lavatory whence these things cometh from on high. What man of you despitheth your humble friend?'

It was a hook for considerable prepared laughter. Draper was staring, fixed and thinking. Williams was taking a bow; Grant uneasy like a man wakened in the night. And then Draper contrived a laugh. The right muscles in his mirthless face moved and stopped the mutiny. Their laughter died out because it had not arisen spontaneously: the supremacy of real laughter wasn't there. Williams sat down.

'Ted's right,' said Draper. 'Sometimes this is a dirty, shitty job.' He made a dignified exit followed by Grant. This scrappy affair marked the establishment of Draper. Revolt had consumed itself and in the unthinking his plausible act had brought out a useful, shallow sympathy.

'Draper's right, to be fair,' said Westbrook.

'Fair, my fanny!' Williams looked round his supporters. 'This is only the beginning, boyoes.'

But his supporters had changed sides. Many condemned him for their own misplaced laughter and when a bell sounded only Williams and Griffin remained.

'Wonder why we never had a bloody revolution? What England wants is more Welshmen, man. Or a kick up the East Anglia.'

Frank laughed. He was relieved that Draper had made only one reference to him.

'And while I think of it stop reading so many bloody books. You'll bust your eyeballs.'

'To hear is to obey.'

'You don't want to be blind *and* barmy.'

CHAPTER 8

'TAKE young men in uniform, boys mostly. Makes 'em look young. Terrible. I've seen it twice. When I was in France. . . .'

'Father!' shouted Mrs Cooper. 'No anecdotes, *please*.'

'All right, all right. I can take a hint. Your hints. I'm in the way; you don't need tell me that. I'm full of words and wind, aren't I? Well, I am. It's my age.' The old man writhed in his chair, knocking the teacup off the arm. 'There, look what I've done!' He sounded pleased, as if he had proved what he had been saying. His daughter knelt down to gather the pieces.

'Look what your grandfather's done.'

'What's that then?' asked Anne from the window where she was reading behind the barricade of the back of the settee.

'He's broken my last cup.'

Anne shifted position and looked over into the room. Her mother was holding up fragments of flowered china. The old man, motionless in his chair, appeared guilty. There they were. The two preceding generations locked in a childish combat but for the noise and screaming. Anne felt the last month's list-lessness all at once, like a hole in things, a void dragging at her stomach. Her mother, the old man: these were puppets, drab fictions.

'It's only a cup.'

'It's the last one. All the others are broken. It was a wedding present.' She cried. Hopeless.

Anne went over. 'For goodness' sake.'

'I'll be all right, dear. I'm sorry. I don't expect you to under-stand.'

'Don't be so sentimental.'

'At my age sentiment is all you have left.'

'Age! Age! Mummy, really. You and grandpa are a pair.'

66

'It's my hands. They're not right.' The old man, explaining and apologetic.

'You've upset him,' said Anne quietly. 'And all for a cup.'

'It's more than a cup. I was a young woman when I first washed up that tea service.'

Anne took a big breath. Her next words must be stiff. It was too bad, this fuss over a cup.

'No it wasn't. An old, cracked cup, that's all it was. A dirty piece of china.'

And now more snuffling, and the old man producing a tobacco-stained handkerchief.

'You're growing so hard-hearted, Anne. You're not my little girl at all.'

That did it. 'Mother, why don't you differentiate between what matters and what doesn't matter a damn?' Priggish, sixth-form, yes, but she didn't care. 'Your marriage is breaking and you cry about a cup!'

Mrs Cooper laid her head on her father's knee, darkening the grey cloth with sprouting tears. Anne knelt, putting her arm round the trembling shoulders. Now she wanted tears, but there were none. The old man's ever-moist eyes, there perhaps were tears, but Anne's were dry. 'There, there,' she said.

Mrs Cooper recovered, dabbed, laughed at the ruined make-up, looked at her daughter like a child awaiting instruction.

'I shouldn't have said that; but I feel so pent-up lately.' Calmly, Anne took a few seconds to locate a suitable phrase. 'You know how it is sometimes.'

'Of course, darling. I'm thoughtless, aren't I? Silly old harridan of a mother. I know I am. I'll make us some tea.'

Trite little sentences, magic achieved. The old man had only half understood, sitting uncertain there, old man's flesh. In the kitchen her mother was happy. Catharsis. Only Anne herself was unmoved—the unmoved mover.

In the window-bay it was now too dark to read. She lit a cigarette and watched its smoke slipping off into the dusky air. Peter was busy again to-night. He was trying for a Cambridge scholarship, going there in a few weeks' time, going up. She put him there in the cloisters or whatever it was they had

67

there. And he was walking in a black cloak among great pillars of stone. He'd probably get in all right and Cambridge would set him up—let him fly his full extent. He was a hawk. She knew he would be lost to her for ever. But it was a case of not knowing what you had lost until you lost it. She would have liked his company to-night. It was, what, three, four weeks since the party? If she loved him, the night of the party had changed it. She had lost spirits; become morose, obsessive. Was that love? Now Peter was always dressed in black for her, strange. But he was handsome so. He was removed, independent; no longer was he brilliantly ingratiating. And her destiny as a woman . . . she was tired now. Half in love with easeful death. Keatsian mood. This was, after all, a mere overdose of Literature. And as for company, Sheila would come round.

Finishing the fag, she declined Sheila with thanks. Perhaps Frank Griffin was indicated: she liked him and he amused her. He had figured in the party's other odd happening: the old man, who had placed himself at the window, reminded her of it. It had been childish of him to turn off the mains like that, but he was no more childish than her mother, than herself. He needed cheering and the thought unfroze her. Cheer yourself up by cheering others: what you did came back an hundredfold; there was a whole religion founded on it.

Anne kissed his cheek. 'Oy,' she said, 'I'm taller than you.'

'I'd go away; I ought to. I know when I'm not wanted. Your dad doesn't like me. I forget I've no right now to speak my mind.'

'Let's run away to one of those places you used to tell me about. Shall we?'

'I made most of those places up, ducky. I never went further than Gibraltar and Norway.'

'Somewhere where the sun always shines.'

'You go out and have a good time. I enjoy that. I'll do here, looking outside for a bit. I can get down to a bit of doing nothing now and enjoy it.'

She kissed her grandfather again and left him, feeling better. It was possible he did like stillness and silence and that he could forget how old he was. Few old people perhaps were unlucky enough to retain young energies and be crucified on old age. She took tea in the kitchen, chatting to her mother about potted plants and the price of coal. Recovery was complete there, too. Anne felt like Florence Nightingale. It was better to leave the house on such a note. The car was forthcoming with an injunction only to take a scarf.

The roads were pleasantly empty and the light was following the sun to the west in a definite gradation, stage by stage. It was a nightfall governed by low, heavy rolls of cloud. The effect was an indoor one. She was driving along wide roads flanked by low, century-old buildings, as under a canopy. The clarity of the outlines and the absence of people exhilarated her and put her in possession of what she saw. On either side the orange streetlamps burning, burned only to make artistic contrast at this time, adding no light to the road. It was as if the Corporation had forgotten utility and squandered the rates on beauty. To be out, alone, driving the car was enough in itself she found.

But then by chance she saw the corner shop of Griffin & Son. She pulled up. It looked as dead as ever. The daytime frontage might blossom with commercial news but in the evening there was only sightless glass in front of a green blind—that and the painted name.

She hadn't seen Frank since the party. All she had heard of him from Peter was that he had been made a prefect and had made himself a recluse. Here was one of life's little ironies. Mohan said that Griffin was cut up when he found out he was serving under Draper but she knew that the irony went deeper: Frank had taken Popkin's place. Still, great men are made when others fall; and school office was of no real importance. Anne herself was school vice-captain and set no store by it. Frank, though, might be tying himself in knots of contrition in there. What with Popkin and the kiss at the party, he might well be suffering agonies. And, if he was, it was her fault. Poor Frank!

'It's the curse of my beauty,' she said, stepping out of the car. There was a light scudding wind and it was colder than she had expected. To knock at the side door and risk the parents' hospitality and Frank's churlishness a second time undecided her. She scanned the building and noticed the pale blob of a

69   C*

face at one of the upper windows. She waved and the window was opened. Frank looked out.

'Hullo, Juliet,' she called.

'Hullo. I can't remember what she says.'

'Ad lib, then.'

'What are you doing here?'

'Just passing. Drawn here by invisible threads. Does it look as if I'm at the bottom of a tomb? Juliet said Romeo did. It's significant. You can pretend you're still swotting by dabbling in conversation with me.'

'You look cold.'

'But healthy. I take Bile Beans.' She *was* cold and getting a crick in the neck. 'Want to come for a ride?'

He agreed to come.

'You were ready quickly.'

'I came as I was.'

'Good.' she started up. 'I was getting browned off.'

Frank was nervously keeping his eyes on the road.

'Relax. I hardly ever crash.'

'I'm not used to cars.'

'They're not one of the things that matter, anyway.'

'Tell me what does.'

'You tell me.' Anne looked at him and swerved.

'Careful!'

'Sorry. I'm quite safe really.'

'Safe!'

Anne switched on the sidelights. It was a big car, rather plush, but the household's second best. Mr Cooper was a rich man, he thought.

'Pity it's not light,' she said. 'We could have found a landscape to suit our mood. I know of a ruined cotton mill hidden away down olde English lanes. In Dickens's time they used to import waifs from London to work there. They got them by stories of good food, worked them to death in a year and buried them by the river. Then there's another place with acres of slag heap and brown water like the end of the world. That's what we look for in landscapes, wouldn't you say? Pegs to hang our morbid sensibility from.'

'I thought people went to cheer themselves up.'

'Ah, you belong to the aspiring bourgeoisie. The Coopers are a house in decline.'

'I only like arty coloured films about the countryside.'

'*Ars longa, vita brevis.* It should be the other way round. The real country make you hungry and wears your feet out. You get the best angles in the pictures and a complete change of scene next minute. That's why art's more satisfactory than life: no sore feet. Wow! you must be admiring my intellect, I think.'

'I admire you altogether.'

'I shouldn't,' Anne said, sadly. Then, 'Tell me about school, Prefect.'

'You know about that?'

'Peter told me.'

'You know I was tricked into it?'

'Were you?'

'I didn't know about Mohan and Frazer resigning.'

'He told me you didn't.'

'Things seem to be getting back to normal. Popkin's pretty odd though. Sometimes he does funny things. He hardly speaks to anyone.'

'Give him my love,' said Anne.

Griffin stared at the girl in amazement. He could study her profile intently; since the first swerve she had kept her eyes on the road. Faint light dusted the outlines of what he saw. Her face was now beautiful but expressionless. Her words, so overwhelmingly cynical and callous, had been delivered like official disasters—summonses, call-up papers—with no ill-will. He was angry with her again for disturbing him. She collected him like a parcel and remained so guarded from him, so damnably withdrawn. Their exchanges were only wit, a counterfeit intimacy.

'Why don't we talk seriously?' he asked.

'Sooner or later, Frank Griffin, you always want to celebrate a solemn mass.'

'Keep that sort of joke for Mohan. I kissed you, remember.'

'Only by mistake.'

'What if I knew it was you and not Glenys?'

'But you didn't, did you?'

'I thought it was Glenys.'

'Good, truth-telling boy.'

'One day you might say what you mean,' said Frank, angry and stupid.

'Perhaps I do.'

CHAPTER 9

IT was the term of the cross-country run: the junior on Tuesday and the senior on Wednesday afternoon. Until the Monday of that week those in the sixth-form had relaxed, knowing themselves immune, able at last to decide for themselves whether to enter or not. Some who had suffered five annual runs declared themselves willing to undergo a sixth; now it was voluntary they said they had no objection. Many really meant to take part. The previous ordeals had settled in their minds as an epic residue where comic incidents involving others were remembered and the racking of their own bodies forgotten. On Monday morning, however, Hare announced that all would participate. 'The old tag *mens sana in corpore sano* is as true to-day as it was in Juvenal's time,' he said. 'And it has merit, even for our sixth-formers.' Some blamed Draper; others pointed to the visit of Her Majesty's Inspectors. By Wednesday all but the morally strong-minded and the physically incapable were reconciled.

Frank joined Mohan and Frazer on the starting line. The day was bright and chilly, heaping white cloud into a blue enamel sky. Along the line there was the familiar smell of old sweat from seldom-washed running kit. Faces looked different set above the red, green, yellow or blue house-shirts. Nervousness showed in sallies of wit and less inhibited, less real laughter.

'Bill's health is so rude,' said Mohan, 'that he ought to be made to apologise for it.'

'It's high time you did some physical exercise. What are you doing, Griff?'

'Limbering up,' said Frank.

'Looks like you want to go somewhere.'

'Not on this run, then.'

'Do you good.'

'This is the first thing Hare's done which Bill approves of,' Mohan remarked, punching Frazer in the stomach. 'Bet I beat you.'

'You will now just to spite me. You and your bloody nervous energy—dressing up as Death and all.'

Draper trotted by in new kit. He was a good runner with the runner's leanness of limb and visible muscle. To-day he was everyone's friend and nobody's boss.

The worst stretch came first. When the starting line had been settled, the whistle would be blown. There were two hundred yards of uphill playing-field separating the runners from the gate. This sorted them out, giving encouragement to the leaders and hopelessness to the rear. Although he hated it, Frank felt some touch of desperate elation in the last stationary moment; if only because he was one of such a crowd. He was part of their tension. Bull looked at his stop-watch, placed the whistle between his lips. They were off.

The leaders broke away immediately. The race was between a dozen, no more. The rest were only there to make up the field—to swell the casualty list and augment the winner's glory. Some ragged cheering from the junior school sent them off. They'd had theirs and could afford to be enthusiastic. Around him, Frank saw familiar faces, expressionless. Now they were all different people. He who could run was a hero; though the rest of the year a fool. Frank looked for thoughts to tide him over. He pictured Anne—a woman behind every exploit; he remembered something—a self-comforting thing from previous years. They were charging horsemen, whose armour or red tunics glowed. You sat your horse easily but with your whole being on edge. Light there, you let its power pace beneath you; and like this—riding above your body—the gate was reached and your feet hit tarmac. Breathing easier, Frank was pleased not to be last. He overtook several down the hill.

The first checkpoint was manned by the new French assistant. Excitable Gaul. The country, so near school, was unfamiliar, with its small fields and ragged hedges. The French assistant had said that, after the Continent, England was like

74

a 'rough-haired beast sleeping'. He was thinking only of the hedges but the most revolutionary members of the group had felt a welling-up of patriotism. So England likes herself thought —sleeping. When she awakes, watch out!

This was the sea-mark of the town and for every haystack there was a wood-yard or scrap-iron dump. The water they crossed by a metal bridge was neither industrial canal nor rural stream. Birds sang; but traffic was also audible. Now that Griffin had found his pace, he was his childish horseman no longer. Distant slag heaps reminded him that, had it been light, Anne would have taken him to the ruined mill or the mining country. But instead they had driven around for half an hour with nothing to say to each other. Anne was ruining his work and spoiling his sleep. He blamed neither her nor himself. He hadn't thought it out. Success with her—and it was impossible—would be a betrayal of Mohan. He saw himself already as Hare's Judas and thought that life was beginning now in earnest with moral problems, self-denial, wrenching yourself straight along the guiding edge of scruple. He was pretty miserable, but how could you be good and self-respecting otherwise? Fancies about Anne were cut short. Always there was Mohan. And here was Mohan, walking ahead of him.

'I left Bill to it. Stone in my shoe. I'm walking.'

Frank slowed to a trot. To walk would not do. He must keep up the motions of running.

'Draper ahead?'

'Sure to be; he's out to win. Personal feud with Williams.'

'Got a job on.'

'You go on. I've got a stone in my shoe.'

'So long, Captain Oates.'

Mohan laughed. Frank resumed his pace.

The second checkpoint was being kept by Hutton, a young, hopeless maths master who was being murdered by the brats in the third form. The runners had to cross a barbed-wire fence. Hutton, the idiot, had draped his good raincoat over it. Compassion might have made him do it; but this was Raleigh's favour-currying cloak. Hutton made himself despicable by throwing himself on the mercy of merciless schoolboys. He had

75

so mismanaged things that even feeling sorry for him degraded you.

After the fence the course ran straight for some way up a slight incline. Griffin had left the stragglers behind and was in sight of the main body. There was only one other runner before him on this stretch. Frank gained on him. The other was clumsy but dogged. His motion and the anonymous house-shirt made him unrecognisable. Frank reckoned to know all the upper school by sight. The problem of this identity was a spur. They met at a stile. Popkin had been the stranger.

Popkin clambered blindly over and back into his ungainly stride.

'Hold on.'

'What do you want?'

'Nothing.'

They thudded along side by side. After the strangeness of the starting line and the torment of the first mile, bodies settled into the routine and you were stimulated, your mind freed. Thought took on an epic quality. Frank's relationship to Popkin now that they were running together had a wider significance. A future essay might incorporate something on the physical nature of epic.

Frank said, 'I didn't know you were good at running, Tony.' He said it to be friendly, but as he said it he analysed his motives. He was condescending to the unattractive Popkin, bracketing him with Hutton. And to mention running after the incident in the park might be taken the wrong way.

'I'm not blaming you,' said Popkin at length, the length of twenty yards. 'I'm not bearing malice for what you did. I could get my own back but I've gone beyond that. I choose to suffer.'

Frank had nothing to say.

'When something like that happens, you sort of grow up,' said Popkin. 'You get over the normal needs.'

'How do you mean, Tony?'

'I mean insight through suffering.'

'Do you mean all this?'

'You don't understand,' said Popkin, never moving his eyes from the middle-distance. 'You and Anne and high-and-mighty Mohan.'

76

'Tony, are you all right?'

'I am all right, but I'm different now. That girl Anne gives herself to a fellow whenever she looks at him.' He laughed, short and desperate. 'I was fooled with the rest of you. Frazer and Mohan had their glory. They don't know how ignorant they are.' Popkin turned his head. Frank caught his foot and stumbled. He imagined he had seen insanity in Popkin's eyes.

'I'm putting on a spurt,' he said and doubled speed. Soon he had put a safe stretch of meadow between himself and Popkin's terrible world.

Frank was stiff for a day or two. He had come in high on the list—twenty-something. It was inexplicable. Only he knew that Popkin had done it. He was pleased that after a while he could smile at the explanation he'd arrived at: the fact was, he was better at running away from things than towards them. And because of the race he found it easier to concentrate on work and get Anne out of his mind. He could spend hours in his room sorting out Disraeli or searching for the *mot juste* in rendering a French unseen. He was an academic after all; real life, the things which mattered, were arrived at by intellectual application. When he came out of a book, he was nicer to his family and in return nothing was said about reading at table.

One evening he had let up to make tea. Both parents were out on one of their rare visits to Mrs Griffin's sister's where they would watch the same programmes on a different screen. It was a pity they were not like the rest of the street, happy pub-goers once or twice a week; but it was a change to have the house to himself, to be in sole possession of its brown and yellow familiarity. He was surprised when Graham walked into the kitchen. 'I thought you'd gone round to Aunty's?'

'Nope. I got out of it.'

'Good for you.'

'It's not that I don't like her. But, you know.'

'Have some of my tea then: the cup that neither cheers nor inebriates.'

'Cowper,' said Graham, pronouncing it as spelt.

'Said Cooper,' said Frank. Long study maketh pedants. 'I didn't know you were an Eng. Lit. expert, Gray.'

'I'm reading some things myself.'

'I didn't know.' Frank was humbled. His own brother was a stranger; reading Literature with no outside encouragement, no exam in view. 'I can lend you some books. You could have a bash at "O" Level.'

'Our school doesn't do G.C.E. Anyway I'm leaving to go into the shop.'

'Is that what you want to do?'

'What dad says is right. I didn't pass the scholarship.'

'That doesn't mean a thing. We ought to talk more. Perhaps I can help you.' As he said it, Frank wondered how. What did it matter that Cowper's name was pronounced like Anne's, when you set against that Graham's unaided attempt to read poetry? A sentimental admiration for all self-educators and for the wisdom of the uneducated swept over him. He re-assessed the old pensioner in the pub whom he had forgotten.

Later he re-assessed himself. The study he was immersed in was perhaps an escape from life. Poetry was about life, novels were about life but they were not life. The smell of gas in the kitchen, the friction with his father—these were life. Then, quicker to lead you astray, Graham and the nameless strugglers; Anne—the panoply of love and war—life again. Those few words with his brother had reordered his thinking.

Lately it was true he had made some real progress, and not merely in examination-proficiency. He'd done some hard and painful thinking. Such thinking *was* painful: it stretched you. He had been discovering Marlowe and was seeing things through those towering, desperate eyes. Next week it might be someone less torturing, but for days he lived heroically—in his brain.'Like Shelley's, Marlowe's sensuality was intellectual,' he wrote in an essay. But what did he know of sensuality? What was it all worth? He wondered if the sudden sensual-intellectual mix-up over Anne was going to lead to nothing more than a few epigrams in his school essays.

CHAPTER 10

THE winner of the senior cross-country had been Williams; Draper came second. It got about that Williams had cheated by cutting off the last corner. It was confirmed by the next group of runners several hundred yards behind that McCormack had only just taken up position when they got there. As Williams and Draper had made record time, the music master had doubtless thought he could spend a few minutes on the way listening to birdsong. Draper cautiously let out that Williams had been just behind him, then, when he next saw him, some way ahead turning into the school gates. Because of McCormack's inefficiency, nothing could be proved. Draper was testing his ground. Then Williams himself let it be known that he had cheated. Draper had to choose between turning a blind eye and being thought a rotten sportsman and a liar for spreading the tale or insisting on a full enquiry when Williams would brazen it out and a major scandal ensue. Politic, Draper chose to say nothing.

One day about a week after the race they both happened to be using the library. A good number of others were present.

Williams was talking to Mohan but in a loud, public voice designed to carry round the room. 'I enjoyed that race; the best man won of course. At home we have to run over the mountains to get a drop of drink on Sundays.'

'Stop boasting, bloody mountain goat,' said one of the studious.

'Can't help being the man I am.'

'You can pipe down in the library,' Draper said.

'Sour grapes never got anyone anywhere,' said Williams, stepping up his Welsh accent. 'That was said to me once. And do you know what I replied? "They got Hannibal over the

79

Alps," I said. That was quick, man. It's agile we are in the valleys.'

Tactically, Draper had lost the initiative but the time had come for a public statement. 'Most of us here know how you won, Williams.'

'Accusing me of cheating? Was it a corner I cut off? Well, well, well.'

'Shut up,' said Draper.

'Man, you ruddy creep, you. Say I did cheat, it's because you're not worth beating fairly. '

Draper closed the atlas he had been using and got up to go.

'I don't want to know your twisted reasons,' he said.

'He's Jugg to a tee!' Williams was dancing up and down in jubilation as Draper left the room.

'For God's sake pipe down,' said Westbrook, 'I'm working.'

Grant confronted Williams. 'Cheating isn't funny,' he said. 'I'd advise you not to boast about it.'

Williams yawned. 'Go and have forty winks, Grant boy. He won't be taking this to Jugg, not for once he won't.'

Grant followed Draper out of the swing-door.

'I'm getting rid of them,' said Williams. 'It makes my bloody blood boil!'

'Sending Celts to Methodist chapels, what else can you expect?' said Mohan.

'Thank you, Peter bach. The epigram from Rome, you are. Why do you put up with Draper, you, the hero of this revolution?'

'That was between me and myself.'

'That means between him and his maker. He keeps his conscience in his wallet.' They watched Popkin go and looked at each other.

Rain sniped down as they left school. The sky was massive spectacular silver, going black at four o'clock. Frank wheeled his cycle, talking to Mohan. An unmade drive led them down, with the playing fields to one side and the back of a housing estate on the other. Smaller boys whooped, capless. Mohan ordered one of them not to run; only to be told that he was no longer a prefect. The descent from the school on its windy hill to the road home was a daily affront to Hare's rule. His pupils scented freedom on that slope and charged away under his windows like hounds.

Music and the sounds of tea-time came from the houses on their right; whilst on the left the playing-fields were umbrous, deserted, like a battlefield—the levels of that unnatural landscape seemed so gloomy. They sniffed at the coming night. The city's lights were growing around and below them; winter stabbed at them and Frank rejoiced. Suddenly he was as wide as that scene: a feeling of promise swept him to its height, width, power and light. Knowing the promise would never be fulfilled didn't matter. He could have shouted. In his throat he did.

'What's up? Indigestion?'

'No. I'm happy.'

'That's much more serious. No Englishman should admit to that without qualification.'

'No qualifications,' said Frank. 'Not even being English, Midland English, mid-twentieth-century Midland English.'

Mohan smiled. It was impossible to get over to him any of the momentary exultation. Frank pulled himself together; Mohan was talking.

'Have you spoken to Popkin lately?'

'No,' said Frank.

'He said something crazy in the library to-day about my conscience. I'm getting some non-conformist's thing about it, myself. It's very depressing.'

'What did Popkin say?'

'Oh, nothing much. I have terrible fits of depression, you know. All the saints did. Why did I resign for instance? Was it pride?'

'You've got to take things as they come,' said Frank.

'If you can't do right without this built-in absurdity clause, why bother?'

It made Frank uncomfortable to hear Mohan in such an uncharacteristic mood. He looked tired, wan in the failing light. His fair, lank hair was plucked by the cold wind.

'You're in for the 'flu.'

'Sin is a stomach-ache, damnation a virus. You're right. I'm full of it—'flu I mean. We're working too hard. We ought to organise something, an outing: you know, picnics and red waggon wheels—like the memoirs of an Edwardian childhood. Where is there to go in winter?'

'Drinking?' Frank suggested.

'We don't want more talk. Climbing up mountains. We talk too much. They train us to dissect all the time. We're too clever by half, aren't we?'

Frank agreed and mounted his bike. By going further round he could have had ten minutes more of Mohan's company. But he wanted to be off and alone.

'See you to-morrow.'

Frank called a farewell and got going. He had thought Mohan so possessed and self-assured but now his own limited but secure views were dissolving. He had been charting a number of mirages and they were disappearing.

There was an outing a week or so later but Mohan—whose 'flu had finally put him to bed—wasn't one of the party. It was arranged by the Joint Sixth-Form Society, whose experienced hikers had picked on a part of Derbyshire where, the radio promised, snow would be falling. The hike was an annual event with a special aura of drink and seduction. That Hare and the girls' headmistress permitted it at all was a wonder. Possibly they felt justified in ignoring what took place at the weekend; or perhaps the thought that such goings-on went on in another county comforted them. Or else they didn't know about it; or else they didn't mind.

Frank looked on it as a big day, a symbolic day. In all his life he had never made such an expedition. Previous holiday-trips had all been family affairs—a day run to Belle Vue when his father had muddled the tickets and had tried to bluster through by standing on his dignity; the summer fortnights at Skegness.

The corner where the coach was to pick up the final passengers was on a hill, the shoulder of the city. Frank got there early and watched the road, anxious lest the coach slip by unnoticed and with it his new life. Realising how early he was, he looked about him. Where there might have been a wide view over towards Derbyshire were the tall obstructions of derelict and half-dismantled lace factories and the shapes of new but drab buildings. He had heard that people ordered them by the yard direct from factories and he started to dwell on the state of modern culture, etc. But there was plenty to take his mind off that. Behind him was a pub called of all things the Sir John Borlace Warren; there was a shop kept by one Cyrus Hazard and another by Olivia Jude. Then the people in the streets were humanity when you looked twice and not just 'modern humanity'. An old woman had sold a flower to a natty gent and was fixing it in his buttonhole. A hearse went by at an undignified thirty-five. No cars followed. Its sombre drivers were making time for a smoke. Beauty well-shod paraded by.

A minute to go. He started worrying. Then one or two other hikers arrived and, on time, apparently with no intention to give him the slip, the hired coach pulled in. The automatic door opened and they clambered aboard. The old faces, new and fancy anoraks, rucksacks, cigarette smoke. Frank looked round for Anne. There were few empty seats. He couldn't see her. The vehicle jerked forward. He crashed down in a place by the door. Grant, reading Finlay's *Introduction to Physical Chemistry*, had the window. Just across the gangway he saw Lucy.

'Hi,' she said. 'Where's William Frazer, the wretch?'

Frank said he thought Bill wasn't coming but he wasn't certain.

'That's great! Communing with Nature simply isn't me.' Lucy seemed different to-day, the crust of her assurance broken. 'Griffin, darling, do you have a cigarette?'

He said he didn't smoke. Somewhere behind him Anne was sitting. But he was trapped between Lucy's cadging and Grant's chemistry. Seated at the front, he could only listen to the general babble, catching at odd, recognisable threads. Draper, jovial, was there and he could hear Williams in high form. When Frank tried to look round the head-rest prevented him.

'Your dress is pretty *casual*,' remarked Lucy. 'You *always* wear those shoes.'

'Do I?'

'It's hardly *kit*, is it?' She threw a sweet at Grant and asked him if he would mind awfully changing places. Frank she told not to move. Stifling a yawn and still reading, Grant climbed over his knees. Lucy scrambled heavily across him in the other direction. 'I like windows,' she explained. 'Kit! what a spiffing thought! Of course you men have shaving tackle to fall back on. You could have got yourself some boots though. Your feet won't thank you. What do you think of these?' Lucy was wearing jackboots, stockings and a short tweed skirt. 'If you think Good-bye to Berlin, I don't care.'

'Sensible,' he said.

'And smart. I feel like a Hun. Why can't people settle down to decadence and enjoy it? That's what I keep telling Anne. She's here somewhere by the way. Peter's not coming, is he? If you neglect me, I shall quite understand.' He was left to work that out. Beyond the window they saw no snow but hills and grass; the miles of brick scrubland had given way at last.

The setting-down point arrived unexpectedly. Hiking experts tried to disclaim their geographical commentaries. The party disembarked.

'Snow!' Those with boots stamped and rubbed their hands. The uplands were white. Derbyshire rolled back from the road with all its minor ruggedness, its feasible mountains. Personalities were overlooked: Draper and Williams discussed the route.

'All these rucksacks—you'd think we were going up Everest.'

Frank turned and saw Anne. He looked up at the snow and then down at his shoes.

She laughed. 'No eye for detail.'

'That's me. It's a pity Pete couldn't come.'

'Isn't it?' Or perhaps she said 'Is it?'

'Weren't you on the hike last year?'

'No snow last year.'

84

The coach drove off in a cloud of diesel fumes. They were to rejoin it several hours later in a village over the main ridge. Directly after it had left they started out for the snow. The grouping of the party was arbitrary. There was a general feeling of anticipation and most were content to exchange words with those they hardly knew, and had no interest in. Later they had other hopes; but on this preliminary trudge they could afford to talk about boots and sandwiches.

The ascent was harder going than it had looked from the road. Frank was loosely attached to Anne's group: Lucy, Glenys, Sheila and Grant. Sheila and Grant were in conversation; Anne shot Griffin a significant glance. He was reminded of the Conference when she had tried to get Sheila off with Popkin and, though he made the appropriate eyebrow movement, he couldn't take these things so lightly.

Anne was wearing an old pair of jeans and a sweater. Either she had dressed deliberately to emphasise her natural beauty, or—and this was quite contrary—she hoped to avoid attention in Peter's absence. Frank couldn't believe a girl, a girl like Anne, would ignore appearance, even on a hike. Perhaps his role was to be that of helpmate and protector—his original one of Mohan's *aide*.

These complexities did not fill his mind for they had crossed the snow-line into a world of white perspectives under a hard blue sky.

In this world people both gained and lost significance: they were clarified and reduced; made into miniatures, at once less looming and more individual. The most drably dressed of them shed the camouflage of moments before.

> More individual on the snow,
> More in communion, being so.

Frank was taken up with the idea when a snowball smashed into his neck. A wedge of it went sliding down his back. Then his skin was burning under his shirt. To get at it he had to fling off his coat and tear away his pullover. Desperately, he tried to hook out the melting agony, succeeding only after a

85

wild and ludicrous dance. The end of itching and the sounds of laughter registered at the same time.

He filled the white perspectives with his anger. Attacked and ridiculed! It was impossible to be sure of the aggressor. Was it Draper? He was guffawing louder than any.

Griffin advanced towards him with clenched fists. He had just selected the side of Draper's head for the first blow, when his own ear was filled with softish snow. Anne! He ran after her, pursued by more delighted shrieks. Anne was agile. As he gained on her, she turned aside, leaving him to blunder into drifts. Under his feet the snow had packed inches; he was a clumsy bull in a blinding arena.

Powered by fury and fear, he at last got near enough to catch hold of the girl and send her rolling down a slope. He crashed after her, grabbed a handful of snow and forced it inside her shirt. She struggled madly beneath him, then went limp. He bent his head and kissed her, fierce and clumsy.

As he withdrew his mouth, he noted the contrast between the snow and her loose hair—fair, animal auburn on soft, crystalline white. He helped her up and dusted off the clinging snow.

'I suppose I asked for that,' she said.

'I'm sorry. I saw red. I'll go back and get a service bus.'

'Don't spoil the effect. I quite enjoyed it.'

'Did you?' Frank was incredulous.

'Didn't you? That's twice you've kissed me and suffered agonies.'

'I didn't mean to; I shouldn't have.'

'Wow! I must be a *femme fatale*.'

'You are. It's not your fault.'

'Mumble, mumble. You moral philosopher. I only threw that snowball because you looked so solemn. Cheer up.'

'No one saw it, anyway.'

'That's right,' said Anne. She flung back the hair which was lying on her shoulders like epaulettes. 'Aren't you lucky? First Popkin obliges by carrying the can; then your little attempts at rape pass unnoticed.'

They moved towards the others across the soiled snow.

Anne's words had slapped him in the face and ruined the white perspectives. He stopped walking but she went on. She could join the others or turn back: it was up to her. She halted. Faces were looking at them but the distance was enough to ensure privacy of speech. 'Are you sorry?' he asked.

'Good God, what for?'

'What you said.'

'Is it a written apology you're after, to bandage up your bloody little ego?'

'You silly bitch,' Frank said.

'Thanks.'

'I'd be pleased to be seen raping you as you call it. I'm too decent to take advantage, that's all.'

'You're too decent to live,' she said.

Then Griffin became detached enough to see that her mockery was justified; except that what she was mocking she had made.

'I happen to be Mohan's friend for one thing. I'm not blaming you for affecting my reason.'

'For what?' Tone gentle and intrigued.

'For affecting my reason!' he shouted. 'That sounds literary, doesn't it? You can't help it—I can't. What Popkin did, he did for you, remember.'

The others had stopped for a drink from their flasks, that and to strain ear and eye. As the two loiterers trudged into the circle, they arrived as strangers, objects of speculation. In Anne's vacuum flask there was a mixture of coffee and broken glass. She showed Griffin and said: 'There are snags in everything.' The way she said it made him happy and the others sitting nearby curious.

Now they were ascending reaches of unbroken white. Furrowing across them gave a heady feeling of promise, as if life and the world were like this—as clean and on such a scale. The expedition's objective was in sight and they were able to measure their progress by it. Some ran and others fell back as the slope increased. A great pillar of stone waited on the crest of the ridge. It was there as a war memorial and had stood some forty years immortalising the dead. On it were carved their hundreds of names: officers facing south—perhaps to get the best of the sun—others listed by rank, north, east and west. For miles it was a landmark and from its foot you could see the contours of half a county. They crouched out of the wind, exhausted and smoking themselves to death. It was pleasing to arrive at such a monument. A reminder of human futility, it was at the same time a human claim: man's seal on the man-free hills.

'Two minutes' silence,' said Lucy, 'while I think great thoughts.'

'It's too late for patriotism. I'll never be carved up there with those boyoes.' Williams, who had teamed up with Lucy, put down his anorak to make her a seat. Normal pairings were for-gotten on these hikes. It was catch as catch can. Griffin sat with Anne. He was trying to find a way of re-opening the earlier incident which didn't let his mind rest but anything he said she had the power to turn round and send back at him. Yet she kept with him and seemed pleased to. She was impenetrable and beyond his understanding. He had no experience here, no path ahead, nothing.

Draper, unusually affable still, joined them. 'Share my lettuce,' he said, proferring an orange.

'No thanks,' said Anne.

'Thought Joan Morley was coming?'

'I think she was, until she heard you were. That happens to be the truth, so don't blame me.'

'You've all got your schoolgirl intrigues. Isn't that right?'

'Of course.'

'Quite complicated ones, some of them.'

'The more sophisticated of us.'

'And you're a sophisticated one?

'As one Machiavellian to another.'

Frank was uneasy. He didn't like it. Draper's face was ugly in its cocksuredness. And he was still a little afraid of him.

'Mind if I sit down?'

'Ask the dead.'

'Sharp, aren't you? How are you liking it, Griffin?'

'It's quite good.'

88

'Get yourself a safer girl next time. Snowballs I mean. How's Peter Mohan?'

Anne said: 'He may have taken a turn for the worse and died for all I know.'

'Hard-hearted lot, aren't they?' said Draper pleasantly.

'Are they?' Griffin said weakly.

'You ought to know.'

'Cryptic in your insinuations, aren't you?' said Anne.

'Sometimes I am. Cigarette?'

'I've given them up.'

'Since when?'

'Since then.'

'You like other vices better?'

'She doesn't like being cross-examined,' said Frank.

'That so? I don't reckon Popkin did neither.'

'We'll set off, if you have no objections.'

'You do that, Anne.'   ·

Gentleman mountaineer, Griffin assisted her to her feet. Still seated, Draper appraised the manoeuvre. 'You're quite a girl,' he said. 'I suppose that's why a fool like Popkin kept his trap shut.'

The way down from the pillar was steeper and flanked by rocks. The snow here had another sort of impressiveness, one in keeping with the failing light. Rocks and bare trees had made the fall uneven and patchy; intermixed were the dark shades of stone and wood. A small unfrozen stream followed the path, chinking like money.

Even allowing for the downhill slope they were walking faster.

The faint gloom of the place helped imagination. A ravine filled with heavy light was the opposite of their glaring mid-day and minds became more self-absorbed. Frank, worst-shod and uncomfortable, imagined himself one of a primitive tribe of hunters. Others in boots privately led military patrols. Lucy remained herself.

'Lead, kindly light!' she whooped. 'Get me to the bar on time.'

'Let me get it down me!' shouted Williams who was support-

89

ing her arm. 'The graves of my fathers will be full of movement and jostling. Turning over, I tell you!'

At the village they stamped off the snow and the quest for health and spiritual beauty. The Green Man—'Super! Fertility rites!' from Lucy—was open and theirs for an hour and a half. There was a long room, a good fire and an accommodating landlord who let them have the room to themselves. 'I know you youngsters like a drink,' he said, happy in the knowledge of how much drink bravado would be buying.

Frank, who was quite shocked at the wild change from sobriety to license, concentrated on warming his feet and drying his socks. Out of the way by the fire he could forget Anne and Mohan and Draper and try to fix the quality of the hills. The day had provided him with an image. He went into the future until the present was a clear image from the past. He was thinking about Time when Lucy boxed his ears.

'Poor Anne's simply being eaten by wolves at the bar,' she said. 'And *please* throw those socks on the fire or something.'

Williams thrust a pint of draught cider in his hand. Grant and Sheila were kissing; Lucy went off into a spirited dance. Over the room a post-mortem was being held on a lad whose head had turned after half a pint; from elsewhere the wisdom of drinking on a full stomach was being advocated. Suddenly Frank changed. Finicky moral scruple and poetical maundering vanished like trapped water breaking in his ear. Anne had been drinking and smoking at the bar with a group including Draper. He joined them. The group, mostly friends of his, discreetly withdrew. Draper had gone into the yard.

'Good evening,' said Anne.

He took her arm. 'Tell me something.'

'Anything, my lord.'

'Why do you go on like this? Pete's ill.'

'He's got a touch of 'flu.'

'You don't care for anyone.'

'I don't really see how you can say that. But I don't want to argue with you.'

'I don't.'

'Then don't, honey. Let me get you a drink.'

90

'Did you hear what I said back there? I love you,' said Frank, 'I think.'

'I hope not. I'm not worth it.'

'I can't bear to look at you.'

'Please.' She touched his hand. 'You sounded genuine.'

'These people are trash,' he said. 'Compared to you, they don't exist. I don't.'

'Don't make me special. I'm not.'

'Break it up, you two.' Williams appeared, flushed and Celtic. 'We're revelling. This is the druid's circle, not chapel. Keep your introspection for the bus.'

'What a vee good idea! Dim lighting and passion. Gee!'

Williams put his arm round Lucy's shoulder. 'At last I've found the Scarlet Woman,' he said.

The ride home was traditionally orgiastic. By some agency unknown the vehicle's interior lighting was extinguished. There were enough couples and recent pairings for the protest of the few who would have preferred to read to be so patently hopeless that it wasn't made. The thirty miles of darkness was an hour for kissing, accompanied by discursive chatter or by pledges of air. On this journey Frank sat next to Anne. Time, under the impetus of the outing, had wrought changes; Lucy and Grant were elsewhere. Anne was between him and the flying glass of night.

'Now,' he said, 'we can talk.'

'Why talk? Why not do as others are doing unto each other?'

'There's Mohan. Besides, that's not what I think of you.'

'I'd rather have snow stuffed down my neck than be on a pedestal.'

'This is different. Not like that,' he said angrily.

'Oh dear. The Real Thing.'

Griffin was silent. He had made no clear statement to her; he had none to make; yet somehow, anyhow, his feelings had come out slipshod. To leave it there seemed best. More talk would lead to no solution. Anne was too independent to manipulate. He didn't think of her as a coquette but he remembered Popkin's words on the cross-country. Yet, as well as the moral knot, there was a growing pride in himself. Now he was an initiate. Anne had given him stature as well as pain. Weeks ago he had been a boy; now he was older and less wise.

'What did you want to tell me then?'

'I've made enough of a fool of myself already.'

'No you haven't,' she said. 'What's wrong with spiritual gestures?' She got hold of his hand. 'It's not our fault we're living too late for them. Man was a spiritual being and now he's a mechanical contraption. Heart and soul once; now fingers and brains.' Her fingers caressed his wrist, tickling the inert flesh. 'How about another kiss, honey? No one's looking.'

The third time was luckier.

'I'd say you quite liked that,' said Anne.

'I did,' said Frank.

CHAPTER 11

THE weeks before Christmas were marked at home by a growth of goodwill. Mr Griffin became almost jovial. Christmas, it was true, increased the takings in the shop, but Frank liked to think his father's expansiveness was bigger than money. If not, why did he give away boxes of dates to the regular customers? Frank made the effort to be pleasant and started helping out on Saturday mornings. He had not served in the shop since he was eleven; his mother had quietly insisted that he did not; consequently on the first morning he was at a loss with reckoning bills and where to find things. It was hard to make out his father's attitude. He hindered by giving too much help; said the work was below Frank's capabilities; and implied that he had years of soapflakes and jam to make up before he could master the art of Grocery. But on the whole he was solicitous. They found a sort of community in packing orders and checking stock.

'Thirty,' said Frank from the step-ladder.

'Thirty-four, the pickle.'

'Sorry. There's four hiding round the back.'

'That's better, son, I *can* keep my stock in order.'

At such times Frank was pleased with himself; and Mrs Griffin was pleased when her men came in for lunch talking shop. As her husband's temper improved, his routine slackened and he would leave Frank in charge and do the jobs about the house which were man's work.

Frank enjoyed being behind the counter: it meant the improved feeling in the family and it meant talking to the customers. Charles Griffin had always been critical of his clientele. At the back of his mind there was an untarnished image of Baxter's, his uncle's shop in the city where he had served his apprenticeship to Grocery. Baxter's had sent out its goods by van to a retired admiral and the better country parsonages. Now the premises housed a bit of a dress shop but he always pointed them out. To him they contained the ghosts of Gentry; to the rest of the family merely frippery costing more than a sensible woman would dream of giving. Frank liked the present customers and saw them as representatives of the life unthoughtful; unlike school where everything was trimmed to a syllabus; unlike home where everything was a matter of profit and loss. Mrs Jones's stories about her old dad's part in the General Strike were epic to Frank and dialect turns of phrase in among scraps from the telly, poetry. Carefully, he kept his mouth shut to preserve the frail bond with his father. Christmas, it seemed, would dawn as it should on a united household.

But one mid-December Saturday during a slack period when Mr Griffin was in the house seeing to something, the old man who had told Frank about the Great War entered the shop. In daylight and the publicity of walking he looked much older. He seemed to have aged in a few weeks but Frank recognised him at once.

'How are you keeping?' he asked.

'Eh? Not so badly. 'Ev we met before, youth?'

He mentioned the pub; but the mind that had forgotten so much had forgotten that also. The old man appeared uneasy. It entered Frank's head that the old man wanted to keep the one thing he had left: anonymity. So, business-like, he asked him what he wanted.

'Tobacco for rolling fags. I roll me own.'

Frank placed three brands on the counter. 'Take your pick.'

The customer hesitated. 'Is it soe'd by the quarter?'

'That's the smallest we stock. Half an ounce, is it?' Frank checked. 'Half an ounce.'

The old man turned away. 'I don't smoke them meks,' he said, making for the door.

Frank snatched up a big two-ounce tin and vaulted over the counter.

The pensioner was fumbling with the door-latch. In a second

94

the tin was in the flapping coat pocket, the door unfastened and held wide.

'I can't tek it, youth. It's charity.'

'It's not charity.'

'I can't tek it and I will not.' His famished hand lunged down into the ripped lining hunting for the tobacco. Still holding the door, in a position parodying shopkeeperly subservience to wealth, Frank was growing desperate.

'Take it!' he said. The word 'charity' was again forthcoming. 'You silly old fool!' Frank was shouting. 'Hasn't your life taught you anything? That's not charity. We've got no right to give you charity.' The old face was frightened; he saw it and stopped. 'Please take it.' Frank bundled him out and shut the door.

What was fountaining in his mind? Closing his eyes, he put his forehead to the cold glass. Was it good or stupid what he had done? The old man, stupid or good? The sharp reaction was soon over. He went back to the counter.

There, flanked by tins of fruit in the doorway connecting house and shop, as in the portal of one of the gaudier Egyptian temples, his father was standing. Hands on hips.

'That your notion of keeping shop?'

'What?'

'I witnessed the whole episode from start to finish.'

'You did?'

'When I'm ill—or studying—you can come down here and give away my stock.'

'I'll pay for it; I meant to.'

'What'll you pay it *with*?'

'I've got the money you give me for helping.'

'Paid back with my own money. Settles it nicely, don't it?'

'In your own bloody coin,' said Frank. 'What harm is it to give that poor old bloke a bit of tobacco?'

'What coin shall I pay you back with one of these days? I'm warning you, lad, your road of going on if you want some free advice is going to end up buggering you. You're like some little tin god you are. Well if you don't know what happens to people like that, I've told you.'

95

Frank said nothing. His father's words might be true, were true; the money was all out of his own pocket. Giving away stock was bad trade and cold charity.

'I'll take over now. You amuse yourself. Read your books.'

'So you don't want my help?'

'That's it.'

'I thought it was working nicely.'

'Yo'd best keep a still tongue in your head. I'll not be balancing with you here.'

'Balance away!' Frank swung into the house—a childish exit. Graham in the corridor stood aside. Muttering wildly, Frank stormed the stairs. He enjoyed his desperation because he could see beyond it; he was detached even if he stormed and cried. He paced his room up and down, acting it out. His father was odious; his position here untenable. He'd break off the academic grind now at this late stage. Work honestly with his hands. There they were: someone had called them a labourer's land. In independence he towered over his past actions. Quaint honour over Anne, guilt over Popkin, reconciliation with that impossible shopkeeper—finished! He broke the shackles of conscience, shunted the yoke of dependence from his shoulders . And there he stood among the crashing iron.

Outside, the lunchtime trolley-buses were grinding by, loading and unloading a city's humanity. He could look back on his melodrama. No rash action would come of it. *King Lear* and French dictionaries; ten-shilling prints of the Impressionists out of his father's jars of jam: all this, under his masters' guidance, invited him to the university and there and thereafter to civilised independence. He was too self-conscious ever to walk out and try his strength on farms or building-sites. By and by he saw his cursed introspection flowering from subtlety to subtlety. He remembered the box of brown snapshots in the attic: his ancestors. Where they had watched conscience, he watched sensibility—a small modification: rashness wasn't in the family.

Towards end of term the chosen few went off to examinations and interviews at Oxford and Cambridge; and returned uncommunicative. Post-mortems were conducted by Hare who was told by Barbender, a laconic chemistry youth, that he, Barbender, had asked during the vital few minutes whether he was making the right impression. 'I wanted to know,' said Barbender, 'so I asked them.'

Hare, paling, had replied to the subsequent rehash of his own integrity pep-talks 'with a sort of groan'.

Mohan brought back an acceptance on the strength of his interview. For a week or two everyone talked universities.

Draper met Mohan by chance in town one evening. He offered to buy him a drink and Peter, though not much looking forward to it, felt it meanminded to refuse. His university place had helped him break with school; a month's withdrawal into isolated hard graft had left him detached and tolerant.

Draper guided him into the nearest pub, got the drinks and settled him at a window table. It was midday, the pavements full of shoppers.

'We can watch the birds,' he said. 'Cheers!'

'Good luck.'

'I'll need it. We're not all brainy like you. Congratulations. Cambridge is just your place.'

'The same as any other place.'

'It's two hundred a year to anybody. Then there's the intellectual quality and all. New horizons like Jugg says.'

Draper drained off his glass and gave away a cigarette. He leaned forward confidentially. Mohan expected 'as man to man. . . .'

'You interest me.' Draper flicked back his long, greasy hair. His eyes were green and brown and fixed on Peter. 'I'm not a pseudo-intellectual but I do a bit of thinking.'

'We all are. Pseudo and intellectual, mate.'

'I know you don't think much to me but I like being chief functionary where you weren't bothered. You're a Catholic, aren't you? You go to confession?'

'I've never confessed that much to anyone.'

'You know that book by James Joyce? I've always wondered about priests listening to girls. I'm dirty-minded.'

'You know best.'

'That bloke there,' said Draper. A stylish young man was buying whisky. 'Look at him. Queer as a nine bob note. What makes blokes queer? Women are queer enough you'd think. Know Joan Morley?'

Mohan nodded. 'Slightly.'

'I liked her. Quiet as a mouse and not much to her. But they get you all ways. Your ex has got Griffin all right.'

'My what?'

'That girl Anne Cooper, she's knocking on with Griffin; but you must know that.'

'You have got a dirty mind.'

'Take it easy. Pete. You gave her up. She's knocking on with Griffin. They were at it on the hike. If you don't believe me, what about when they went into the park that night? Popkin copped it but they all went along together. He just tagged along. I saw it. What they were after's not far to seek.'

Mohan said: 'What campaign are you running? I think you told Jugg, Frazer and I were resigning.'

'I'm not perfect either,' said Draper. 'I reckoned you were keen on intellectual honesty and all that.'

Mohan stood up and put a shilling on the table for his drink.

'Thanks for everything,' he said.

Leaving the money where it was, Draper got up. 'Honestly, Pete,' he said, 'I didn't want to stir it.'

CHAPTER 12

MR COOPER pushed aside his plate and belched. 'Arabic thanks,' he said.

'Did you have a good day, dear? I forgot to ask.'

'You did and I didn't. I was hoping you'd changed the routine. I had a bloody day.'

Anne said: 'I thought it was to-day they photographed the local dignitaries.'

'It was, my girl.'

'Wasn't sitting in on that a change in your Town Hall routine? As you don't seem to like mummy's routine, I conclude you don't care much for yours.'

'For a girl you're logical. You take after me.'

'Thank you.'

'Only I was more circumspect to my parents of course. No, the annual team photo is routine again, only on a lower frequency. I've set it up and sat in on it for eight long years. They field a stupider bunch every year. Arranging that crowd of fly-halves and silly mid-ons gives me a pain, I assure you.'

'You've mixed your sports,' said Mrs Cooper's old father with a note of triumph in his voice.

'Figure of speech. Permissible. Would you like a metaphor from painting? I'm reminded of those religious things where a group of the wealthy commissioned themselves to appear round the Virgin Mary. Go into any gallery and there you see them passing through the eye of a needle.'

'Italian pictures?' asked Mrs Cooper.

'Italian, French, Dutch. Money speaks louder than words.'

The old man finished his sweet, minutes after the others. 'I didn't think to see this Christmas,' he said. 'If I can keep alive ten days I'll see it.'

'You'll see me out,' said Mr Cooper. 'I'd forgotten Christmas. As my power of coping with the money side increases, my goodwill diminishes. What present would you like, love?'

'Anything. You know it's the thought that counts.'

'I was asking Anne, actually.'

'I'm sorry, dear,' said Mrs Cooper.

'Nothing,' said Anne.

'Come on. Daughters are supposed to importune their fathers with kisses and warm slippers.'

'Are they? I didn't know.'

'It's one of the major pleasures of fatherhood. Cross my heart it is. What would you like?'

'I've not thought about it.'

'Cajole me, you hard girl.'

'Tell your father what you'd like, Anne.'

'Well,' said Anne, 'I'd like to know that myself.'

'When you were little,' said her grandfather, who had been leaning forward to catch every word, 'you wanted to be an old maid with lots of money and cats. Do you remember that, Mavis? Perhaps she didn't tell you. She told me that ambition —didn't you, ducky?'

'I grew up since then.'

'I told you! She remembers.'

Anne refrained from putting him right. The deafness which was a cushion for him—a defence-mechanism of old age—was for them the opposite: a sharp reminder that most of what's said doesn't bear repetition.

She abruptly left the table and her father raised his eyebrows. That was always his last comment—the Englishman's eyebrow—one of the few public-school and Oxford mannerisms he still allowed himself. To-night she had no sympathy for him. His epigrams sometimes struck a response in her and she could laugh. Her father was good company, sometimes. But to-night he was dull metal, a corroded version—acid and bitterness—of what he perhaps was once, at Oxford in the early 1930s. He seemed old and his wit was like her mother's make-up, grossly excessive by a tiny fraction of an inch. Anne went out to walk away her mood.

She walked quickly along familiar, ill-lit roads. One star was throbbing and there was a moon. It was windy. The night was sad and desperate. A few minutes took her to a place of vantage where she could look south over the Trent valley to hills whose low slopes showed no lights. Nearer, the ground was spilled with glinting bangles and the river itself was visible in dull silver slabs. The black air buffeting her face was warm. In this city lived all the people she knew, under this moon. They were strangely existing somewhere around her; the bodies they lived in were taking different measurements now from hers; none perhaps assessing the night. She was pleased to be alone.

Back in the matchwood room she had left, situated amongst its minute furniture, her family would be talking or listening to the radio. Anne thought of them, those married people and the old man. She was nearly nineteen; they had been just a few years older when she was born. Abstract marriage from them; extract them from marriage. It couldn't be done. The cement had hardened. Looked at one way, they were the composite thing society required: man-and-wife; yet they were ill-matched. Bits kept sticking out of the perfect unity. They were neither one nor separate. From here you could imagine yourself reaching down like a giant and picking up from the rich deposits of the Trent, a handful of mud, houses, fences and trees; squeezing them into a ball.

The unfailing topic of her friends was marriage—when you married you were home and dry. It was their ever-after, she thought contemptuously. A cosy version of the afterlife—more fulfilling because there would be children looking up to you; responsibility, a husband and children. If you didn't marry a worthless man. And, if you did, Romance promised you bigger things: Reform. It made her tired. Anne rejected the general belief; declined to think about something as soulless as marriage. The very word was ugly, rhyming only with carriage, miscarriage—half rhyming with sewage. Official word for official state complete with licence. And the weddings she had attended had been so silly: the smell of furniture polish in new, insipid churches; the jocularity of fathers, a cert for 'something blue'. She wondered how her contemporaries could look forward so much to a ridiculous ceremony ushering in a lifetime's petty civil war.

Though her eyes were still on the moon and star, she had not seen them for minutes. There were more stars than before. Their faint constellations were algebra to her, reminiscent of the half-erased lessons of the Science Sixth which could be seen every Tuesday during European History. A girl in their history set was a palm-reader and astrologist. The hand Anne was keeping warm in her coat pocket had been pronounced 'secretive'; there was a decade of stress in store for her, Kate had said. Kate's technique usually managed to take in even the rationalist members of the Science Sixth. But it was another future to be discarded along with the future of marriage. You just couldn't say. And the night, instead of exulting her, made her uncertainties more trivial but more depressing.

Having Peter and Frank on her string did nothing to help. She had no wish to make that sort of choice.

The functional had been disguised with conspicuous mistletoe, holly, veteran paper streamers. It was the Sixth Form Social when a term's dancing classes were on display and the untutored tried to catch up by getting the expert to draw diagrams. The first hour was formal and excruciating. Hare was present and performed with the headmistress of the girls' school. There was awed silence. Hare, a graceful dancer, made the diagrams inadequate. Mohan had famously characterised Hare as a being born with no talents whatsoever. As he grew, the young Jugg had watched humanity attentively. What he lacked he had contrived, first rigging up an intellect, then a sense of humour. As time went by he adjusted himself to perfect working order. So with the dancing one supposed—the precision wanted life. And if his audience was tailoring the man to the coat, not one of them was aware of it; most were too busy trying not to laugh.

Next the Head went out of his way to speak to his prefects. He asked Williams how he was doing and included Frank, who was with Williams, in a remark on the weather. The light, opaque eyes travelled over their attire—neither was wearing a suit—but Hare made no comment. He went on like the Queen to talk to someone else.

'Frazer's bringing Lucy tonight,' said Williams. 'Still, that's how it goes. I thought I was doing fine with that slice of Eve.'

'That what?'

'Milton or some bloody thing. Do you dance, bach?'

Frank said he couldn't.

'Bloody silly they look. We'll go for a drink.'

When they came back there was a more appropriate atmosphere: more dancers and more spectators. Griffin tried desperately to see if Anne had come but spotted only Sheila flaring in red on the arm of Grant. At the door he and Williams discussed politics. Williams's father remembered the bad old days and Frank was treated to a description of the hunger marches, the singing and the burning of banisters on the firebacks. He had heard it all before but he was in a conspiracy with Williams to fabricate an intelligent conversation. Anyone could see that they weren't joining in because the school hop was below them. When the last banister had been consumed, they watched the stiffer or more unexpected dancers: ballroom dancing had its comic aspect. They were part of the usual chatter on the sidelines.

One or two of the younger masters had come along, which was good of them or perhaps merely would-be politic in the hope of catching Hare's eye. They were rigorously off-duty and at ease. Sooner or later Williams and Griffin were talking to Saunders—Geography and Junior Maths.

'Change not to have a bar,' he said. 'Means of course I can't dabble in the art. I need Dutch courage for dancing. But it saves cash.'

'Is it like dances at the university?' asked Williams.

'At most it probably is.'

'Which one were you at, sir?' Frank was scanning the hall for a sign of Anne but he could do his bit to keep the conversation afloat. For the first time he realised that people talked without purpose.

'I was at Cambridge, actually. Evening dress and the woman shortage.'

'Cambridge, was it? Going for Bangor myself. Well, I mean I've got Ordinary Level Welsh so I might as well use it.'

Anne was dancing with Mohan. The feelings tearing at Griffin's inside were a foreign body like rough iron in his guts; but mind and voice were unhindered. He swung the talk to Geography, asking whether it was an art or a science. Saunders thought both. History grew out of it—look at the Welsh. Williams struck a pose and uttered his native tongue. Smiling, Saunders swept through Meteorology, Oceanography and Palaeontology.

'The world's our oyster, even the Arts with a capital "A". Imagine Michelangelo north of sixty degrees. Or think how things would have differed if northern Greece had been an alluvial plain. Literature, Philosophy, Western thought, the whole caboodle.'

Specialist's excitement had inspired him to the collapse of language. Delight with the obvious animated his dead, oval face. Griffin, who really regarded Geography as a shifty non-subject stealing everyone else's chickens, brought up the siting of towns. The schoolmaster listed rivers and hills which had invited towns to channel and flatten them. This was what he was paid to discuss with youths five years his junior and his manner relaxed. Fords gave way to bridges, Anne danced with Mohan, the clock proceeded.

When the dancers took chairs, Frank crossed the floor leaving Saunders in mid River Conway. They seemed pleased to see him whereas, dancing, they had not smiled.

'Hullo,' said Anne. 'Not seen you the whole evening.'

'I saw you,' said Frank.

'I didn't know you were a dancing man,' Peter said. 'I'm not, am I?'

'Well, you kept off my feet this time. He's really quite good at almost everything.'

'I can't dance at all.'

'It's not difficult,' she said. 'How about it? This is our tune.'

'Go ahead; but keep off each other's toes.'

'Waltz,' said Anne. 'One—two—three. You can hear it in the music.'

Frank looked down.

'Shackle yourself to the rhythm.'

Frank tried to obey but had no conception of the means.

'Never mind. Keep shuffling.'

'Anne, what am I supposed to do?'

'Keep shuffling.'

'Not that,' he said angrily. 'Apologise about the hike or what?'

'Why have you stopped?'

He kicked back motion into his hopeless feet. Around them sailed stiffly erect practitioners. Afar off a call for jazz.

'I'm sorry, but what's the idea? Are you attached to Pete?'

'Legally?'

'You know what I mean . . . Morally.'

'Good God! Is anybody?'

'Is it fair on him? Or me?'

'*Three* beats to the bar. One—two—three. Concentrate.'

'Hell. You enjoy the set-up.'

'Not particularly.'

This was, so far, the best of Anne's excuses for obliqueness and the worst setting for Frank's putting his incoherence into words. Like his dancing, his points had jerked out bittily.

'Shall we give up?' He had involved Anne in a collision again. So much for his idea that the impromptu dancing lesson was her way of talking privately to him. Her way as ever was wilful misunderstanding. They trailed back.

'I watched with awe,' said Mohan.

'He's worse than you are,' she said. 'If we maidens can't trust your manly lead, no wonder the country's going to the bitches.'

'There; you should have swept her off her feet.'

'Off his hands, he means.'

Their banter was ballasted. They had quarrelled perhaps—time for Frank to step in openly. Or Mohan had got to hear about the hike. Frank had never come to terms with what he felt about Anne; she had been more corrosive than positive in his mind. Their meetings had all been dance-floor collisions and love in him was variable like the needle on a dial. Now it read zero and he was calm.

'I was deep in talk with Westbrook when Anne made me dance. The Universe.'

'Now I've got Frank to play with,' said Anne, 'you might as well go back to the Universe.'

Mohan smiled. 'I will,' he said. 'I never like leaving things half-done.'

'Shall we get on with the lesson?' Anne asked.

This time Frank concentrated on ballroom dancing and improved. He distinguished the waltz from the foxtrot-quick-step which he received as a mongrel entity different from the waltz. This was enjoyable. There was no strain between them. He could think of her without torturing himself or—better than thinking of her—he could look into her flushed face and feel the stray lock flailing there with a new intimacy, as though the hair were registering directly on his own senses.

The Griffin Christmas was the same every year: faces, decorations, dialogue. Frank had less patience with it than before. He thought of Anne and his failure to have things out with her; of leaving the dance in a group, a tribe, a nation of chaperones—Mohan among them. He tried to picture what she was doing this morning. The only share he had of her this festive season was a card—Brueghel reproduced in a good cause.

The Day was mostly sitting about with television—the Great Leveller which has ousted Death. The house was full of cold or colourless people he had nothing in common with except—he supposed—genes. This blood was a good deal thinner than water. There were only two relatives, on his mother's side, who afforded any ancestral hope. There was Alfred who drank and was vulgar and Tom long since off to New Zealand but not by all accounts yet clear of his cloud.

Mrs Griffin senior was there: tough, opiniated, seventy-nine. She measured all things on her temporal yardstick; Frank's mother plainly merited little of her time and himself, less. Old

Mrs Griffin was spoken of with admiration and was privately wanted to die.

When Frank had been observant, to pass the time at previous family meetings, he had seen in her some explanation of his father. In her presence the owner of business was subservient, hearing out her scheme for turning his premises into self-service with motivated customers and canned music; saying nothing. Yet he wanted 'class' in his trade more than profit and regretted his customers' dropped h's as much as their shaky credit. He was more old-fashioned than the old woman. Mrs Griffin senior abhorred 'going off the rails' but she re-laid her tracks every decade: her criticism did not come from the sidings of the past. The present age was one of private affluence; she was aware of it and thought her son slow.

The ordeal of Christmas brought the brothers into greater sympathy but that was all. When Graham left the room to read the book Frank had given him, Uncle Alfred said: 'Our Graham's improving in favour. He's getting to look like I remember Tom.'

'That's nowt to boast on,' said Mrs Griffin senior, 'even if it was true, which it isn't. 'E's destined to be one of the ugly ones of this world. 'E's more like my George was, face like a box. All bone. Young Frank's more your side; Graham's got the Griffin face.'

'I'm sure they're both well-featured boys,' said Mrs Griffin junior.

'I didn't marry George for 'is beauty. I married to raise station. 'E wukked. 'E'd've turned our Charles's copper into gold.'

'I'm sure we don't do too badly,' said her daughter-in-law.

'We went to chapel in a motor when motors was something. I came round 'ere on public bus. At my age.' So Mrs Griffin senior clinched her argument as she always did by getting in the last word. There was something ever up her sleeve. Sixty years ago perhaps it had been beauty; now it was nest-egg and age. Nest-egg she played rarely; it was her ace.

'Can I get you a mince-pie, mother?' Charles Griffin asked to end the silence.

'Send the lad.'

Frank duly rose. In the kitchen he struck his fist against the wall and muttered obscenities. In trying to exorcise Anne's burning ghost, he forgot his mission, returning empty-handed. The annoyance and laughter in the living-room seemed to wreathe out of the wallpaper as he stood gaping and listless, reviled by such people.

CHAPTER 13

'I've been watching you, girl. Tell your old grandad what's up. Don't tell me it's none of my business; I'm too old to have any.' The old man had entered Anne's room in his noiseless Turkish slippers. 'The door was open so I took it you weren't half-undressed. Come on, girl—sit me down or send me packing.'

'I'll make tea with my fabulous electric kettle.'

'Proper boudoir you've got here.' He meekly awaited the tea which he extinguished when it came in one boiling, milkless gulp.

'Now. It's one of my hearing days.'

'Nothing to tell,' said Anne, joining him on the velvet ottoman.

'It's boys; you don't want to hurt some boy's feelings. Aren't I right? You shouldn't be so pretty then.'

'You, turning off the mains switch. There was a stupid mix-up and I got kissed.'

'That's not very serious.'

'Now I've got two suitors,' said Anne. 'It's stupid. What the hell can I do with two suitors?'

'Take your pick. The world won't end for the other one. Young men need taking down in the order of things. If you don't know which one you want, set them some test or other.'

'Did you have to do a test?'

'I had rivals. Moths round the light. Your grandma was a desirable woman. Mulcaster and Roberts, I remember. All the fellows wore moustaches in those days.'

'You won her on the upper lip.'

'Bless you, I was the only one to get to 1918.'

'Don't worry about me,' said Anne. 'I've gone off love.'

'Let the lads fight over you.'

'You Romantic! Don't you know we all play safe to-day?'

'Life's exciting. I'm still what you might call mildly excited now I'm old. It's air and electricity. That's not dull. The trouble with my Mavis and your father is they've forgotten they're alive. So don't talk about playing safe; not while I'm around to hear you.' Away he went in noiseless slippers.

Alone, she was restless. On the dressing-table lay a Christmas card which she had not added to her mother's display. The middle page had been removed and, as a substitute for the printed goodwill, there were four handwritten lines.

> Polish the teeth that live in your skull
> Use all your skill to be beautiful
> Hope your bright hair and limitless eyes
> Will wreck you a lasting paradise.

It read like an incantation, a vicious one that disturbed her. That someone had copied it out and sent unsigned was a whiff of evil. For most of Christmas afternoon she had hunted through her father's books. It was one time she couldn't make use of his Round Britain Quiz memory. Perhaps the sender had made it up; worse if so, more venomous. The handwriting was spiky and unknown. Peter could have followed up his dressing as Death with such a postscript and, judging from his behaviour at the social, he had heard something of the hike. But it was far beneath him to do such a thing. And Frank? It was neither of them. Some third person then—some stupid girl's idea of a joke.

Anne changed her dress and wandered about her large room lightly touching this and that; tidying the wardrobe and drawing the curtains. What if, instead of giving her grandfather tea, she had been entertaining a lover? She needed one—to complete the boudoir. How to manage such an evening? Peter or Frank for example—not as boyfriends or potential fiancés—but for a lover; something extra for herself. Adages of husband-catching, which permeated the thoughts of her friends, seeped in. But that wasn't what she wanted. To 'take a lover' under your parents' roof counted as an extreme thing but it fell between the extremes of wife and whore.

It was a civilised idea; but the reality would push it out of shape. Peter or Frank was acceptable. She felt a disquieting excitement with one and an affection for the other. She could picture either on the ottoman with pleasure but—the necessary betrayal of the absent one left aside—how clumsy it might be in fact. But why should people see it, she half see it, as unthinkable? It was not the oversophisticated daydream it seemed. On the contrary, the idea was simple though setting and occasion suggested the decadent splendour of Parisian salons. Against it set the unthinkable married state! She saw the whole gamut of the emotions socialised by convention, refined and coarsened by that refinement.

She could sit down and write two letters, one to Peter and one to Frank, outlining what she intended and giving a time. Then she could wait and see who came. It would get round the need to choose between them and neatly cut out yards of confusing talk; where words were twice changed going to and fro, love would be straight intercourse. But then they might both turn up, clutching their invitations. *Ménage à trois* would never survive the shock. Still it was good to preen on. The trouble was she just didn't want the things her age and sex were entitled to want. Anne didn't know what she did want, there alone with imaginary lovers and a torn-up threat.

When the new term started, Frank avoided Mohan and concentrated on his Advanced Level subjects. He found it easy. Routine was a good hypnotist if you went along with it. One of his duties as a prefect was to collect the dinner money. Hare had instituted a system of financial responsibility. An economist, he was aware of the dangers of 'unalloyed academic education'. He was said to have obtained his headship by bringing out a book called *Pounds, Shillings and Sense*. There had been a copy in the school library until someone unknown had annotated the chapter on famous economists with a vignette of 'Erasmus Hare B.F.'.

The money was collected every Monday by the duty prefect from the form masters. The duty ran for three weeks and involved collection of cash and records, addition of grand total, checking of actual total with recorded total, signature and handing over to the office of about £100. The office then did it all again. About two hours were consumed in this way together with as much numeracy as was called on in a normal fortnight and more nervous energy than was usual in a month. In return there was a stepping up of one's sense of responsibility and more chance of survival later on in 'the world outside'. Frank was sitting exhausted in the prefects' room.

Frost like hands was covering the windows and, beyond, the school buildings were fluid water-colours. Frazer was doing something to his football boots.

'Pity you don't play,' he said. 'You don't know what you're missing.'

'We do,' said Mohan.

Frazer was whistling. 'Good dubbin this. Supple as a girl's lips.'

' "The poetry of earth is never dead." '

'Keats,' said Bill, pleased with himself. 'Now what suggested that to your twisted mind?'

'You, a clod. You seem to enjoy cleaning those boots.'

'Not cleaning: dubbing. Or dubbining. It's my feet I'm thinking of. Animals keep their fur clean, Catholics their souls, me my boots. What about you, Griff? What do you keep clean?'

'Eh?' Frank was in a corner with a book.

'You don't have fur, football boots or—according to you—a soul. What do you spend time on?'

'History, English and French,' said Frank easily.

'Sounds a bit limited,' observed Mohan.

'In one of his bloody dissecting moods,' said Frazer. 'Just because you're in at Cambridge. Why can't you train to be a surgeon, like me; learn to cut up something useful. I can just picture you and Anne on a date, talking metaphysics. Girls are anatomy according to me.'

'There speaks the most sentimental Harry in the place.'

'Seriously, can't you see them, Griff? Anne's too intelligent; she needs some great clodhopping prole like you or me.'

'He means well,' said Mohan, accurately.

Frank was colouring. Mohan had attempted to help him out as if he knew about the situation. Not long ago moral consternation might have come in but now all Frank wanted was to keep himself to himself. Already his behaviour had become strained in Mohan's presence.

'I'll get round to the changing room,' said Bill. 'This year they're a scruffy bloody shambles half the time.'

'Goodbye, commander of men. We'll stay here and keep warm.'

Draper opened the door; he hesitated, embarrassed it seemed. He might have walked in on an amorous couple and not just three of his schoolfellows. He made a half exit, came back firmly into the room and shut the door. Leaning against it, he folded his arms and smiled.

'Wotcha,' said Bill. 'I was saying what a scruffy lot the first fifteen are.'

'Are they?' said Draper. 'You two shouldn't be using this room, Jugg says.'

Frazer laughed; Mohan said, 'By name?'

'That's right; Mohan and Frazer he said.'

'I hope you were rude,' said Frazer. 'My locker's here.'

'Alternative lockers are being provided.'

'Well, you can't argue with Jugg,' said Bill lightly, picking up his boots.

'I concur in this instance.'

'You what?'

'I happen to think efficiency's what's needed. Having you always here disrupts things. When the small fry come in with lines they know you're not prefects. It's undermining.'

'Well, well,' said Mohan. 'Once I'd have said you were an aberration but I've a nasty feeling you're the norm. You come in here humming and hawing and wearing Hare's adjectives like epaulettes. You're a politician.'

'The trouble with you, Mohan, is that you can't stand organisation—getting things done. You're sort of impotent.'

'Do you mind?' said Bill. 'Pete's my friend. If you want a punch-up, say so.'

'I'm not looking for trouble.' Draper unfolded his arms. 'I don't want trouble. I need only've said what Hare told me; Hare's the headmaster. I added what I thought because you asked me. I'm behind Jugg on this. Griffin here knows the truth about that Popkin eyewash. You resigned to bugger Jugg about; you're a pair of anarchists. And while I remember, Griffin can witness the fact that I've passed on Hare's order.'

'Like hell,' said Frank. He was uneasy about the extent of Draper's knowledge but had to say something.

'You will if it comes to it. You're the same coward you were in Arts III. I know what you are. Don't kid yourself people change.'

'Draper, old cock, I know you can't help being brusque, big-headed and a bastard; but you're not yourself to-day; you're worse.'

'You did this job before, Frazer. Do you think I don't know that?'

'What I know,' said Bill, 'is that you either want a brain-storm or you've had one. The "job" you're always on about is sod-all. So are you. Keep your nose clean with your mates and let Jugg stew. That's my advice, cock. I'm off.'

'Big-hearted Bill,' said Draper when Frazer had left the room.

'He is. To a fault.'

'P'raps he's right. What's it matter if everything goes to hell?' He straightened some books on the window-sill. 'Oh, Griffin,' he said offhand, 'Jugg wants a word with you.'

'What about?'

'He doesn't tell me everything.'

'When's he want me?'

'Whenever you care to call. I gave Anne Cooper a note for that Joan Morley. Was it delivered?'

'Who are you asking?' from Mohan.

'Just asking in general.' Draper's eyes swept both of them with a not very pleasant grin.

The Head said: 'Ah, Griffin. There seems to be some discrepancy in the dinner money. Miss Turle's sorting it out. Can you assist?'

Frank shook his head.

'Her present theory,' said Hare, fumbling through the carefully littered papers on his desk, 'is that there are two pounds more in the bag than on the sheet. Take a seat. They used to reckon usury unnatural; strange to our way of thinking but the idea of money's breeding money was repugnant to them owing to its inanimate nature. I find this talk of fast-breeder reactors similarly disturbing. Griffin, your money appears to have bred in the darkness of the dinner bag.' Hare smiled by adjusting the wrinkle geometry of his long face. Humour. Q.E.D.

Frank, grateful the the mistake didn't lie in the other direction, apologised for his stupidity.

'But it's not book-keeping, is it? It's not Economics.' The last was a phrase they had all adopted since the lower school to be used whenever the ordinary make-believe Englishman might say that something wasn't cricket. It resurrected Frank's early fears of Hare the dictator who never was. He apologised again.

'My scheme,' said the Head, 'as you must know, is a modest attempt to counter what is becoming an increasingly prevalent type of criticism tilted at the educational service: that we are out of touch. Other headmasters whom I know personally resent it. And, as they are only classicists or historians, you can gauge my feelings. Economics is not enshrined in Adam Smith; we have no room in Economics for mildewed pedestals!' He looked at Frank with the concentration of an American trying to fathom the Mona Lisa. So he had looked at him years before when Frank and Draper had been caught fighting and cross-examined by Hare prior to detention. Greta came in from the office.

'Ah,' said Hare leaving his desk. 'I fancy Miss Turle has come to a decision.'

'Shall I go, sir?' asked Frank.

'Certainly not. Remain here.'

He left Frank and Greta together in his study. Greta was

good-looking and good-natured in contrast to Miss Turle, the school secretary. Frazer had recently tried his luck with her but her engagement ring held.

'What's it all about?' said Frank in not more than a whisper.

'It's the dinner money. Turle's gone barmy counting it up. She's been on it ever since you turned it in; the cash is down or something.'

'But Jugg said it was up.'

'Probably been some mistake.' Greta was busy back-combing in the cunning mirror which the head had set to pry round his door. 'Turle's such a *methodist*. People like that never get anything straight.'

'He's taking his time about it.'

'Birds of a feather, them two.'

Griffin had a growing sense of fear: the neutral uneasiness of waiting for dentists, interviewers, chiefs of secret police. When Greta asked after Frazer, her question came from the distance of unhurried normality, out of the easy-going regions he was leaving. He told her that Bill was playing rugby.

'Nice lad. I liked him for giving old Hare notice. Turle was away; I heard the whole thing through the keyhole.' Greta examined her fingernails and her moral censor added: 'I don't make a habit of it. Only when Turle's away. Here's his nibs.'

Dismissing her, Hare fell into his chair. This time he did without historical background and contemporary allusion. 'Now tell me, Griffin, where is that three pounds ten?'

'But you said the cash was up,' said Frank.

'I know I *said* that.' Hare spoke with the emphasis of fictional detective inspectors who use verbal trickery to trap their suspects and draw out the guilty truth. The Head leapt up, brandishing his limbs.

'You have betrayed my trust!' he shouted. 'First Popkin and now you.'

'You've got the wrong sheets, sir.'

'The wrong sheets! Do you imagine we are as easy to cheat as the gas-meter? I don't know your home background; I don't wish to know. Your final total does not accord with the added figures; there are several clumsy alterations. You betray my trust *and* insult my intelligence.'

'I'm honest,' Frank said. He might have denied being a thief but his protest came out as a more general and less valid claim.

'What *am* I to think? Do you have trouble with arithmetic? Are you trying to pass it off as mathematical?'

Frank asked to see and was shown the figures. He was amazed to see that they had been altered and said so.

'You catch the outraged tone admirably.'

'I never entered this total. Because it's on a separate page it makes it easy for them. All they'd need is a few duplicated sheets.' Suddenly he felt tired and unconcerned like a teacher with no more patience to use up. 'Those are not the figures I wrote down, sir.'

'It seems to be the same writing implement and the same hand.'

'It's a cheap biro. There were plenty of my figures for them to copy.'

Hare stood with hands thrust into the trouser pockets of his expensive but well-worn suit. He had the judicial air. Moral indignation had given way to intellectual involvement with the problem; the expression on his gaunt face promised impartiality.

'You use the third person plural; advisedly I should say. Like certain sections of society you find it indefinite enough to offer you an excuse for your own weaknesses. Can we limit the reference of your "they"? I admit the cheap pen and the ease of forgery.'

'I don't know who it was.'

'You suggest,' said the headmaster, who was by now plainly enjoying the complexities, 'that another piece of paper was substituted?'

'It must have been, sir.'

'Now, these sheets are issued singly; the duty prefect has just the one copy he needs. Every Monday that sheet, duly completed, is returned to the office to be checked by Miss Turle. Procedure is governed by a well-defined punctilio.

Where did your persons unknown obtain their vital spare? Are you implying they blew the office safe?'

Frank doubted the punctilio; if Hare had been intent on preventing forgery, why hadn't he introduced a simpler, fool-proof system? It would be futile to take him up on administration; so Frank tried to understand what had happened.

'Two sheets could have been given out by mistake and the extra one used.'

'Good; that limits our suspects. The criminal is a prefect. Not you, Griffin, but another of my school's officers. The thought is very comforting.'

'Are the sheets numbered? That would tell us the date.'

'Of course they are not numbered. I have just explained the system.'

Frank stared at the forged figures as if they would tell him the name of their author. 'I left the money and papers in my locker when I went to the toilet for five minutes. I locked it but the lock's a common sort. It wouldn't have been difficult to undo.'

'Doesn't this sound unconvincing even to you?'

'Yes, sir. I know it does.'

'Locker checks! It's spreading like some blight,' said Hare, speaking to himself. 'Think. Has any boy's behaviour invited your suspicion?'

'Draper,' said Griffin and regretted saying it immediately. The head's concocted impartiality had betrayed him into open speaking.

'On what grounds?'

'Well, none really,' he said miserably.

Hare picked up the green telephone and asked for Draper. 'There,' he said. 'I shall ask him, Griffin.'

This was worse than waiting for Hare to return from Miss Turle; worse than when as a junior he had queued with other small absconders; worse than any dentist. Draper did not keep him waiting long.

'Yes, sir?' he said with a deference that was novel and disgusting. Frank dully wondered how Hare would introduce the topic.

'When were you last on dinner money?' asked the head-master.

'Last term, sir.'

'You were issued with the correct forms?'

'Yes, sir.'

'No accidental duplication in the issue?'

'No, sir.' Draper answered without hesitation. They spoke the same language. So far, all had been tact; Griffin was listening out for the confrontation. The suspicions which he had not so much entertained as glimpsed from afar were thistle-down if it came to facts. But Hare remained unexpectedly economical.

'Have you set eyes on any dinner money since your last duty? Think and be quite direct with me.'

Draper looked at Frank with a contempt which Frank felt was justified.

'No, sir. Why should I have?'

'Exactly.' Hare's eyelids fluttered dismissal. 'Thank you.' Draper marched out.

'Three pounds ten. We seem no nearer making it up. I'll make you an offer, probably improper. I mean repayment of the sum within the week.'

Frank felt a surge of gratitude for this generosity coming down, inexplicably out of character, like grace.

CHAPTER 14

BEFORE the week-end Frank had changed his mind. His change from a fluid state of wondering where to get the money to a blaze of righteous anger which lit up Hare's motives as petty sidestepping was sudden. What settled him for a fair trial was not so much the abstract dame, Honour, as the concrete lout, Draper. A day or two after the accusation they met, nearly collided, after school.

Griffin was coasting down the hill by the hospital when the school captain drew level. What was said suited the circumstances. Draper told Frank he was a sneaking cad, if not in those words. Nervously aware of the 500 c.c. ticking over at his elbow, Frank called him a thief. By the time they had reached the roundabout their positions were clear. Draper was going to bust him once and for all; in return he would see Draper in the courts first. He drew up to regain his breath. Machine and Draper diminished rapidly down the boulevard.

Despondency swathed Griffin's decision not to pay; he wondered how he had ever thought he could extract himself for three pounds ten. The surrounding landscape remained immune. Neither depression nor decision had any effect on it. There was King Lear raging outside the ice-cream and stationery. No storm. The same pillar-boxes, lampstandards, hospital, new estate, playing-fields filling the saucer of land he was in. Overhead the sky was grey, featureless, immutable. He was caught in a trivial web: the shop, old Mrs Griffin, Anne, meaningless complications at school. The meanness of everything had him fast; voyages into Shakespeare and the French dictionary were futile escapes; the real world was so—colourless, solid, debilitating. The only positive thing in it was his refusal to pay Jugg what he now thought of as a sort of moral blood money.

Of course three pounds ten was a small price to avoid the risk of expulsion, investigations, more stupidity. But Jugg had more to lose than he did: to have another school captain crumble would not be a good advertisement for the autocrat who appointed school captains. If in the showdown Draper's guilt came out, any trouble would have been worth it; and it was high time Frank got Draper off his back once and for all. He would never pay Jugg that money. St Frank the dragon-slayer. He pictured high-toned scenes but they didn't come off.

He got through tea and when the television was switched on went upstairs as usual to work. Graham's door was open and he went in to have a chat with him. But his brother was out and he remembered that he was delivering groceries. Since Christmas he had been working in the shop and errands were part of his daily routine. That morning as Frank left for school a special bicycle had arrived. It was a trade type with a monstrously heavy-looking basket over its small front wheel; Mr Griffin had picked it up second-hand. Frank remembered the scuffle and excitement as he went out: the grocer sizing it up; Graham's noticing the previous firm's name still on the metal plate under the cross-bar; his father's. 'Put our name on, son. Take a while over it; you're the artistic one.'

He had forgotten all about this morning: his eight hours of other life had intervened. But now Graham had no other life. He idly looked round. Books, several about prehistoric animals, were piled on the table; on the wall a picture his brother had painted. Promising or ordinary? Frank had no eye for pictures. He wished Graham was there to talk to. Because he was out peddling their father's meagre wares, his belongings had the forlorn look of relics. Frank reverently turned over the books. The Cowper he had lent him, a Penguin Blake which he must have bought for himself. At the bottom of the pile Frank came across a desk-diary—Christmas present from Grandma Griffin; gobbets from Samuel Smiles Monday to Saturday and a rest on the Sabbath. The first page was blank except for the note:

'Start in Shop'. Overleaf there was something in the form of
verse:

> I have two friends
> One is tabby, one is black.
> They are two cats
> I have no other friends.

Start in shop. I have no other friends. This was the brother he
did not know, lonely, introverted, wasted; Frank had pried out
what he had suspected. Because he had not passed an examination when he was eleven Graham was to be a grocer; he himself
by grace of the examination ladder was not. Set for a university
course, he was nearly out of danger. He looked at the diary;
documentary evidence was something he was used to. It was
how you dissected the pickled dead. But knowing that Graham
was lonely and adolescent was different; it didn't help. Frank
wasn't doing an essay about him and Graham was not dead.

An hour or so later he went down. No Graham. Mrs Griffin
was worried, turning on her husband, missing the thread of her
serial. Frank volunteered to go and look for him. Mr Griffin
said that the boy was old enough to look after himself: he was
working for his living. His son took no offence, his wife no
comfort. There was a little crisis in the air.

Half an hour afterwards Frank was cycling through the cold
streets. Imagination burdened him with disasters. Graham was
under a bus or hurt in a fall. Graham was dead. The delivery
bike was too big and clumsy for safety. Or suicide. A canal he
crossed helped him to the thought. I have no other friends.
Reality intervened at the doctor's. This had been Graham's
main call. When the doctor's wife came, he explained his
mission.

Yes, she said, the boy had been and two of the eggs were
cracked. She would fetch them. She seemed to think that Frank
had replacements in his pocket. The eggs appeared on a
saucer, leaking apologetically.

'We always light boil—ninety seconds,' said the doctor's
wife. 'If we fried, there would be no complaint of course. It's
stomach-juices or something, John says.'

Frank told her of the worry at home over Graham; clucking with sympathy, she promised to scramble the doctor's eggs. Good nights were exchanged.

It was gone ten and his mother on the doorstep. There was talk of the police. Mr Griffin, still outwardly calm, was inwardly sagging under his wife's accusations. 'Sending him out like that,' she said, 'in the dark on a bike made for a man. You need your head seeing to, or your heart.'

'Stop carrying on, Jane. The lad would've phoned if anything was amiss.'

'*Phoned*! How can you phone from the ambulance, the mortuary?'

'Steady, mam,' said Frank. But it was late; he was as worried as they were. The words in Graham's diary took on a new and real pathos: his epitaph. Frank was made guilty of wilfully failing to befriend his brother while that was still possible. At the same time he knew he was indulging in melodrama. But the mortuary in his mother's mind seemed complete down to the last cold detail. She was weeping.

Her husband said: 'If there'd been an accident, the police would've phoned.'

'And how could the police have phoned? How'd they know who they were picking up when they picked up our Graham?'

'It's all on the bike, number and all,' he said triumphantly. 'Graham did it himself this morning.'

That did it: she sobbed uncontrollably and was becoming hysterical when Graham rode up on the hated machine, number and all, and not a scratch on him. In the midst of their relief and anger all he had to say for himself was that he had 'been for a ride'. He had been reading about the stars and it was a clear night.

When the parents had taken their fuss off to bed, Frank made cocoa. Graham knew far more about the stars than he did and was delighted with his sidereal observations through National Health spectacles.

What had seemed a newspaper tragedy to the mother and father, a tragedy of loneliness and despair to Frank had been nothing of the kind. Graham was happy and self-sufficient. A policeman who had stopped him for having no rear light had helped him locate and admire some constellation. By chance he was the one member of the city force with a home-made observatory in the back garden; Graham could go round any fine night when he wasn't on duty. When his brother went to bed, Frank was left with a changed view of him. All that godlike help which an accident seemed to have prevented—mere patronising! Graham was as independent as a cat. Working in the shop didn't worry him: he was too much of an individual to be swallowed up by something so unimportant. Heads had come down tails. Fear of the shop was a part of his own uncertainties. His compassion for Graham, for the old pensioner, for Popkin had more to do with him than them.

He couldn't sleep on this. Frank looked out his lined anorak, mounted his bicycle and set off for nowhere, under Graham's stars. Both lights worked perfectly and no policeman flagged him down. If one had, it would not have led to astronomy but to a fine. Three pounds ten. Near the shop most of the houses were in darkness. Here people had to start work too early to be up at this time. A sociologist could make a survey after eleven-fifteen of lighted windows. Behind some such house his brother's policeman had built not a garage or a potting shed but a place to eye the stars. On the great back of the planet where life and cities grew like a tiny layer of mould, a policeman off-duty was sitting among roads and greenhouses fixed on the stars.

He crossed a deserted main road into a region of bigger houses with more lights on. It was the way to Anne's house. Unlike Graham, he needed to be going somewhere; perhaps that was why he'd never met such policemen. Outside the Coopers' he stopped and wondered why he had come. According to his theoretical wealth/lights ratio, the place should have been blazing like Blackpool front. It was dark.

He gazed at the building as at a corpse. Anne was in there, inaccessible Anne. She was the unsatisfactory equivalent of his brother's stargazing. Yet she had appeared beneath the window of his room. He thought of the petty politics at school, the whole scrappy chain of events culminating in the dinner money affair. Anne was involved with every link of it. There was no one but Anne to discuss it with. He wanted to discuss it. The stand he was about to make was heroic and heroism needs onlookers, or drink. A light went on upstairs.

Frank worked out the light in relation to the remembered structure of the house. The light stayed on. If it was in Anne's room as he thought it was, she had possibly gone upstairs from the back. It was eleven-forty. Frank went through the open gate and stood on the lawn. If he could get her to come down and talk things over, his action would be more significant when he told Hare on Friday. A search revealed nothing smaller than a stone to throw at her window. What had Romeo done to attract attention? He'd sung, hadn't he? Come into the garden, Maud. No; Shakespeare had made it easy: after a minute or two Juliet had appeared. Anne was unlikely to step out on her window-sill. The obvious thing to do was to go back to bed. Frank found himself half way up the wall.

He was clasping a well-made drainpipe. On a level with the lighted window he rested. His position was easy, feet firmly placed on an ample wall-bracket. Removing a glove with his teeth, he ran his fingers over the surface of the pipe. He felt smooth, unpainted lead. It was square and solid and almost too good for draining mere rain-water. His hand admired its texture; he forgot where he was.

It looked a short step across to the ledge. Again he acted automatically. Now he was spread-eagled on the rough brickwork. One foot remained tucked against that comforting lead; but the other was nicked on the alien window-sill. Hands were palmed flat on the wall, one glove gone. He couldn't move. The glove worried him, lying at the base of the wall, one finger pointing upwards. Minutes passed.

His balance depended on arching in his spine. The bracing position induced confidence; a feeling of equilibrium which pleased him. Then slight twitchings in the muscles gave a warning. His back would go from concave to convex and fling him off. In no position to change his mind, he whistled softly and then more loud. His plight was not really his own fault: it had happened, ridiculous and unplanned like the snow business.

First he worried about who would open the window: the old man perhaps, Mavis, the unknown Mr Cooper. At least the old man was deaf. Next he worried lest no one heard him and he fell. Weak points were showing up all over his body. Soon he would slither down the wall like a broken crab. He whistled very loudly and called.

The sash-window slid up and three feet from him, just below eyelevel, a face looked out; it was Anne's.

'Good God! It's you,' she said.

'I'm stuck.'

'What are you doing?'

'I'm falling off. Do something,' he said in mannerless desperation.

'Hang on.' Anne disappeared. Now that rescue was coming, his danger increased. Muscles were less stubborn; mind less independent.

'You still there? Look, can you wait while I get a ladder? Or do you want to grab hold of this broom?'

'Broom.'

He clutched the broom handle; snatched his foot from the safe unpainted lead and lunged at the window. She seized his coat and went down under him. His shoulder hit the floor. He was in a lighted room, gasping.

He shook his head and got to his knees. As for something to say, there wasn't anything.

'Are you all right?'

'I think so,' he said.

'Not hurt?'

'I don't think so, thank you.'

'A cup of tea?'

'Thank you.'

'If you will come home before the milkman, I'm afraid it'll have to be plain,' she said.

'Thank you.'

'You haven't seen my fabulous electric kettle.'

'I am really sorry about this.'

'I thought you had changed your routine for once. You're one long blinking apologia.'

'Sorry.'

'Sit down and shut up. And take that windcheater thing off. It's not cold in here. Excuse the dishabille; I was going to bed.'

Anne's nightdress—simple-styled thin white material like a day dress in Jane Austen—gave Griffin something new to worry about. On the green ottoman he examined his brick-roughened palms; looked everywhere but at Anne. He was pleased to let her take charge.

'You do have a flair for drama, Frank. Hackneyed but technically accomplished; just the thing for the telly. Here we are. Heaps of sugar to get you over the shock.' He dumbly accepted the tea, having to look at her to receive the cup.

'You must be cold,' he said.

'Women are tougher; built for child-bearing they tell me. Drink it. What's the good of taking something for shock when the shock's worn off?'

He hadn't known her so hard-bitten or seen her so femininely defenceless. The contrast synthesised in a conclusion; or he jumped to one. His coming had unnerved her. That and/or the tea set him up.

'Come here, you, and sit down. You mustn't catch cold. Get near the fire.'

She joined him on the couch; relaxed into a smile. 'You are an idiot.'

Hard head, soft body. Frank had never been so ignorant of what she was. She was shivering.

'You are cold,' he said, solicitous.

'Am I?'

'Perhaps it's shock. I don't know why I climbed in. It was something. . . .' He looked into her accurate, greenish eyes, held. His mind could not place what had brought him. The drainpipe, literally. He remembered the smooth moon-coloured surface with a feeling of weight in it. The palms of his hands, where they were not scarred with the brickwork, were bloomed with lead.

'What *could* have brought you?' she asked, more arch.

'Dinner money.' His garden reasoning came back.

Anne laughed not quite under her control.

'That's ridiculous.'

In all seriousness Frank tried to explain. He paraded brass tacks: Draper, locks, duplicated balance sheets, Hare's duplicity. Anne yawned. She started smoking.

'That was what brought you?'

'Yes. I know it sounds stupid. I admit it.'

'Why don't you ever admit to anything else?'

'There was something else.' He started to dissect the business of Graham's astronomy. It made less sense than the dinner money; for one thing, Frank had only a dim idea of it himself. He broke off.

'You look like something out of Jane Austen,' he said.

'Something nice, I hope.'

'Something very nice,' he mumbled, setting down his cup, preparing to go.

'Jane Austen isn't in the syllabus.'

'I'd better be off. Thanks for the tea.' He got to his feet. Anne was looking up at him.

'You came,' she said.

'Can I go out the front door? I'll shin down the drainpipe if you like.'

'And plummet into the parental bed.'

'Anne,' he said, 'I am sorry.'

'Come here.' She kissed him. 'There you are: forgiven.'

Her kiss altered the situation like a signature. Frank's arms round her back were vibrant and autonomous. His body lived. The brain—like some over-civilised, depraved, intelligent commander—bathed in the pleasure of losing control. They made kisses deliberately, without hurry. The labyrinth was full of light.

'Now you can't go, honey,' she said.

All his education was telling him that discussion preceded action.

'You might regret it,' he said. It sounded masterful and played for time.

'In that case I would have turned you out, wouldn't I?'

They returned to kissing: kissing led on where more talk would have turned back. Frank calmed his hands on her body.

Anne was not so disturbed, though catching her sweet breath. She made a start on his anorak, then switched off the light. He got free of his heavy clothing, kicked off his absurd great shoes. They came together in scraps of moonlight. He thought of conscience; found himself not guilty. This was love. He used his mind not to observe but in an effort to control. Anne under him was receptive, gentle, helpful. But it was so untried that mind was overthrown. Bodies molten. Spilled.

They lay comforting one another with small caresses. Anne said:

'For a first time that wasn't bad.' Her voice was her usual one.

To Frank in a never-never land it sounded too practical, too mundane; though all he had for words was the melting slush of remembered romance. Talk was unnecessary when contact was through hands. The resultant feeling was one of great separateness and not the fusion he had imagined; yet it was not severance and now he liked Anne more, or loved her. His consciousness had advanced. The mind's excitement came as a backwash: towering, absurd. They had been picked out by that great flashlight. The Earth was hurtling through space carrying them on its skin. From where he was lying he could see the moon; it gave the pitch for his madness. They were its creatures, something it had imagined, he thought—their faces moon-mash over the hard skulls. They lay motionless under the sheet and the thin lead-foil of the moon. Anne nipped him with her slender fingers.

'What are you thinking, love?'

'That it wasn't so bad,' he said.

'I thought you were good. Thank you, Frank.'

Tenderness grew as they became more pleased with themselves.

She said: 'Think what it must be like for the chaste honeymoon first-nighters; like taking part in a music-hall joke.'

'Honeymoon before the marriage,' said Frank.

'Just honeymoon.'

Griffin watched the leaden moon riding through cloud. Poetic image and rocket-base. It brought no madness this time.

'We must start thinking about marriage,' he said.

'Frank! I'm surprised at you. What a suggestion!'

'You seem to forget there might be a child. I don't mean that's why we ought to get married.' In this case the clumsiness followed the event. Realising how crass his words must have sounded, he took comfort from the expected womanly amusement at his muddle. Instead Anne said: 'You seem to forget I'm not daft.'

'I'm sorry.'

'You're sorry for all the wrong things.' That was feminine enough, cryptic. 'You're just like Peter.'

Mohan had gone out of Frank's mind.

'I felt guilty over him on the hike,' he said. 'This is much worse, isn't it? I've betrayed him.'

'I don't see how you can. You go on as though you're knights of the round table. Which makes me a sort of medieval lollipop. This was between us; nothing to do with Peter. I've betrayed him, if you like. But it never worked with him.'

Did she mean in bed? It was the cue for jealousy, etc. Frank felt a weak, an almost obligatory pang. 'You mean sexually?' he asked.

She laughed. 'No, I don't!'

Hasty apologies; but this time they weren't needed. All was affection and womanly amusement when he'd thought he had made a worse blunder—insulted her honour or something.

'Pete was a bit overwhelming somehow. I could never be frightened of you, honey. He's more fascinating than you are, of course.'

When Griffin left by the drainpipe, he did so silently and with precision. He retrieved his glove and got home at half past two.

CHAPTER 15

FRANK entered Hare's study with a brief knock. Things had completely turned round for him since Monday's accusation and his half-hearted decision not to bail himself out of trouble for three pounds ten. Anne had been the catalyst changing all his thoughts and actions.

The headmaster looked up from his desk. 'What is it?'

'I've come about that money, sir.'

'Come back at lunchtime. I am very busy.'

'It won't take a minute, sir. I stole nothing; I'm paying nothing back.'

'I beg your pardon?' Hare's surprise was better managed than most of his dramatic effects.

'It's impossible for me to do as you said, sir.'

'But you have done it. I have the money in this drawer.'

Griffin said nothing.

'The incident is considered closed.'

'But you can't have.'

'Thank you, Griffin. Say no more. I am a little tired of boyish moral oratory.'

Frank left abruptly. The cunningly-placed mirror showed him Hare's scholarly head already bent over his papers In the fish-tank he laughed. Hare must have paid up out of his own pocket. Three pounds ten had been the bargain price not of his continuance at school but of the headmaster's avoidance of scandal. If every man had his price, that was Hare's sum, not his. Or Miss Turle had made some monstrous clerical error and there had been no theft. Greta, tight-skirted, her small belly pouting deliciously, was coming along the corridor towards him. She smiled. He asked her whether Turle had broken down weeping when the mistake had been discovered.

131

'It came in postal orders this morning.'

'Who from?'

'Search me; there wasn't any letter.'

'Nothing at all?'

'Just three pounds ten. Search me; this place gets more like the blinking Kremlin every day.'

'Thanks a lot, Greta.'

It couldn't have been better, he thought, gleefully striding back to the library: Draper had caved in, for all his blustering. Reconstructed, their exchange on the road assumed more firmness of stance on his part than he had actually shown. Anne gave him new bearings on all old landmarks.

In the library Mohan, whom he had not seen for a few days, was unavoidable. Idly perched on a table and bookless, there was no creeping by him. As Frank had mentioned the dinner money business to him—chiefly as something to say to allay his increasing uneasiness in his presence—he reported the latest development.

'It's pretty odd,' Mohan agreed. 'I suppose you're right: it must have been Draper. Poor twisted blighter.'

'He's sod enough for anything.'

'I'm thinking, or did I say, of leaving when I can get round to it. There's not much point in hanging on here.'

'Leaving?' Griffin sounded as he felt and didn't mean to sound: pleased. Acting was needed. 'How do you mean, "no point"? You're in a good, leisurely position.' He was half expecting a passionate outburst of accusation; but Mohan's tone was easy, with no edge at all to it.

'I'm through into university; I'd like a change. School's gone sour on me. Things like yours just now. Bitterness. I don't enjoy it. It sounds wet but I want to believe people are good. I've made some friends.'

Again Frank was dissatisfied with himself. Looking at Mohan's handsome face, he was reminded of that time at the swimming bath when they had shaken hands. That was their heroic era. Things had gone the other way.

'If I stay, I shall be disenchanted with the uses of this world. I musn't turn into a Jesuit, all harshly abrasive. I envy you;

you've got nothing on your back. Not like us poor pseudo Catholics or even old Welsh Williams staggering around under a load of inherited claptrap.'

'Don't we all?' said Frank.

'Agreed. We live in nets. I think girls are probably better at living than we are. What's your opinion?'

'What about?'

'That's not like you. I've just made a highly questionable and meaningless statement about girls. You let it go.'

'I don't know if they're different. They've got their own nets.'

'Hair-nets.' Mohan laughed. 'Give me a metaphor and I'll follow it to the ends of the earth. I had a symposium with Draper before Christmas; girls again. I got taken for his father confessor.'

'That must have been interesting.'

'Wasn't really. A dirty mind, impure and simple, was all he revealed. He was honest about it, though. And he has a chaste passion for one Joan Morley—I don't think you know her. It almost redeemed some of the other things he said.'

'You hadn't told me about this chat,' said Frank.

'It ended abruptly, snapped off by me, I'm afraid. He reckoned you were playing about with Anne.'

Frank mumbled something non-committal. His face went neither red nor white. He carried it off. Conscience slept; mind was wry. Any playing about had been the other way round.

Mohan was folding and unfolding his arms and yawning. 'You know, I'm bored. Both occupations gone: no detentions to give, no exams to pass. I may as well buzz off. Are you doing anything this evening?'

'No.'

'Then why not come along to a groovy cultural evening? Here you are: one free ticket. We're all meeting in the pub next to the Playhouse at seven thirty.'

When he had gone, Frank examined the ticket. The play was one he had heard of: *'Tis Pity She's a Whore*. He thought of Popkin's opinion of Anne; gave up. Mohan had not engineered the ticket by way of satirical comment; he hadn't put on the play; even the ticket was impersonal: one of the weekly issue to sixth forms.

The title of the play ensured a sell-out. Ford had made his point; old Shakespeare's what you wills and as you like its meant an Arts Council subsidy.

The pub was brimful with the cultured of the province. It took Frank—in his one suit and less unfashionable shoes—a long time to reach the bar. The school's contingent was ensconced in a corner. He saw Frazer first; Frazer waved. Then the curly black of Williams's head occluding Mohan's fair—a few girls.

'Hi,' said Lucy. 'Sit on my knee. I need a buffer state, darling. You'll do nicely.'

'She's a proper Poland. She ought to be partitioned.' Williams was babbling.

Frazer said: '*You* tell us what this play's about. Pete for once doesn't know.'

'I've told him it's incest; but he won't believe me.'

'How can you have incest if the characters are in dustbins.'

'Christ!' said Williams. 'Hasn't he been telling you it's not modern.'

'Dear Bill thinks it's by Beckett,' Lucy explained.

'Beckett's decadent, isn't he? You told me this was decadent.'

'Bless him. We're not the only ones to be decadent, darling. It goes round in circles.'

'What is she talking about?' asked Frazer.

'You're so obtuse,' said Mohan, 'that no one can get away with anything.'

'If we were all as clever as you. . . .' Frazer trailed off.

'Look who's here!' whooped Lucy. 'We thought you'd been abducted at the bus-stop.'

'Am I late?'

Frank was facing away from the congested entrance but the three words were enough for him to recognise Anne's voice. He had half expected her to come, and to be with her in public was a necessary test. A sudden nervous depression handicapped him before the trial commenced.

They had two minutes to beat the curtain and half way down the aisle they were frozen by The Queen. A gent in evening dress shooed them into a row in the same random order. Chance not symbolism sat Frank between Anne and Mohan.

It was a lavish production. The stage was full of high impossible Italian names and authentic doublets stuffed with smoky lust. Ford's verse laid it on with a silver trowel and the actors lived it up. Everything was sinister and significant.

Frank, small and real, was miserable. He was only half following. Anne's smile as they sat down had been no more than a social salute. Her hands, clasped tightly on her lap, were nothing to do with him. He slumped, more morbid than Ford. On one side of him was Anne, on the other, Mohan. He imagined lines of force between them, pencilled in Ordinary Level Physics style. Towards the interval he felt bodily exhausted. His body was tenser than when it had hung crucified on the Coopers' brickwork. He nearly got up and went out; at the interval he would get up and go out; a second half like this one was unthinkable.

Curtain.

'Is there a bar in this place?' Bill asked far too loudly and a split second before speech was in place.

'You are a groundling,' said Lucy. 'Yes, there is.'

Frank didn't move. Let the others go and chatter; he wanted to suffer.

'Come on,' said Mohan. 'It wasn't that good.'

He joined the stream.

The bar was typical of theatres: the old lady behind it had been put there for dramatic irony. She had difficulty with hearing, with change, with bottle-tops. The fifteen minutes dwindled. Bill started groaning.

'I didn't know you were coming, Anne,' said Griffin. 'I wish we were by ourselves.'

'Why? I like the others.'

'It's unbearable.'

'Don't be silly; of course it isn't.'

135

'Going around in great flocks.'

'Don't make things awkward, honey.'

Williams appeared with a small tray of drinks. 'Madame, Monsieur.'

'I don't want one,' said Frank rudely.

'Moving i'n't it, this play?'

Frank said: 'It's overdrawn rubbish put on for people with nothing better to talk about.'

Williams asked Lucy for her opinion.

'It's divine. I only wish I had a brother. Isn't decadence splendid? Haven't I always said so? Look at Bill talking to Peter about football! Bill's so *un*decadent.'

'Middle-class rubbish,' said Frank wildly. 'Like the present-day lot. Those characters are just mechanisms for raping each other. As if sex is a crossword puzzle.'

'Please,' said Anne.

'That's exactly what sex is, darling. It's just like politics or anything else: something to be witty about, if you can. Wit's all we poor moderns have got.' Lucy had made her major statement.

'You don't understand anything,' said Griffin.

'For goodness' sake don't be so stupid.' Anne spoke the words in his ear. She was affectionate, kindly, soothing. It made him angry.

'Too much of a Philistine for you, am I?'

'Good God,' said she.

One drama at a time. The second bell went.

The last acts passed quicker for Frank. The interval had made things worse but now he was more actively wretched. He had a post-mortem to be getting on with. And when he had played himself out there was the play to watch.

They found room at last in an alcove of a cellar. The coffee-bar had opened in the twilight of milk-bars and had prospered. It had taken over the upstairs, the backyard, both next-doors and now the cellar. The 'atmosphere' was everything and nothing: fishing nets, sombreros, matadors' cloaks, cigarette machines, a Louis-Quatorze-type clock, more fishing nets, black leather jackets, students. Frazer ordered six coffees. The girl, flustered and rushed under her Max Factor, stilettoed her way up the narrow stairs.

'I shouldn't like her job,' observed Williams. 'Not that I've got the right figure. You'd be good, Luce. I can see you in the part.'

'It pays,' said Mohan. 'Think of her grandmother as skivvy to some lace tycoon. Now she has cash, she has glamour: everything in the world.'

Anne said: 'I'd rather be a servant observing my betters through the keyhole. She just gets observed, and rather rudely.'

'So I'm rude,' said Bill. 'What Awkward Annie here wants is a nineteenth-century coffee-house or whatever it was. You're all the same, you arty intellectuals. Monkeys picking at your fleas. Take a warning from old Pete; you don't want to end up like him.'

'We're not intellectuals though.'

'There she goes again. Disagrees with every blind thing.'

'We haven't got the money,' said Frank.

'For what?' Anne asked.

'What you said: to be real intellectuals.' Frank felt happier, a bit. This time Anne had chosen to sit by him and in the talking he was on her side.

'You need it to be decadent, if that's the same thing.' Lucy, perched with improbable delicacy on Williams's knee, pegged up her theme for another airing. 'Poor people are debarred— so are healthy brutes like Bill. No, darling, being slovenly's not the same.'

But coffee arrived and no one was interested in her theses.

As always, Frank had his own to ponder on. What sort of relationship existed now between Anne and Mohan? Their words and gestures gave no clue. That they had cast off from each other with no more ado than Bill and Lucy was unlikely. Yet he could detect no sign of intimacy. To an outsider, he reflected, there was none to be detected between himself and Anne.

It was a tired question, too tired to get an answer from.

He was jerked out of it by a voice from the stairs. 'Hold it! Thank you. I'd like very much to go over a few songs. They're pretty hip: folky without being square, if you can believe it. Ludwig Koch hasn't recorded me yet. I'm bumming around just two towns ahead of him. Here we go. Relax, there's no collection.' On the bottom step the boy jerked upright and ran long, ringed fingers over the strings of his guitar. The old bardic device made people stop talking. 'I'm perhaps one of the few folk left so I'm going to start with my own composition. It's about my old mother, gawdblimey. It's not Freudian by the way; it's not about Freud's mother.' He started singing, not so much accompanied by his playing as entangled in it:

'A story I'll tell you as true as I'm here
About a young woman who got drunk on beer;
She got drunk on wine and she got drunk on gin
And once got so drunk that's where I came in.

Her morals were lousy; the blackout was on,
The buzzbombs were buzzing all over London;
A soldier I think or some military man
Took hold of her hand and so I began.'

The singer was smiling to himself and executing a fiddly bit on his guitar when a big man tapped him on the shoulder. The big man was in a dinner jacket—incongruous, there where nothing was out of place.

'Was that you singing?'

'That's right, dad.'

'I'm not licensed for singing. Saturday nights is different but I got skifflers in on contract. Cut it out.'

'This is art, not skiffle.'

'Cut it out's all I'm asking.'

'Dad, all I did was sing. We're human beings sharing experience in art. Admit it.'

'Shame!' shouted Lucy. 'Let him sing.'

'This isn't an easy job I've got,' said the owner pacifically: then, to the singer: 'Get yourself in a group if the customers like you.'

'I'm not commercial.'

'Come and talk it over in my office.'

138

The boy followed the big back meekly upstairs. On the top step he looked about him, puzzled; he was gone.

'Artistic integrity,' said Anne.

'My coffee's cold. Let's get out before we have any more performances,' said Bill.

For Griffin the problem of homegoing was more crucial than after the Christmas social. Did Mohan assume he was taking Anne home? If so, it was up to Anne to make things public. Lucy wanted a hot-dog from a small handcart which looked folky against the plate-glass and neon of big business but was probably kept by one of next year's millionaires.

'I'm like a dog with lampposts with things like that,' she explained.

Anne offered anybody who wanted one a lift home in the car. Everyone but Frazer accepted. Frank shared the back seat with Williams and Lucy. As the car started up, the hot-dog fell to the floor and Frank helped to retrieve it. But that was the end of communal activity. They shrank into the corner leaving him sitting old-lady-upright like someone taking refuge in a strange town's cinema landed in the back row. He was well and truly isolated from Anne. Was it significant that Mohan was sitting in front? He was tired of himself but his mind worked out a map of setting-down points. It was convenient to drop Williams and Lucy first; but then geography left it up to the driver whom she took home next.

Lucy and Williams managed to climb out, arms round waists. The roads outside seemed to be leading them to the shop. She would deposit him and finish the evening with Mohan. Let her. The whole evening had confirmed him in thinking theirs was a love-affair without love. She was a player on other people's nerves, heartless. Inert as a parcel in transit, he listened as one listens to conversations on buses, academically.

'I thought it was still on: Lucy and Bill,' said Anne.

'They're not very bothered.'

'What tangled lives we lead.'

'Don't we just. I live here, clever girl! Coming in?'

'Ask Frank.'

Mohan swivelled round. 'He seems to be asleep.'

139

Frank was pretending to be asleep. He had no definite object in doing so.

'We'll get along. Thanks for the offer of refreshment.'

'See you at the City Strings then.'

'I'm not even sure about that, Peter.'

'Not Bartok?'

'Won't promise.'

'Good-bye.' They kissed briefly.

Anne accelerated violently. Frank opened his eyes. He said— the first words he had spoken in the car:

'You kissed him.'

'I beg your pardon?'

'I said you kissed him. A bloody funny idea of people's feelings you've got; I've learnt that much.'

'You're fantastic.' She skidded round a road-island.

'Slow down!'

She stopped. They were at the shop. 'What the hell is wrong with you?'

'It's not me; it's you,' said Frank. 'You're totally irresponsible emotionally.'

'Totally irresponsible emotionally.'

'That's right, make me sound stupid. Just because I don't accord with your rather flashy idea of witty, cultured behaviour. Things are different, Anne. We're lovers.'

'You own me; is that it? My lord and master. You had my precious maidenhead.'

'Of course I don't,' he said, though perhaps that was what he had been thinking. She was snuffling in her handkerchief. 'Hush,' he said, softening and pleased to. 'Don't you cry, love.'

'I've got a cold coming.' Anne blew her nose. She had a cold coming; everything was going wrong.

He touched her shoulder. 'I'm jealous of Pete.'

'You can't trust me very much.'

This was better, more like the book. 'Of course I do, but did you have to kiss him?'

'He's a friend. You never look at things from my angle. I'm sorry if I didn't stop to consider your precious sensibility; something more important's happened. That's why I was late

140

for the play. And why I don't particularly want to go home.'

Egoist! Frank's one hopeless idea was that she was pregnant. He said: 'But it's far too early.' This time he was lucky.

'It's nearly midnight. I ought to go home. Grandpa had a stroke this afternoon.' Now she did weep. Tears had always devastated Frank. He was at it with kisses and handkerchief across the well-padded back of the driving seat. He called himself a moronic fool and felt himself one, on other grounds. Anne's grandfather was the assertive little man he had met on his first visit.

'He'll be all right, you see.'

'He's too old. He'll die.'

There was nothing to say. Frank was unmoved on the old man's account but his illness had been useful to improve the evening; it was a godsend. When he said how sorry he was, he thought he was speaking the truth. 'And it's been worrying you the whole time,' he ended.

'It changes one's viewpoint,' said Anne, rather primly. 'I didn't mean to hurt you; I didn't mean to kiss Peter. Such things don't matter a lot at the moment.'

Frank was on the kerb, apologising through the driver's window.

'You're quite right; I am selfish and insensitive.'

'Anyway you're happy again now you're saying sorry.' She smiled, the tears still wet on her face. Frank experienced a great pang of love or sentimentality. Kissing her, he felt he'd done some good at last. The old man's stroke had been a perfect let-out.

'He'll pull through,' he said as she started the engine. 'A game old chap like him.'

CHAPTER 16

HAVING put the car away, she walked up to the front door as quickly as any doctor on his morning calls. There she hesitated. The house was silent, dark and still as death.

But her father was in the 'civilisation room' as they called it, the drawing-room which served as music-room and library. He was reading in the pool of one standard lamp.

'Did you have a nice evening?'

She took off her coat relieved. Even her father could never open the conversation like that if the worst had happened.

'How is he?'

'Fairly peaceful, I think.'

'He's not in hospital?'

'No point; you can't move them about at that age.'

'Is Mummy with him?'

'Yes, she is. I called in a nurse.'

'Oh.' Anne hung up her coat and came back; she wanted to delay going up.

'He can't last long. Don't have any false ideas about miracles,' said Mr Cooper. 'Rich men can pass through the eyes of needles but everyone dies.'

'I thought he had died when I came in.'

'Perhaps he has. It's half an hour or more since I saw him.'

'Can't you give your callousness a rest for once?'

Mr Cooper looked up at his daughter, raised his eyebrows. He appeared as he always did: formal. Never conventional, never standoffish, there was something never to be relaxed in his soul. Anne had thought it a shield borne against others or against himself. 'Callousness' was only her definition for the moment, to suit the present circumstances.

'This is just the time my callousness should remain. My view of life is consistent, if nothing else. Do you want me to go contrary to my nature because an old man's dying? You'll get more honest as you grow older.'

'I don't want that sort of honesty.'

'You've no choice, love. Did you enjoy the Playhouse?'

'Lousy.'

'The play or the production?'

'Everything.' He would drive her upstairs with his fine distinctions.

'How's the work then? It must be epochs if not æons since we had a good chat.'

'I don't know. Did the doctor say he'd go into hospital?'

'I told you, Anne. They only do that for a politician or a well-known. Medicine has to in such cases—to save face, not life. Otherwise the public would have no faith in them. No public, no futile gestures.'

'How's Mummy taking it?'

'Upset, of course.'

'I'll go up to her.' To reach the door, Anne had to pass his chair. As she went by, her father caught her hand.

'Why must you?'

'Of course.'

'Your mother will be down shortly; I'll fetch her myself. The nurse is there.'

'But to see grandad.'

'What point in that?'

'I love him.' Anne tore her hand free but he was up, gripping her shoulders; speaking harshly, out of key, out of character.

'Go up. But, if you do, understand your motives. You're like me though you deny it; you're my daughter. The reason's because the sight of his twisted face will hurt you into grief—the more, the better. For your own sake, that is why you're going, not for his. It's unenlightened self-interest, believe me. And for God's sake don't whimper. I'm not your lover.'

'You're detestable!' She broke free and ran from the room.

The door was ajar; inside, night-lights and a medical smell. She was on tiptoe. Her mother and the nurse were sitting at either side of the bed like unmoving, mantelshelf Florence Nightingales. The bed's great expanse divided them and in the

143

bed the sick man made a tiny, insignificant hummock. The nurse got up and intercepted her on the threshold.

'He's quite peaceful and your mother is asleep. You go to bed, dear. I'm trained for this work.'

'I must kiss him good night.'

Her shoulders were held more gently and insistently than just now.

'Bed. Quick march.'

'I'm going to him. Please let me go.'

The nurse did not. 'I'll bring you tea in the morning.'

A loud rasping sound came from the old man. 'It's coming every few minutes,' said the nurse. 'Gases from the stomach.'

Anne freed herself and went to the head of the bed. Her grandfather's face was curiously distorted like one modelled on a sagging balloon. She saw a lop-sided caricature of the sprightly old man. Another of the sounds broke out; it had no connection with any human or animal sound. Death was going on, terrible to watch. But the thing in the bed was not her grandfather: it was something unrecognisable. She felt neither horror nor grief.

'He can't recognise you; he's unconscious. I didn't want you to see him.'

'I'm not a child.'

'I'm used to it, dear,' said the nurse—comforter of sick and hale. 'The old fellow's quite peaceful.'

'I'm not; that was why I had to see him. It's a good experience.'

'Your first deathbed shocks you a bit. I've been by them regularly now for twenty years.'

'He's going to die then?'

'It slipped out. Quite soon, I'd say.'

'Good.'

'It looks terrible but he's going the best way.'

Anne went to bed without having kissed the old man. She slept the night through and dreamt no dreams.

On the outskirts of the city you could gauge the advance of

spring by flowers as well as by women's cotton dresses. In fact a whole department was maintained by the council to coax up daffodils in the dancing cloud of diesel fumes.

The school permitted spring to dress its little planted trees but Hare's permission ended there. The first week of April was so hot that a deputation of four prefects went to plead with him for open-neck shirts. Frank was one of them. Since the dinner money episode of weeks before he had not entered the Head's study.

Grant put their case in his unhurried but confused style, ending:

'So as it's so hot, sir, we felt it would be better for work. The summer term it always rains except when exams are on. The youngsters are taking their ties off anyway; and always giving lines devalues the effect, sir.'

Hare settled in his chair and smiled with pleasure. This was his sort of show. Frank cursed: it would be too late to go home and change; he would have to meet Anne as he was.

'Study has many enemies,' said the Head. 'Parents for example, some parents, and especially those who go through life without a neck-tie. Adolescent romances are another enemy, and so is sunshine.' He scanned the delegation, giving them a moment to digest points A, B and C. 'My feeling here is that ties are analogous to shaving in the army: they are a disciplinary prop. Did you speak, Griffin?'

Frank denied it. To object to Hare's nonsense would only give rise to more and make him later. He had yawned.

'Against my better judgment, I have conceded the open collar in Summer Term; I see no reason to abandon my judgment entirely.'

Grant restated all his former arguments, expanding them, getting more muddled. Hare replied with a short lecture on discipline. Frank, comforting himself by thinking of some vague-conceived medieval process called 'trial by boredom', yawned again.

'Griffin, why are you yawning?'

'I don't know, sir. It must be the heat.'

The meeting seemed to have ended. Frank fished out his cycle clips and stood up, as much relieved to be going as he had on the previous occasion. He was politely holding the door for the other three when the Head called him back.

'Close the door and sit down.' Hare sank out of sight behind his desk. Frank wondered if he were doing up his shoes or looking for money on the floor. Just enough of the polished scalp was visible to perform a blessing over or to be the target of a downswinging blow with the glass inkstand. Hare surfaced with a silver cigarette box, smiled, seemed to be offering him a cigarette. Shattered, Frank helped himself and craned forward to receive a light. Now anything was possible—expulsion, perversions. The four-twenty bell sounded.

'Out of hours,' said Hare with some relief.

'Thank you, sir,' Frank said, inhaling deeply.

'You might scrub your finger-ends, Griffin; smoking is not a habit you should advertise. You were telling the truth about that theft, Griffin. My pleasure at that has instigated me to break the rules, this once.'

Frank was moved, not greatly, but enough to feel pleased that his headmaster was to be seen as a fallible human being rather than merely as a moral coward. Hare's facial geometry showed pleasure and Frank could reflect it by smiling back.

'I shall explain. When we were confronting each other early this term, it seemed to me that a moral dry-rot had got hold of the school. First I had been faced with the scandal of Popkin last winter. I sack the boy; I choose afresh; you are my choice. But then you appear to collapse—you implicate Draper. The thing is like a stone dropped in water. Yesterday these foul clouds dissolve. You are as innocent as you said.'

'I don't quite follow, sir.'

'Yesterday I stumbled over the truth. Chance put me on to it; that and an observant eye,' said Hare modestly. 'The money when it came did so in a buff-coloured continental envelope. It was disposed of but when I was in the library—a very good new book on the American Labour Acts; but you are not taking Economics—I saw several envelopes of the same type among

146

a boy's papers. That boy was Popkin, Griffin. Please use the ashtray.'

Frank used the ashtray.

'You see my point? The contagion is limited and the school has a clean bill of health. I am recommending Popkin for psychiatric help.'

Frank felt like someone making a stand against the forces of evil whose inside is attacked suddenly by indigestion.

He collected his books from the fish-tank. Popkin had suffered some sort of breakdown, that much was clear. He had suffered at the police station and in assembly but that was months ago; and, besides, it was well known that Popkin had a very unhappy home-life. Psychology was hard to understand. When he remembered how Popkin had looked on the cross-country, Frank thought only of his own state of mind at that time, the way he had changed, and of Anne. He went out into the sunshine; the day was still energetic with spring. Only under cloud can man study and moralise.

Built on a hill, the school caught the wind from the country. A smell, compounded of growth and industrial smoke, came to him. There was no one about and his bicycle was solitary in the racks. He was inevitably reminded again of Popkin. Like Popkin, his bicycle had been taken by the police; like Popkin it could break down at any moment. But Popkin's home background was bad and unsettled. The theft of dinner money was deranged spite, not poetic justice. His rear tyre was flat. He saw Mohan and Frazer coming across the playground from the science block. He unfixed his pump.

'Flat?' shouted Bill.

The tyre would make him late for Anne, dressed in best suit or not. He was in for talking and delay.

They came up the steps. Mohan's hair was bright in the sunlight.

'We'll walk down with you.'

'Puncture?'

Frank said: 'I think someone must have loosened my valve.'

'Price of prefecture,' said Frazer. 'At least they didn't slash your tyres. I caught some little sod doing that to Popkin's old

147

bone-shaker once. Administered corporal punishment on the spot.'

Frank wheeled his lame machine down the long ashphalt drive.

The others talked generally. 'You still thinking of leaving?'

'France, I think, away from here. D. H. Lawrence, Byron, everybody leaves sooner or later.'

'I shan't ever leave,' said Bill. 'I'll get a practice here and join the Old Boys' Association. When you lot are famous, I'll just be happy.'

'And we'll be free when you're stuck in your nostalgia like a fly in amber.'

'That's good,' said Bill who liked a simile.

'Before I go I ought to make a gesture.'

'You could pump up old Griff's tyre here.'

'If you are asked to carry his helmet a mile, carry it twain,' Mohan said cryptically. 'Give me thy pump.'

'I'll do it,' said Frank. They were at the gate, ten yards from . the concrete road. He wanted to get going. Mohan took the pump from him.

'I had a bike,' he annouced, 'when my father was alive. I'd have been about eight or nine when I had a puncture.' He fumbled with the valve.

'Did it hurt?' Frazer asked.

Mohan went on with his story, jerking out the words in time to his pumping. 'He mended it for me. I watched him. When it came to putting the tyre on again, he was obviously doing it wrong. I said something purely out of mechanical curiosity. Told him to keep his hand on to stop it popping out. Lost his temper. Offended his ego. My innocence was wiser than his corruption. There—hard as a rock.' Mohan cranked himself upright and smiled.

'I don't get you,' said Bill.

'Explain the text for him, Frank.'

'Don't ask me,' said Frank. 'Thanks, Pete.'

'I used to think that innocence had the edge over worldly wisdom.' Mohan sounded unusually plain and in earnest. 'My sense of sin is slipping. I've been reading psychology among

148

other things. That's why there's the Index. I've been tempted to subtle intellectual sins: Christianity was a good idea that doesn't work. It seems that not sleeping with your sister is only a social taboo.'

'And the fact that I don't have a sister, thank God.'

'I'll leave you to it,' said Frank.

Having locked his bicycle to a street-sign, Frank went to the Council House. It was the first time they had arranged a public rendezvous in town and he was embarrassed to find himself one of many young people waiting on the steps. The word 'swains' came unbidden. He took his place among the classless young hopefuls, the wearers of pointed shoes and Italianate suits, the be-twilled oxbloods. But differences were only in detail: age and situation made them essentially the same.

They were casual to a man. Some had climbed the steps to study the architecture of the Market Square; others to light a cigarette, out of the late afternoon breeze. Some were here to read the official notice of Quarter Sessions. All had one eye open in case some girl they knew should appear by chance in that perfectly normal place to be at five o'clock. Frank took his turn at the notice board. The date itself was enough to frighten the life out of you: In the Year of Our Lord One Thousand Nine Hundred and so on. By legal magic the Tuesday night sweet-shop job became a conviction on the Fifth Day of April in This Year of Our Lord.

He scrutinised the Square, retreated into a telephone-kiosk, decided against calling her. She was now twenty minutes late. The pubs weren't open so she could not be paying him the compliment of taking Dutch courage. For the tenth time he checked with himself date, time, place. Nearly all the others by now had their coincidental meetings fulfilled. He was no longer one of many young swains in the public eye, but the forsaken swain; a figure for young passers-by to giggle at and a cause of mutual, motherly glances exchanged between middle-aged matrons out shopping together. Or so he imagined. He wondered where Anne was, in what setting; and cursed her.

And then she was there, sophisticated in a light blue shift

dress, and on her head a large, cartwheel hat of navy straw. She dazzled him; he wished he had changed into his suit.

'I'm late,' she said.

'Not really. You look very nice.'

'Late but beautiful like this year's spring cabbage.'

'I like your hat.'

'I don't. Probably shan't wear it again. This get-up's a compliment to you, not a habit.'

'Well, it is a habit,' Frank said weakly. She didn't need to have said it. If you wanted to please someone you kept quiet about it. He was growing nervous. He was landed with a girl to entertain. She was looking improbably beautiful and expensive; and he had no money, no programme.

She was unhelpful. 'Where are you taking me in this fair city?'

'What would you like to do?'

'Peter and I used to ask each other what we should do to be saved.'

'*Did* you?' Her mention of Mohan annoyed him into greater independence. He and she must have catalogued the available recreations right down to the City Strings. But his own courtship of her, if that was what it was, had started where most courtships ended.

Nothing that could be done in public by such an ill-assorted pair suggested itself. Self-consciousness had made them in his mind Beauty and the Beast almost.

'What did you use to do?' he asked.

She squeezed his hand. 'You take the lead. My job is to be amused.'

'Do you want me to walk on my hands?'

'Yes please.'

'Shall we go somewhere and talk?'

'Talk, talk.'

Frank manufactured some determination. 'Follow me,' he said. He took a few steps and looked round. She remained on the municipal steps, laughing at him. New fabric against pretentious old stone—a page from *Vogue* come alive. When he walked off, she followed. They got on a bus stopped by traffic-lights. It took them down to the river. The sun was still holding though dusk was coming and it would be short. On the embankment he held her hand.

Anne said that the river was a good and romantic idea. Frank got the credit but he had brought her here, if he had any motive at all, subconsciously. The embankment was the place where he had come a year or so before to be alone in adolescent misery. That same water, those very trees, the identical boat-hiring jetties had been the scene of old despairs. They were here, if he had a motive, to cancel that region of his past.

'Country life,' said Anne. 'Chilly and green.'

He put an arm round her shoulders. 'How are things at home?'

'Since the funeral? Depressing. It's not the same since he died. That hateful cremation and now the parents bickering at each other.'

Frank tried to envisage death. It was an abstract concept, not too abstract though; everyone knew something about it. Not like God or Character. No one he had ever known well had died. Old Ma Griffin would go one day, but he couldn't see it; Griffin père; his mother; Graham; himself; Anne: they would all go into the fire.

'He was old,' he said.

'He had more life than we have.'

He believed her, though the old man's death seemed to disprove what she said. It wasn't a death he could believe in but the fact of it somehow heightened the feeling of life in him. The night was quite warm; they ought to get down on the grass and make physical love. He took his arm away and looked into the water. He was still only her fool.

'A penny for them.'

'I don't know. It's a pity it's too late for a boat. We could have gone out to the sun.'

'You're waxing mighty lyrical.'

'Stop fencing me off,' he said. 'I thought things had changed when we went to bed together. You don't ever talk straight; you go on as if I'm a witty sort like Mohan.'

'I couldn't stand it if we confided all the time. It's more

exciting to fence a bit. Besides, I'm what I am; I can't help what I am.'

'You could try,' he said bitterly.

'That's a mistake. Be nice to me, honey.' They kissed like any other courting couple. Then she said: 'You try to change yourself. Puritans always do. It's a mistake. One of Peter's good qualities was a kind of easiness he had; he left himself alone. Perhaps it's a virtue of Catholicism: they're quite free really. I suppose, once you can swallow that lot, their church takes it off their shoulders.'

'Why are you talking about religion?' He kissed her again, not wanting to talk about anything.

'I wasn't. I was just comparing you and Peter. I'm a social scientist in disguise, doing fieldwork.'

'It's a good disguise,' he said: happy, affectionate, hitting off his replies. Anne was telling him home truths and he was humbly prepared to listen.

'They've left the oars in that boat. Take me for a ride.'

'It's dark.'

'Come on, Charon.' She raced across the litter-scattered grass.

He gestured to heaven—film-actor's shorthand communication to the audience that the opposite sex is a mystery. Not that there was an audience. He ran after her.

'Row upstream.'

Arthur Ransome was the nearest Frank had come to oarsmanship; but passion made accurate mechanics. The oars were not a pair but he fitted them into the rowlocks and cast off the painter. He was surprised to be in the centre of the dark water, far from either bank and travelling purposively upstream. When they were level with the Garden of Remembrance the apprehension of arrest finally left the scruff of his neck. The memorial's rather Greek gateway and the sun setting behind its scrolled wrought-iron suggested the timelessness it had been designed for; flashed superb across the coal-black Trent.

A bend in the river was making things difficult; suddenly one bank was very much nearer than the other. Frank battled with the oars. They were ill-matched—they had been left out as a trap for such as he—they were male and female: transmigrated lovers. The big masculine oar in his right hand had a will of its own, slicing down sheer cliffs of water. And the other tittered frivolously on the surface. The boat swung broadside to the current.

'Pull the other one from the way you want to turn,' Anne said.

'I am. It's the current.'

She laughed and made her way forward, falling on top of him as the prow grated ashore. The stream arranged them alongside. Tall grass overhung them and in the darkness secret life rustled and plopped. Voles and water-rats.

At least he had navigated them clear of the municipal embankment.

'So this is Hades.'

'I'm no good at rowing.'

'You are, honey. We've arrived—somewhere. Why, I can't even see the bridge.'

'It's like our first evening,' said Griffin.

The wail of a fire-engine crossing the river further down.

'Our tune,' she said. 'You're making romantic statements now. What next?' They kissed, a mutual reflex action. Her straw hat spun into the water and floated away. Frank started to rescue it. 'Let it go. We didn't know each other; you were an embarrassed schoolboy, weren't you, honey? That was before I took you in hand.'

'You're always getting me to break rules.'

'Am I?'

'You know that dinner money farce? Popkin lifted the money and sent it back. Hare found out. He told me this afternoon.'

'Whatever for? The idiot.'

'He's got to see a trick cyclist.' That was his father's sort of euphemism.

'God—the idiot. Tell me, does Popkin write poems?'

'I think so. Why?'

'Nothing,' she said. 'I had a Christmas card.'

'Look at that!' said Frank. The sun dished out a final flare of magnificence on the river.

153

'Popkin's an omen,' she said mournfully.

'You cold? You're shivering.'

'I only shiver when I'm cold. Got goslings hatching—that's what grandad said when he had gooseflesh. Which is why I said it, I suppose. I'm freezing. Be a gent and lend me your coat.'

Frank wrapped her in his blazer. She kissed him; he prolonged it and his blood beat up. He wasn't looking for words.

'Take me back, honey. I'm cold.'

By now the river was dank almost but Frank said: 'It's deserted here. Can't we stay a bit? There's nobody about. Please.'

'That's how Lawrence got rheumatism. Let's arrange something. I want to.'

Going back on the current was quite easy. They landed and tied up unobserved; Frank held his breath until they reached the bus-stop where there was a trolley-bus in, waiting like a donkey with ears laid back.

They took a front seat on the deserted top deck.

'Smells of disinfectant,' said Anne.

They smoked in silence. The conductor, resentful of the walk they had caused him, took Anne's sixpence and Frank's fourpence. Frank tried to give her the money, playing the gentleman too late. He wished he could have gone to her doorstep and said good night but there was his bicycle to think of and anyway she had spoken of arranging something. He was trying to think how he might ask her about that when the bus moved off. A pageant of cinema crowds and restaurants passed before him. They had returned from somewhere else where there were voles and sunsets. And the need to make the mundane arrangements for love were pressing: he had five minutes. He watched the well-lit, well-dressed city and knew himself involved in something with no probable outcome. Perhaps it would continue piecemeal; its problems solving themselves as they arose. Perhaps things would turn up indefinitely. Home background denied it but he was leaving home behind him.

'You must be tired,' said Anne. 'Arms ache?'

'My stop's coming up. About what you said in the boat.'

'Let's get together, honey, somewhere private. Mummy and daddy are going away but that's not till June. I can get the car for a week-end.'

'No money, love.'

'I shouldn't worry. It's only money. I'll get in touch. Off you go.'

He left the bus an initiate. The city was different.

CHAPTER 17

'I CAN'T get rid of that stuff—that yoghurt, Jane. Don't know why I took it. Round here they think yoghurt's a Hungarian footballer. They're only good for fish and chips, half of them; they ought to be put down.'

'Why did you stock it, dear?'

'Because,' said Mr Griffin, '—I don't know why I stocked it. The representative was a nice class of person. I thought the doctor's wife would have it. I still see myself as a Grocer in this filthy area.'

'Don't upset yourself about it. I can use it in a pie.'

'It's not meant for pies,' said her husband, viciously. 'Frank.'

'Frank, your father's speaking to you.'

'What's that?'

'Come out of that book. I'm speaking to you.'

'What did you say?'

'Yoghurt.'

'Pardon?'

'Yoghurt, yoghurt.' Griffin's narrow uneven face went red. Mrs Griffin saw how tight his shirt-collar was getting and diagnosed that young Mrs Baxter, the manageress down at the laundry whom all the talk was about, was letting things slide.

'I don't know him,' said Frank.

'You're becoming mighty insolent. It's a food made with yeast. Didn't you know that?'

'No,' said Frank.

'Well, I've got some I can't get shot of.'

'Charles saw Miss Cooper in town to-day,' said Mrs Griffin. 'She asked after us.'

Griffin said, ' She would know what yoghurt is.'

'Bound to,' said Frank.

156

'Her people might eat it.'

'I'll ask her for you.'

'Are you *seeing* Miss Cooper, Frank?' His mother brought out the question with a sort of middle-aged bashfulness.

'We've met occasionally.'

'You be careful,' warned his father. 'Their station isn't ours; they've got a different road of going on. Her father's someone in the Town Hall; I've seen his name in the *Post*. This country's not yet been turned into the classless Socialist state, thank heaven. It's not that I'm saying they're better than us; I am saying they're different. If you think I'm complaining because you're mixing with a good class of person, I'm not. Miss Cooper's got real breeding, I know that. So don't start treating her like the girls round here. She'll have feelings they only read about in the women's magazines.'

'Christ!' said Frank.

'Frank!' said Mrs Griffin.

Graham came in from an errand. 'Hullo.' He kissed his mother. 'Any tea?'

'Get sat down.' She poured. 'It's not been mashed long. We'll all have a cup. It might quieten your father and brother.'

Mr Griffin was momentarily silenced by the evening paper. Then he read them a letter and snorted. It had been written in support of the scheme for a civic theatre. Graham had no wisdom. 'It would be smashing if they built a good one,' he said. 'Make a change from car parks.'

'That's to solve a problem, son—the traffic on the roads.'

'But lots of people don't have cars. We don't.'

'We don't go to the theatre either,' said Mrs Griffin, pleased with her logic and anxious to stave off her husband's indigestion.

'We mus'n't have one big car park,' said Graham. 'And people watching television.'

'That's an Economics question. You and Frank are getting a cocky pair. There's whole teams of experts these days. Grocery's the thing I know about; I know book-keeping and I know my legal rights as a trader. There's others who know Economics and traffic planning.'

'You're a sort of object-lesson,' said Frank.

'I don't know what you mean but, if the rates are anything to go by, I am. I'm subsidising the lazy swine over the main road. I'm not buying them a theatre.'

'The Coopers support it. Wouldn't you like to please our betters?'

Mrs Griffin flew to the television.

Wednesday evening at home! They were more like different species than flesh and blood, like fish in an old tank full of familiar, hateful litter.

When the commercials came on, catfish Griffin stayed inactive. Usually they were a cue for him to fetch out the little green book in which he noted down the products so as to be accurate with his printed 'As Advertised on T.V.' cards. But tonight he told his wife not to bother opening the drawer for it. Just to underline his ill humour, he said to Frank: 'Given over your studying, have you?'

There was more habit than malice in it but it prised Frank out of his chair and his bored hypnosis.

His mother said: 'Come into the kitchen, Frank. I want you.' She closed the door. 'Your father's got the old man on him to-day. I don't know why it is no more than he does. So I'd like you not to rile him, Frank, please.'

'I didn't mean to.' In this kitchen some years ago a small boy had been upbraided for something undone or wrongly done. But now his mother pleaded to get her way. They were so familiar—the long steamy kitchen, the small woman in one of her busying aprons. He didn't see them. There was the same remoteness about his affection for her; as if he was handling it behind special glass like some dangerous substance.

'I'll keep off his toes. Promise.' A month back he would have taken a stronger line about forcing the old devil to face up to the truth. But now that large talk was less important than being nice to his mother. It cost nothing. He yawned.

'It's not good to study yourself to death. I know it's not too many late nights making you drowsy. Let up a bit. I had a battle to get you kept on at school; now you're there I don't want to see you scrimping on other things. I like you to go out; It's a good thing you seeing Miss Cooper.'

'Call her Anne, can't you?'

'Don't go biting my ears off. The girl's name is Cooper, isn't it?'

'Sorry. It's not that.' He didn't want to explain his flicker of annoyance, to embark on an explanation, detailed but vague; and meaningless to both of them. She wouldn't understand. Worse than that, she would. He had two lives to keep from fouling each other.

'You'll bust that milk jug, you and your fiddling. That was a wedding gift, so it's as old as you are.'

'A bit older, I hope.' He put it down.

'You're cheeky-daft.' She kissed her son. He was embarrassed and pleased.

'Take this Anne out properly. Here's what I wanted you for.' Her excavations under the crockery had produced a triumphant five-pound note. 'Here. It won't break the bank.'

Frank took the money. He held the result of weeks of economising and thought of the week-end Anne had suggested. His mother deserved a better son. He kissed her and put it away, the price of his gratitude and affection. He was still saying thanks when someone's knuckles rapped on the glass of the back door.

'Whoever can that be at this time of night? The insurance came yesterday.' Mrs Griffin unbolted and opened the door. From where he was Frank couldn't see who was there, but his mother's hasty battle with apron-strings told him that class had come visiting.

'Yes?' she asked.

'I wasn't able to make myself heard at the front. Is Frank in?'

'I'll just see.' She closed the door and looked round with a worried expression.

'What's up?'

'It looks like a young police inspector,' she whispered.

'It's Peter Mohan. It's you're the daft one.'

'He had a police raincoat on.'

'Gerroff wi' yo',' Frank opened the door. 'Come in. Wipe your feet though; mother's been cleaning the floor.'

Mohan had on a riding mac. That, his thin face and fair hair gave him the stamp of young officialdom, television version. He shook hands with Mrs Griffin and apologised for disturbing her. She was charmed. This was an occasion; she rose splendidly to it with unforced courtesy where her husband would have fawned. Frank thanked God his father was out of the way; he was simultaneously condemning snobbery and being a snob.

'I'll take him up to my room and out of your road,' he said.

When he had turned on the light and drawn the red curtains, his room looked pleasingly cultural and student-like. With Mohan, Frank experienced rather more social unease than with Anne; perhaps lowliness was one of his weapons against her.

'Sit down on the bed; it's quite comfortable. Or I'll shift these records off the armchair.'

Peter told him not to bother.

'Coffee or anything?'

'No thanks. You're reading Durrell; everyone is.'

'Durrell must be pleased.'

Mohan laughed: 'I'm sure he is.'

Frank stacked the records on his record-player.

'I thought you were unmusical.'

'Most of these are lent. Anne's starting me on Beethoven.'

'And finishing you off with Wagner.'

What Frank wanted to say was 'To what do we owe the pleasure of the visit?' There must be a special reason; Mohan had never called before. They were both uneasy. Cigarettes helped.

'Nice room you've got here. Mine's full of fag-ends: I'm smoking too much. I meant to give it up after the exams but I never did. I thought we were going to be friends.'

'Aren't we?' asked Frank.

'It's my fault if we're not. We seemed to have more in common than we have.'

Frank wondered what he was getting at. 'You make friendship sound pretty serious,' he said.

'It is; more than people admit to. It could be a gift, I don't know. If having things in common is important, what have you and I got in common?'

'Everything except your religion. I mean we're a similar age, at the same school—the same sort of interests, surely.'

'Yes, certainly. You see people as mass-produced by environment, like clay modelled from outside.'

'Not mass-produced; there's always a ha'p'orth of difference. But not very much more between us two.'

'I see things the other way about,' said Mohan. 'That that sort of environmental similarity is superficial; that the real difference is inside in the—forgive me, O Twentieth Century! —soul.'

'All right. So what?'

'So perhaps all we have in common is Anne Cooper.'

'Is that why you came?'

'What are we going to do about it?'

'Can we do anything? We can't have a duel.'

'No,' said Mohan, 'we can't. Again it's my damned fault: I thought I didn't care. Now I find I do. I went into the cathedral here, right up to the confessionals. I nearly talked it over with a priest.'

'Christ!'

'No, a priest. We Catholics always have to go through a middleman.'

'I don't get you,' said Frank. 'I never know when you're being serious.'

'Only when I make jokes. It shook me, giving religion a try. I have this vision of myself in twenty years' time still at my wit's end about her. I tell myself it's crazy—love's not that important, not all-important—but it's no good.' He lit a further cigarette before going on. He was in earnest and finding this self-exposure difficult. Frank felt relief that at last they were confronting the problem, and in such a civilised manner. 'We might think it's all-important now but I can see through it and it isn't. Can you see through it, Frank?'

'I see what you mean.'

161

'If you understood that lot, perhaps we're blood-brothers after all. '

'But we can't decide anything talking. Let's talk about something else. Has Lucy settled for Williams?'

'Damn Lucy. She's a sacred cow, a breeding animal; she's a rodeo. She's not; I don't mean that. Lucy's all right. But Anne's so different. There's a uniqueness about her, a difference. That's what makes it so hard. Perhaps it's something spiritual.'

'Now I'm lost.'

'Not spiritual then: enigmatic, independent, other.'

'Other?'

'I'm leaving school before the end of term and I might leave England as well. North Africa. You've got to get something to put on your first book-jacket. I know they've done away with the Foreign Legion. In other words I'm leaving you the field. I'll hate North Africa but it's preferable to hanging around here like a skeleton at the feast.' He laughed. 'Incredible, isn't it? An Edwardian scene. It is lasting between you and Anne, is it? I won't say she's done it once so she'll do it twice. There, I've said it.Would you marry her? I know we're all too young.'

Frank said, 'I asked her once.'

'And she said?'

'Nothing; it's as you say.'

'She's married someone else while we've been talking; or she'll never marry anyone. I think I'll take up pub dominoes.' It was pessimistically said.

Frank looked at his visitor and could detect none of his old superiority. Somewhere along the line he had overtaken Mohan. Everything that Mohan had said was theorising. In a week or so Anne and he would be together in an adult setting; compared with that, what they had discussed was about as real as the telly programme audible downstairs. Mohan was still living in territory he had crossed and come out of; or so he reckoned.

CHAPTER 18

A FORTNIGHT before Easter; the sun shining.

Frank was to go over to the Coopers' rather than have her pick him up at the shop. To be quite safe, he invented a Sixth Form Conference in Derbyshire which he entitled for his father's benefit ·'Advanced Level and After'. Mr Griffin was assured that this was a step in the right direction of a sound job; in fact he was so interested he wanted to know more. Frank was reduced to inventing Haresque study-groups. Saturday afternoon was to be devoted to 'Examination Technique'; Sunday morning, more ambitiously, to 'The Banks, Life-Assurance and You.' All this—but mainly Sunday morning he thought—earned him two pounds out of the grocer's pocket. He had a shopfront send-off like Dick Whittington.

It took the whole of the bus-ride across town to settle himself—he had been so convinced by his own lies. In his wallet he had several pounds, all under false pretences, and also the necessary purchase from a barber's which had cost him a whole morning in town, looking for courage.

Towards the Coopers' part of town the sunlight was less incongruous. Here the sun got a return from the trees as well as melting Nottingham's tar and showing up the dirt on Nottingham's windows.

He rang at the early Victorian front door. 'If the Regent hadn't been such a gouty old devil, our house might have been Regency,' Anne had once explained. Bag in hand, he stood waiting for her to come to the door. Anne had promised that neither parent would be in; that was why she had insisted on perfect timing: half-past eleven. His timing was perfect.

Yet here was Mrs Cooper, feather duster, apron, chiffon headscarf, the lot. Mavis was in for the morning. It would have taken hours for her to get ready to go out—unless they held mid-morning fancy-dress balls in this district. She was at home; Anne had got everything wrong, or lied to him. Mrs Cooper was eyeing his little bag.When she asked him what he wanted, he knew she had forgotten him and took him for a salesman. Despite his reading of Kingsley Amis, Frank said that he had called for Anne. He said this holding a suitcase which looked like, and in its time had been, that of a commercial traveller. The resourceful hero would have sold Mrs Cooper his pyjamas and retired. Griffin merely asked for Anne and stood gaping. He was shown into the drawing-room.

'I'm sorry, you're one of the boys from school. How stupid of me! Without your blazer, I didn't recognise you. I'll tell Anne.'

Left alone, Frank savoured the taste of disaster. Would it have been better if, as his mother had done when Mohan called, she had shut the door on him? Was it some class difference that she had not, or his failure to look like a young police inspector, or her different attitude to young police inspectors if he did look like a young police inspector? . . .

Mr Cooper was a stranger to him but his likeness to Anne was so marked that Frank might have recognised him on the street. He wished he had been given the chance instead of meeting him on his home ground like this. And what made it worse was the wretched little case still dangling from his hand. He hadn't even had the presence of mind to put it out of sight.

'Good morning,' said Mr Cooper. 'It is for once. My wife tells me the daffodils are out and she's country-bred. You know the sort of thing: croquet on the vicarage lawn, hide-and-seek with Rupert Brooke in the shrubbery—English socialism. Sit down, if you want to.'

He sat down, nursing the small absurd case.

'Care for a drink, a cigarette?' Frank said yes.

Mr Cooper was slight in build, hair lushly grey, temples naked: distinguished. He moved as Anne did, rather quickly, economically. So far the situation was more manageable than he had feared, less nerve-racking than the interviews with Hare. Behind Mr Cooper, large windows invited the eye along the valley of houses and trees which comprised the residential estate. You saw no daffodils but what you did see suggested

164

that many artful clumps were in flower down there. What with the scenery and the sherry, Frank imagined that he had some-how gone one up in the world and was paying a normal social call.

'Cheers!' said Mr Cooper. 'Here's to the week-end.'

'Your health,' said Frank, not very convincingly.

'Tell me about it.'

'About it?' They had forgotten to arrange a common story. It hadn't seemed necessary at the time. They had left each other to make their own *ad hoc* arrangements. Anne had failed to make any. Where was she? With the remnants of presence of mind, Frank made a fairly natural noise, implying that there was little to say. 'Anne must have told you everything of interest.'

'She said it was some sort of conference.'

'So did I,' said Frank; but he was lucky—the implications of that passed unnoticed.

'Pot-holing in Derbyshire. Not a bad sport. You're quite an expert, I believe.'

'I wouldn't say so,' said Frank. His mind in full flight; his masterly insurance seminars were hackwork compared with this.

'May I advise you not to be so modest? Modesty is usually a mistake. You were in the Speak Cavern rescue, Anne said.'

'I'd rather not talk about it.'

'No, no. There you go again. Modesty is far too secretive; if you've done something, sound it abroad. Let me top up your glass. This conference will want to hear about it.'

'Pot-holers don't talk much.' Frank in his shrinking corner of consciousness was rather pleased with this.

'You're not doing badly. Actually it was very unfair of me. I could have chosen something more up your street. Anne's been secretive about you, so I was in the dark. Shall I say she's been modest about you? I wasn't setting out to damage your ego. The trouble was, I suspect, my daughter's feminine failure to get dates and times right. We're better at that sort of thing, for all their fussiness. Next week-end neither of us will be here.'

'I don't understand,' said Frank.

'I think you do, you know.'

'I'll go then.'

'Why on earth do that? I'm pleased to have met you. I mean that; I'm not using it as a sobriquet for the never-darken-my-doors routine. Conventional and unconventional don't figure in our vocabulary here. If I didn't like the looks of you, I'd boot you out. Anne knows what she's doing. Or, if she doesn't, she'll have to learn. That suits me. Don't expect anything else. I'm her father, I admit it, but not a symbol of authority. She's still mourning for her grandfather; you might take her mind off that. He was too full of advice and folk-wisdom for my liking; not that I disliked him. Anne needs some hard knocks. A good brain like hers shouldn't go soft. I'll fetch her.'

Exit, leaving Frank to work him out. Frank had a job on there. Mr Cooper was certainly unconventional, perhaps mad. He seemed to think he was hammering on the anvil of truth. He was a better man to deal with than Hare was; but there was something not quite right about him. What it was Frank couldn't and didn't try to say. Mainly he experienced relief that things hadn't been worse.

Anne was a good brain (Mr Cooper); spiritual (Mohan); loose (Popkin). He wanted to keep an open mind. She may have briefed her father as a joke for all he knew.

'I'm sorry about that technical hitch,' she said. 'Blimey, you could have left that case in the hall. You look like a vet.'

'I wasn't expecting a reception committee.'

'That was my fault. Still, the sun's shining. And you look more like an undertaker than a vet.'

'Your father knows.'

'I know he does; I told him. Discreetly, of course. I told him last night. My scheme went wrong and it seemed best to spill the beans. And he's really been good about it. We're going to a remote cottage. Here's the key.'

'Fine,' said Frank. 'And is he coming with us?'

'I think he's been splendid. After a moment of horrifying doubt he was all understanding and broadmindedness. I'm rather pleased; it's brought us closer together. But you don't look very pleased at all.'

• 'He's your father. I don't get it. No, I'm not pleased. It's all wrong, in my opinion.'

'Your puritan nastiness again. An illicit week-end—fine. You like that: it's sufficiently immoral for you. But now the gilt's been taken off your gingerbread.'

'You're wrong as well,' said Frank. 'Like your father.'

She looked at him, anger and scorn. He could imagine hatred in her face; few faces can be vehicles of that. Yet he was calm in a new way, almost detached. He pictured that fine nose of hers flexed tight and hatred in her eyes, living there like flies; but she was only annoyed.

'Well then, why aren't you pleased?'

'Several reasons. Father's don't pack their daughters off so easily.'

'Mine did.'

'Yours has got some rum ideas.'

'Mine isn't loaded down with sham morality like you. You're ruining everything. Why not call it off?'

'Listen to me,' said Frank, holding her wrists. 'Your father deliberately gave me the once-over, then approved. That's an odd thing. He thinks I'm necessary, as an experience to toughen your mental faculties: that's a very odd thing. And I get the impression that you're using me to prove something else.'

'All because he behaved like a civilised human being. You're so small-minded, aren't you? The shopkeeper class.'

'Granted, the shopkeeper class.'

'I didn't mean that, Frank. But you don't have to be—such a stick-in-the-mud.'

'I'm not. I wish my old grandmother could see me: she'd drop dead.'

'Well,' said Anne, 'don't be.'

'I happen to care about you, not for a dirty week-end. You don't think that, do you?'

'You're improving, honey. You really are.'

'I want to know what you are. You're not like your father.'

167

'He's coming up the garden. Shall I ask him?'

Mr Cooper entered through the french windows, loam on his boots and in his hand a daffodil.

' "Fresh Spring, the herald of Love's mighty king",' he said. 'Your mother wasn't dreaming. There are enough under the apple to keep Wordsworth happy for months. I thought you'd have been off.'

'We were discussing you.'

'Really?'

'You offended Frank here. I think we both have.'

'None meant. That pot-holing business was silly; I apologise.'

'It's more interesting than that. Our whole way of looking at things offends him apparently.'

'He's not alone,' said Mr Cooper affably. 'I must have offended hundreds of people in my life.' He sounded pleased. Frank, reverting rapidly back to the nation of shopkeepers, wondered what he had to be pleased about in that. Now was the moment to walk out on them. Nothing would be nicer than to go off to hear how to take out life assurance and a bank-account. No more discussion, no more dissection of philosophies of life. He wanted to get out, to take Anne away from her father—or to go without her. It didn't matter so much. He was tired of being a stage-prop.

'Our way of looking at things is to see them straight. I'm glad you said "our way", my girl; I think you're right. You have more of my brain than your mother's.'

Frank thought that smug and not so different from Hare after all. He thought he was learning—not French verbs or mouldy old Shakespeare's literary influences—but learning. If he had liked, he could have started on Mr Cooper from the philosophical angle, except that Mr Cooper could have tied him up in knots.

'Thank you for the sherry,' Frank held out his hand.

'Not at all. We'll meet again on Sunday. It's a pleasant part of the country. Fresh air and sheep.'

Mr Cooper took a book and sat down.

They were outside on the driveway. Anne started the car.

The bedroom window looked higher up in the daylight and the gap between sill and drainpipe impossibly enormous.

For most of the journey Frank was silent. Anne, to judge from her snatches of humming and her excited pointing out of landmarks, was pleased with the world.

Their cottage away from the main road was small, stone-built and cottage-like. There was no means of guessing its age but some recent improvements were obvious. The door was canary-yellow set in a black frame and a cradled plant creaked above them in the porch; the hills had been given a touch of Chelsea mews. Within, the furniture was good imitation antique. Everything was clean. Years must have passed since any dust was seen, let alone grass and horsedung from the farm.

'Like it?'

'It's very nice,' he said. 'Who does it belong to?'

'Friend of daddy's. I came once for a holiday with them. It was very boring. We got on each other's nerves.'

'Probably we will by tomorrow.'

'You are a wet blanket.'

'Actor's nerves,' said Frank, 'that's what it is. Does this place have a gas stove? I'd like a cup of tea. Does it have tea? We didn't bring anything.'

'Everything's in. Daddy phoned last night for them to stock up. You mightn't be so nervous when I've put the kettle on.'

But Griffin was very nervous; he couldn't believe himself set up for the week-end in this fashion. It was the sort of place writers retreated to between lecture tours or between the wars. It fitted in with the Coopers' outlook on things, he supposed, but it didn't square with the shop sort of reality or even the dim ideas he had of his own. Anne was pretty and gay bringing in the tea; the surroundings were ideal, idyllic, but still. . . .

'Do you love me, serious Frank Griffin?'

'Yes,' he said. Then for good measure: 'Of course I do, darling.'

That bit of conversation was in keeping here, almost a part of the furniture. It was the first time he had said what he thought he ought to say to Anne, rather than launching off into his truer confusion.

'Then why so surly?'

'I don't know; I thought it was going to be different. Not this cottage, this By-Royal-Appointment feeling from your dad. I thought of a small pub somewhere—something like that,' he said vaguely.

'It's much nicer like this than signing their wretched register. Pretending we're young newly-weds.'

'Things like this should be more spontaneous.'

'It's difficult, isn't it? If you want to celebrate a solemn mass again, let's have it out. Did you want a chummy hike or something? This is an adult sort of thing.'

'You stop talking like your father. Abstractions all the time.'

'To-day's the first time you met him. You're a generaliser. Perhaps its a chintzy honeymoon you want. Be real about it. We're too young for that and we're too old for chummy hikes. Why don't you take things as they come?'

'Precisely,' said Frank. 'It's just that it's come a bit too ready-wrapped. Shall we go for a walk?'

Frank's reaction to the hills was towny. They looked nothing but grass and dry-stone walls but, if you knew what to look for, if only you had the countryman's mystique! So he walked in the open air as we can suppose peasants when peasants were the norm to have walked in cathedrals—bemused but rapt, in awe.

'You're meditating,' said Anne. 'What are you meditating about?'

'I'm trying not to think. Thinking's alien to the shopkeeper class.'

'Ah, I've offended you. I shouldn't have said that. It was stupid, untrue. Give me a kiss.'

He obliged. Anne pushed herself into him. They went on, holding hands.

They went for miles and had a job to find their way back. It was heavy dusk when they saw a light.

'That's odd,' said Anne. 'There's a light.'

'Did we leave one one?'

'Don't be silly. It was broad daylight when we started.'

'Then it must be those nameless ones who stocked up. I hope there's some food in the place; I'm starving.'

'Of course it's not them,' said Anne, who was limping in stockinged feet. 'Stop. I want to put my shoes on.'

Frank handed them over.

'Let me hold on to you. You could have reminded me by the way. I don't know why I wear high heels.'

'Your dad must have rung up again to get them to switch on the lights and turn the bed down. Or perhaps he's come along himself to make sure I do my bit.'

'Don't you think you've worked that to death? I thought this walk had done you good.'

'Come on.'

The yellow door was open a few inches and, long before they reached it, they heard music and voices.

'The nameless ones are having a binge,' said Frank.

'It's certainly very *strange*,' Anne said.

They walked in on a party. Four people were sitting about on the replica antique furniture, filling the cottage with cigarette smoke and drinking beer straight from the bottle. Frank checked with himself that this was the right cottage. It was. He recognised no one, let Anne do the explaining. He ushered her past him with a little too much courtesy, a parody.

'Well, hello. We didn't expect to see you here. Join the party.' The speaker was a young middle-aged or middle-aged young man, neatly dressed and wearing black-rimmed glasses. A plump, an overfed intellectual.

'We didn't expect to see *you*, Mark.'

'We took off from London this morning like a flock of pigeons. That's rather an exaggeration; it was planned a fortnight ago. I mentioned it in a letter to your pa; I think I did. Meet my cronies. Anne, Gerald.' Gerald, fair-haired but older-looking than Mark, gave a tired salute. 'Hilda, Sue. Gerald's from Nottingham; perhaps you know him.'

'We haven't met.'

'Gerald practises as a psycho-analyst; Hilda and Sue act; I simply exist, as you know.'

'Not so simply,' said Sue, who seemed to be Mark's girl.

'This is Frank,' said Anne.

'That's right,' said Frank in rapid confirmation.

'How long have you been down here?'

'We came this morning.'

'For the week-end?' Mark tried to catch Gerald's eye, but Gerald's eye was not to be caught.

'That's right,' said Anne with a simplicity that brought Frank back to her.

'Your pa could have warned you. Of us, I mean. But possibly you didn't ask him.'

'Stop it,' said Sue. 'How can you? You'll embarrass them. That's what you want.'

'Not at all,' said Mark. 'I don't want to embarrass them; they're very welcome.'

'I don't get embarrassed,' said Anne.

'Your friend might.'

'Some people *are* an embarrassment.' Gerald lifted his eyes from his finger-nails. 'You are one of them.'

'Thanks. Gerald practises psycho-analysis; the girls act; I embarrass. Was that a professional observation?'

'No. You're sexually nervous. That was.'

'Never go away with a Freudian.'

Frank wanted to laugh or be sick. He managed to do neither. Would six or seven years turn him into one of these, make Anne one? He found his welling, arrogant unreasonableness comforting.

'Mark owns the cottage,' Anne explained. 'His father and mine were great friends at Oxford.'

'Well, I'm glad you came,' said Gerald. 'We had Mark's problems in the car.'

'Now he wants yours,' said Hilda. 'It's so *strenuous* keeping company with a psychiatrist. So be warned. I can *never* act again since he explained exhibitionism. He tells me women all have a desire to go naked in public. I'll never trust myself on the stage.'

'Everything is a stripping-down,' Mark said. 'Literature, conversation. Social behaviour is a form of indecent exposure.

172

But this is the country. Oughtn't we to be silently chewing straws?'

'How is Uncle George?'

'Rolling in his millions, Anne. My pa has just sold off some land in London's erstwhile green-belt. Gerry'd have a hard time psycho-analysing him. No psyche as far as I can see, just money. It makes me mad the sort of people he mixes with these days. Like the Duke of Wellington—he has an intellectual disdain for his financial equals and a financial . . . You know how it goes. I never understand how your pa gets on with him; he's still a live-wire, isn't he? Mine's just a bore these days.'

'Do you like Derbyshire?' Gerald asked Anne.

'Don't answer him,' said Hilda. 'It'll be too dreadful if you do. He may accuse you of bed-wetting.'

'I don't know if I do or not,' Anne replied. Frank noted her social ease in this madhouse. She made the actresses, who must be years older, seem quite juvenile. As for his own feelings, he was pretending to be elsewhere; he was smoking one of Mark's cigarettes and keeping quiet.

'When I was eighteen I used to walk for hours round here. I came out by bus and walked all day by myself. Are you eighteen?'

'And three-quarters.'

'When Gerald talks about the age of consent,' said Mark, 'you had better look out.'

'Shut up,' said Gerald. 'You were never eighteen or any other age.'

Anne was colouring.

'You behave,' Sue said.

'She can take a joke.'

'I heard your name mentioned the other day. As you know, I knew of you through your father. It was mentioned in an odd context and, rather than suffer any more of Mark's party-pieces, I propose to tell you something of it.'

'Tell away,' said Mark. 'We duly assume a religious air in the presence of science. Though I'm sure I don't know how you make a living. Why didn't you go to America, as I told you to?'

'I do a little work for the Education people, not much, some every now and then. The other day a boy still at school in the sixth-form was sent along to me. Adolescent cases are interesting; fairly easy to deal with mostly. You feel you're getting somewhere. I must say I'm not quite as impersonal as Freud would have liked—I want to stay human. This lad is called Popkin. He's a hard nut to crack. Some sort of paranoia, I think. It's the devil to get to the roots of some of these things. A long job. He talked about you a lot at first; but I think that was only scratching. I'd say the trouble lay further back, a lot farther back.' Gerald had sounded so wise and dependable even to himself that he took out his empty pipe and sucked on it.

Hilda said: 'Isn't there some code about that sort of thing? I mean, it's like *priests*—isn't it—what you do.' Then, by way of explanation: 'I'm in *Measure for Measure,* that ghastly play by Shakespeare, and Rodney Bright—he's got the lead—quite well-known and frightfully clever—he said that was the least convincing thing in the show: the way the old duke reveals all their confessions when he's disguised as a priest. '

'It's not the same at all. I'm there to cure my patients—not to absolve them, for God's sake. Anne here might indirectly be able to help by adding to my case-picture. I don't make revelations for the sake of it. If this patient had come out with things unpleasant, I'd keep it under my professional bonnet. As that isn't the case . . .'

'I can't help you,' said Anne. 'I'd rather not talk about it.'

'That's absolutely right,' said Sue. 'What a fate! Stranded in the middle of nowhere with two awful men.'

'Three,' Mark put in. 'No favouritism please.'

'Frank looks sweet,' said Hilda.

Griffin winced.

Anne said something about the car and hurriedly left the room. When she had gone, Mark and Gerald started talking to their girls. Ignored, Frank followed Anne out of the cottage without needing to make his excuses.

Outside, he felt the freedom he had shared with Graham years ago when they escaped into the backyard during a family gathering. The stars were all there, the air was warm, the cottage from this angle squat and black on the hillside. Now it was romantic and Wordsworthian, like the Lucy poems. Some way off he made out the shapes of two cars: Anne's and Mark's. He expected to find her there, angry or perhaps weeping; he would go over and be careful not to triumph over her: Mark had implied that Mr Cooper had been in the know. He crossed the springy turf, thinking that some good might have come out of it if the famous paternal characteristics had been nipped in the bud.

Anne wasn't there. He looked back at the building. No sign of her. For several minutes he walked about in the darkness. The door opened and Mark shouted, 'Join the party, you two!' Watching him, Frank felt like a sniper with telescopic sights.

He found Anne standing higher up on the hill, a hundred yards from the cottage. She was motionless and said nothing, even when he came right up to her.

'It's quite warm,' he said.

'I feel such a fool.'

'No need to.' He put his arm around her. 'It's just a ludicrous mistake.'

'Everything's futile!' she burst out. 'It's worthless. I feel awful. Those people; but it's not them. It's me.'

'What is?'

'Don't you ask me to explain,' she said angrily. 'I've made a wrong start. Once you do that you can't start again. You can never start again.'

'Perhaps there's no choice about what start you make,' he said, guessing.

'Then what's the point? Why not kill yourself?'

'Don't be daft.'

'Another thing; me and you, we got off to a wrong start. It's my fault for playing with people. You needn't have got involved.'

'I'm all right,' said Frank. 'Honestly, I am. My skin keeps getting thicker all the time.'

'Mine's getting thinner then.'

'Now we're talking worse blinking rubbish than that lot in there.'

'It isn't that,' she insisted. 'I saw my grandad just before he died. He was quite different: distorted. One day he was well and lively, next day he was smashed up. Meaningless things are happening all the time. Why did he have to bring up Popkin just now?'

'Coincidence. Do you think Popkin is haunting us, for Christ's sake?'

'He just represents what I'm talking about. You keep worrying about moral issues; but it's something worse than that.'

Frank put his other arm round her. He was baffled, embracing a statue. He put his face against hers. She was only a girl being silly.

'It's not me you're afraid of, is it?' he said. This was therapy: intentionally idiotic statement. No response. 'Shall we go back?'

'If you like.'

'You make yourself unhappy,' he said. 'It's only a fiasco.'

Indoors all was silent. The bottles had been herded into a corner. Lights were still on but the people had gone.

'How many rooms?' asked Frank.

'Two and this one. Bedrooms upstairs.'

'Your dad's theatrical sense.' Then, dropping that line: 'Are the men sleeping together?'

'What *are* you suggesting?'

'I mean I'm tired. If that's the arrangement . . . '

'We could troop off to the dorms? They didn't come all this way to play at prep schools, dear. Now you look shocked. Are you?'

'No, I'm not,' Frank said sulkily. 'That sort of behaviour's immoral. If there's such a thing as morality.'

'What about us then?'

'That's different.'

'I don't see how. '

'Love makes it different,' he said. Enlightened puritan.

Anne saw a note on the mantelpiece and he fetched it for her, standing dumbly by. Let her read it—it was addressed to her and in her language. She read it through and laughed. She read it again, aloud: ' "Dear Anne, Mattress, etc. in the

176

scullery. Kitchen sink touch, I know. Still, better than bedroom farce. Love, M." Then there's another bit by Gerald—terrible writing, can hardly read it. "Don't get too intimate too easily. G." What do you make of that?'

Frank snorted.

The ancient scullery was the only unrestored part of the building. If Mark's father brought servants with him when he made use of his property as a hunting-lodge, this was where they slaved and slept. He had saved expense. It was a narrow room full of plumbing. Under the sink the piping was like a nest of frozen snakes. The cracked flagstones were now almost entirely covered by a straw mattress and a pile of bedding. A dusty footprint led the eye to the cluttered sink.

'Shall we go back?' Frank was dog-tired. Surely all was in ruins; he had given up arguing, recriminating, wishing they were alone in a low-ceilinged whitewashed inn, caring.

'Of course we'll not go back. Come here and help get the bed made.'

They worked at it.

'This pipe leaks. It's making noises,' said Frank.

'You're what they call nesh in my home town.' Anne suddenly smiled, relaxed. 'I'll sleep on that side. This room's nice.'

CHAPTER 19

Mohan opened his eyes and it was light. Dawn. He guessed six o'clock. He was right, dead on; his watch confirmed it. The time was something he always knew without thinking. The mental clock—or good guessers never get married. Why not? He shifted position, studied the wallpaper. Years ago its funny unreal roses had been devils and dragons, making him fear wallpaper. Fragmented dreams jangled in his head.

A grey bedroom, a little place on the earth. Beyond the window grey curtains of air extending upwards several miles.

To-day was the last of school. Literally the end of the old world—figuratively. He corrected himself. A few old stains on the wall were as familiar to him as the map of the world. When his brother had shared the room, when they were small, they had told stories of blood seeping through the plaster. They were tea-stains, always had been. In the dawn the room was shabbily aged. He stretched his body; toe-joints cracked. Martyr on a wrack.

Now Mohan was properly awake.

Cigarette. He was thinking of Anne; he had even dreamt of her. She was temptation, the Flesh. She was too small and neat to be the Flesh, not cushiony enough. She must be the devil— or was that the same thing? Now he was slipping into a senti- mental haze . . . and setting the bed on fire: a martyr on a bed of blazing coals. Who had fried his way to canonisation? Shoals of them had. It must have been a headache to think up an original exit into bliss. Anne was summer to him.

He was back to his own self-torture. The implements of— of all things—tennis: nets in need of repair, odd racquets, a crowd—Frazer had been there, and net-hopping ebullient Lucy, Frazer's girl then, of course. Plus rather dusty shrubbery.

178

Plus heat. Sweat was crawling beneath the hair on his scalp, sliding heavily down face and back. Anne had been ridiculously becoming. He picked at the phrase.

She played better tennis than any of them. But within an ace of winning she had lost interest, given up. Love on a tennis court. He spoke the words. Said aloud, they suggested West End musicals, John Betjeman, Henry V. Still, that's where it was. Anne, hair held back by a wide white ribbon; Anne playing tennis. Perhaps that was his trouble—this collecting of images, people held by moment and place; this wearing of people like decorations. She had left the tennis court. She had left him finally. And here he was: clenched teeth, clenched toes, aching leg muscles.

The faded curtains split a little further, shedding fine mustiness on the air. It was before birds or milkmen in the street. A time of strange beauty. In North Africa or wherever this might come back to him bringing nostalgia.

Politics were under discussion as a change from football and sex. Williams was analysing the break up of capitalist society. He had seen the light shining out of *Das Kapital*. Under the uninspired flag of common sense, Grant was arguing with him. Mohan listened. Grant was educating Williams without knowing it, making him re-state his generalisations in more viable forms. They were embattled over equality by the time Mohan got round to leaving them to it. On this last day solitude was more necessary than remaining in the prefects' room, held by its familiar attraction as in a trap. He would never know how Williams clambered up Grant's cliff of disbelief; he would never know what came out of hundreds of other beginnings. Soon Williams would become one of the Marxists whom Marx had asked God to save him from; then, emerging from that system, he would be—like himself—a sort of ex-Catholic and in a quandary.

The playing-fields he was walking round seemed bigger under the dull sky and desolate like the sea. It was appropriate for making his own farewell. There was plenty of time for the inevitable handshakes, the good wishes, the expiration of interest in their eyes, because—though you were still in the building—you were really a ghost, someone who had left. Your epic farewell was a little jolt in routine. The school, as the school song hinted, went on for ever. It was a microcosm : Hare was right. And as such it had its own citizens. Looking across at the buildings, he wished it did not hurt so much to be leaving.

The second time round he snapped out of it and went back over the first fifteen's pitch, walking with determination. It was his first non-sentimental journey of the morning, to the lavatories. He made for the toilets which had been tacked on to an outside wall as a sort of afterthought to provide for spectators. Frazer referred to it as 'the grotto' and reckoned to think out his essays in privacy there, jotting down notes on toilet-paper. Mohan was using the urinal when Draper came in. They stood side by side in enforced proximity. He had hoped to get through the day without seeing Draper. He had nothing to say to him and associated him too much with his loss of Anne. But silence was impossible, even in England. Something—a remark about the weather, if nothing else—was needed to reduce tension.

'It looks like rain,' he said.

'It's pissing down,' Draper said. 'Think I've got cystitis, or is that what females get?'

'I meant the weather.'

'Don't get shirty. Thought you liked intellectual humour. Isn't it to-day you're leaving, Pete? I'll be sorry to see you go—that's without a word of a lie. I didn't like that hard-boiled piece of yours. Why fall out over a bint though?' Draper, who was taking care not to splash himself, didn't look up. 'Now that pig Griffin's having her. I'd like to part friends with you. That's the truth.' Fastening his zip, Draper regarded Mohan out of sandy eyes.

'This is the right place to see the last of you,' Mohan said with almost melodramatic disgust.

'You treat me like a Jew or something. I'm your equal. You think I'm dirty-minded—I'm a realist. You're an idealist or some bloody thing. It's beyond me. I know it spoils you. Perhaps its rubbed off on you from that Cooper bint. A mate of mine saw her last Sunday driving Griffin in that car of hers. John Masters. He saw them early in the morning coming back from a love nest I shouldn't wonder. There's nothing wrong with my mate's eyes. That's the truth. Face up to it.'

'You feed on infection.'

'Pull the other one,' said Draper. 'If anyone's bacteria it's you idealists. Shit-shooting conshies. And I kidded myself you had gumption.'

'What if I landed you one, Draper?'

'I'd laugh in your face. Christ, you have gone to bits. You really have. Fighting over a bint that's not even yours.'

'Get out of my way then.'

'Get past me.'

Draper, blocking the doorway, put up his fists like a prize-fighter. His face was animated with something like good humour. His body though was insolent, eloquent, sarcastic. It was that which got up Mohan's blood.

It was years since he had struck anyone. As prefect, he had stopped a number of fights. He had stood in an undergrowth of little boys, holding two little boys at arm's length. He had addressed the little animals in the good old liberal style. Some of his phrases came back and his hands remembered the pounding energy he had held in check—because it had sometimes taken a lot of lecturing to stop them fighting again when he let go.

The blow caught Draper on the chest. He gasped but neither moved nor hit back.

'She's not even your girl. What's up wi' yo'?'

'Get out of my way.'

Draper punched him on the breast-bone. 'Tit for tat,' he said.

Lighter in build, Mohan went back against the shoulder of the urinal partition, bruising his elbow. He had heard of shin-kicking contests in Cornwall in which two men delivered slow and stately blows at one another until one dazed with pain fell like a tree. He took a swipe at the side of Draper's face, but

181

it was deflected by a quicker forearm. Standing motionless again.

Both were breathing heavily like animals or lovers. It felt unreal to be there. The white tiles around them; outside, a gauze of rain falling soft and grey. Words were impossible but so was further action. Mohan shrugged his painful shoulders, trying to call it off. Draper's knuckles flicked across his mouth. There was blood, pungent and odd-tasting. Peter clutched at the towel. which rattled round a few inches on the roller. It was marked 'Education Committee'.

He was weak on his knees. His chin was like a punch-ball adjusted to the other's fist.

'You should've done boxing, Pete. I did.'

He wiped blood off with the back off his hand. Unaccountably he felt a sort of respect for Draper. His stunned wits clearing, he wondered if he were some subtle masochist. He was not. Draper had played fair for once; that was all. He nearly offered to shake hands with him, as if the drizzling playing-fields outside were those of Eton; but an odd reflection stopped him short. He had shaken hands with Griffin once after swimming. He put his hands away in his pockets. They had exchanged a more appropriate farewell. It was just that he had glimpsed for a moment in Draper a sort of honesty he hadn't noticed before. Draper remained objectionable, double-faced, lewd.

Mohan said, 'We'll call it off, then.'

'You've got pluck,' Draper said, 'but no technique.' He went off key rather easily.

'I'm not staying the afternoon, so I'll say good-bye.'

'So long, Pete,' said Draper, stepping aside to let him pass. 'Thanks.'

Popkin listened to make quite certain that both had left before pulling the chain.

There was still enough morning left to get round and see

182

people. He met Hare in the fish-tank. Benign smile and out-stretched hand. Mohan shook it. The headmaster's face pro-claimed a man certain of his own intrinsic virtue and worth. Yet dislike of him was something to cherish. Peter had been betrayed into seeing good in Draper; but he didn't want Charity to make a sentimental fool of him.

'I wish you well, old son,' said Hare. 'You ornamented the life here. I look forward to reading of you in *The Times* when your mark is made. I am sure the day will come. We are having your name put up in gold leaf on the honours board; the work-men are in next week. It should look well.' The Head pumped tentatively at Peter's hand throughout this speech as if he was a plastic surgeon testing a stitched-on arm. 'Your mouth is bruised.'

'It's nothing. I walked into something.'

'Yes, you always were one of our intellectuals.' Hare dropped the hand and stepped back. He had either run out of things to say, or else a new school rule had just suggested itself to him. He was said to spend half his time thinking them up and the other half enforcing them. Good-byes re-said, he hurried away. The impression was that of absent-minded cleric: salt of the earth. He had been despicable to the last. Peter could take away dislike intact. It was the name in gold leaf and nothing else which had turned Hare's sunny side up.

He went on to the staff room, was invited in and given a cup of tea. Masters found time to chat pleasantly before rushing off, clasping piles of exercise books. Some of the older men— engraved on his mind as types of absent-mindedness, academic devotion or bullying—said they envied him. No reasons were given. Mortgages perhaps, routine, no savour in the spring. They had followed the same road but he wasn't yet a school-master; could still be something better in the end.

Mohan's final calls were on the people he knew in the sixth-form. But he didn't make them. Those like Frazer, the ones he cared for, he would be seeing again—they were more than school-friends; and as for the others, he preferred to let them go down with the ship. Griffin was the only person in the building whom he didn't know what to do with. He was on the point of collecting his coat when he saw Frank down the corridor. Frank was walking away from him, slowly, reading a book. It would have been perfectly possible to catch him up; do more handshaking.

Mohan grabbed his raincoat, took a last look at the locker-room and left.

It had been an inconclusive morning. He wished he saw the future rose-coloured as the older schoolmasters did, who had had their futures and remembered their hopes. But he had left a past and had no idea what was coming. There was no link between. He had lost his faith but—perhaps because he had been a Catholic—he still wanted things like tradition, context. It would have to be a labour of personal reconstruction: an ant rebuilding its smashed nest. If so, he hadn't made much of a start. He only just avoided colliding with a bus.

It was raining, he noticed—there was a film of cold water developing on his scalp and dropping from his nose. He walked without thinking. Famous writer, theologian, politician revisits the scenes of his youth.

The rain stopped. The sun appeared. A complete stranger told him the sun had appeared. An infant-school teacher had told them that the rainbow was God's promise not to flood the earth again. He looked up for a rainbow. There was none.

Whether it was the sun or the promise of God—whatever it was, he surged with happiness. He was free! The next complete stranger he met he smiled at. The complete stranger, a well-dressed matronly woman, quickened her step. He wasn't thinking.

He had covered the two miles to Anne's school in about twenty-five minutes. Hardly thinking, he turned in at the gate and went up the short drive. The shrubs flanking it were ever-greens—everblacks here in the city, sombre and small. For some reason they reminded him of *Twelfth Night*. Anne had been Olivia in it two years before, since when she had given up acting as intellectually dishonest. It was some comfort to him that she was more mixed-up than he was; but he duly noted the tennis courts, the real ones, the stage his mind kept setting. Some small girls going by tittered. They looked more like little animals than boys of their age did—somehow less restricted. At the corner of the main building he met Lucy.

'Peter! What are you *doing*! You don't know how female we all are. It's suicide to come in broad daylight.'

'Have you seen Anne?'

'Yes, she's eating sandwiches in the Pre's. Seriously though, if the old Bird sees you . . .' She glanced round. Miss Jay was that sort of headmistress.

'I've left school so I'll chance it.'

'Man of the world, I say!' Lucy sounded genuinely impressed. 'But watch it,' she warned. 'The Old Bird's capable of anything these days. She was carrying on with the German mistress and the German mistress went and got married. At least that's the theory.'

'Thanks. I'll use the back stairs.' She had put ideas into his head: he felt himself a desecrator of alien mysteries. The stairs and corridor hung with aged photographs reeked unhealthily of ideals. He could imagine sepia schoolmistresses unwrapping their subjects from layers of tissue-paper; softly and ardently seeking the perfection they only found in death. He halted before a group of ladies, dated 1911. His own face was lightly interposed. There they sat, arms folded across their bosoms, facing the camera as they had faced the future, gravely. Who were this imposing team?

He was standing there in pointless revery when someone touched his shoulder. He turned guiltily.

'Impressive, aren't they? I heard you were here. This place is like Stalag Luft III.'

'I was wondering about them.'

'They made us what we are.' Anne spoke appropriately; she was wearing the protective colouring of school uniform—grey blazer, grey skirt. She was a schoolgirl. He felt foolish.

'I saw Lucy. She made me feel like a trespasser. Perhaps that's what I am.'

'Has someone taken a swipe at you?'

'It's nothing; doesn't hurt. I got involved in a surrealistic fight. I've left school. This morning. I came to say good-bye.'

185

'That was sweet of you.'

'I don't think so.'

'We can't talk here.'

A few juniors came by with straight faces, pursed mouths, beady eyes fixed forward. Out of sight round the corner, they let out a shrill squall of laughter. Anne raised her eyebrows and smiled. 'See what I mean?'

They agreed to go for a walk.

When they were out of the over-splendid back gate, she said: 'Phew! I never knew why you liked school; I don't.'

'Illusion of comradeship at our place. You just have competition.'

'What are your plans?'

'Nothing much. What about you?'

'You know how it is,' she said evasively. He didn't. The restraint between them was difficult to gauge. There was no reason why he shouldn't take her arm as he had done before so easily and so often. They were the same people; but her tone was formal—guarded yet not cold. There existed something, a half-dead intimacy on the point of reviving, or dying. They had the length of a few pavements for death to be certified.

'I'm ditching religion. It makes you morally neurotic. Evil, as you once so wittily said,' he said, skillfully avoiding a pram, 'doesn't exist.'

'I think now that it does. But it's not metaphysical.'

'You're right; it's not.' He stopped.

Anne laughed. 'Isn't it a pity?'

'Why did we have to break up?'

'Tell me about your fight instead. I'm curious. You weren't fighting Frank, were you?'

'Over what?'

'No idea.'

'Look, I'm half decided to leave the country. North Africa. It's an idea, don't you think? Or is it too much like *Beau Geste*?'

'Wasn't he crossed in love or something? Don't tell me that's your reason.'

'What do you think?'

186

'I wish I could walk out on myself.'

'You've changed,' Mohan said. 'I notice it, not having seen much of you lately. I've changed too.'

'And you notice that with seeing yourself all the time?'

They had reached the arboretum. It was sunny and green inside the railings. They sat on a bench near the pond.

'That old parrot died,' said Anne. 'It said it was over a hundred.'

'The parrot did?'

'No, you idiot, the paper.'

'You liked that parrot,' Mohan said.

'It reminded me of grandad. I like very old things if they're not stupid.'

'Was it my fault that you went over to Griffin?'

'It was the parrot actually.' Anne remembered what had caused her irresponsibility that first evening with Frank. She had wanted them to see the parrot out of hours, the now-dead parrot, only because she had once visited the place with Peter and the gardens had drawn her again with the memory of that afternoon. She had thought herself in love. But now the dream of love was over; she was mixed up with Frank, miserable.

'Are you deeply involved with Frank?' Mohan said. It cost him something to ask. She could see that. Their liberal education made everything hesitant and oblique. Her father was right: the truth was brutal and uncommon. Why didn't he come out with what he wanted to say?

'Circumstantially I am. If you must know. We "went to bed" twice.'

'I knew more or less. I was prepared against it. It's twenty to two; I mustn't make you late.'

'There's no hurry. You'd rather I hadn't told you.' She examined her manicure. 'I don't want to symbolise anything, thanks.'

'If I came for anything, I suppose I came to get you back.'

'But now I've told you I'm maiden no more you're not interested.'

'I'm the same.'

'True love! The all-forgiving God.'

'If you like. Don't be so conventional and stop casting other people's parts. I wanted to see you before I left England. We got out of gear; there wasn't a big scene and a final ending. Perhaps the thing between you and Frank is just temporary. The point is I love you, if you'll pardon the word.'

'I'm hateful.'

'Come off it. Now you're hamming. Now you're being silly. Here's my handkerchief; it's clean.'

She was remembering all sorts of things: her grandfather, the parrot, the meaningless week-end in Derbyshire. Peter was dabbing her face but keeping his arms to himself. Why was the burden on her always? Why had she always to permit and to choose? She wanted life to make sense and order but it was a jumble of hopeless compromises. If Peter had gone off with his illusions, she could have made out with the other one; or extricated herself. She had sickened of love but it was too late just to opt out. These clamouring individuals wouldn't let her, were always forcing decisions out of her. Brutal truth didn't get a look-in: she was more hazily fair-minded than anyone. What would follow on from saying yes to Peter? She returned his handkerchief and stood up.

'Did you mean all that?'

'Yes,' he said.

'Give me time to decide. I promise to let you know as soon as I know myself.'

She left him sitting by the lake. The solemn moment passed.

Now there was Mrs Copley to see and the poetry of John Donne to unravel—splendid, reassuring Mrs Copley who had been known to smoke in lessons—splendid, reassuring John Donne full of manageable sex in three-hundred-year-old aspic.

CHAPTER 20

SUNDAY was the worst, the most claustrophobic day of the week. Every aspect of it was foretold from the *Sunday Express* to old Mrs Griffin's coming to tea. But to-day things were slightly better; true the *Sunday Express* had arrived but it had been taken away by the boys' parents. The old lady had taken to her bed and, as she had made a virtue of her activity, her staying in was viewed as significant in family circles. Bert had come up from Southampton and Bert was a man who invested his money. Soon Frank and Graham would have to report to the bedside. Mrs Griffin—swept along in a partly alien current —caught herself wishing that her sons had made a better impression on the old woman or had, at least, not made such a bad one. But this Sunday they were left behind to paint the ceiling of the shop. That was doubly beneficial: it was the sort of excuse the old woman would understand and it was a victory in Jane Griffin's endless campaign to keep the menfolk amicable.

Graham was happily at work on a trestle whilst his brother mixed the paint and thawed out the brushes. The prospect of working together was pleasing to both.

Beyond the plate-glass, Sunday was apparent in streets which had gone back fifty years to a former leisureliness and sparsity of traffic. Inside the stock had been covered; Graham said he was reminded of a mortuary but his comparison was too fanciful.

The ceiling, which looked quite small, proved enormous. They spent an hour putting on the first coat and getting better at dodging the drips. Then came a short break to let it dry.

'You know, there's something good about physical tiredness,' said Frank. 'These days tiredness is mostly mental and nervous. Wasn't it Ruskin who said that labour was noble?'

'Did he include delivering groceries?' Graham asked, good-humoured.

Frank was annoyed with himself for making the sort of remark to Graham which he had developed as a cultural fill-in for use at school. He suddenly felt he knew nothing: he was carefully tying up a parcel and he had forgotten to put in the contents. It set him back. Logically, talking to his brother should outline the contours of his knowledge; talking to Mohan, Anne, his teachers, should map out the extent of his ignorance. But it seemed to be the other way round.

'You're quite noble on it, Gray,' he said.

'I get along. School didn't teach you much really. Half the teachers at our school weren't really interested except as a job. It's different at Grammar Schools.'

'I'm not so sure,' Frank said. He would have liked to confide, but he couldn't. The main thing on his mind was off their common ground: the complication of life was emotional for him now, not intellectual. He was alive in his entanglement with Anne Cooper, not in his studies. All that was too confused to discuss with anyone; and he was shy. The intimacy they had developed did not extend to private lives. It was a real friend-ship though, and perhaps more nourishing to Frank than his others.

The second coat went on more quickly and smoothly.

'It's a good job,' said Frank at last. 'Dad ought to be pleased. I don't suppose he will be, though. He won't say anything.'

'Dad worries too much. When there's no customers in he talks to me about the rates and things. He says someone's got to do the worrying. I think he hasn't got enough responsibility towards himself.'

Talking made the action of painting more satisfying and family matters were a more suitable topic than either literature or love.

Graham gave Frank's life balance and he found pleasure in discussing things with him, a pleasure heightened by the pres-ence in the background of his other more uncertain and exciting life. And in other company it worked the other way about. Without him, home would merely be something to revolt against, he thought, concentrating on the tricky bit round the light-fitting.

'Bill?' Anne said in the telephone. 'I want you to come round.'

'This is Dr Frazer,' said a Scottish voice. Having Bill's would-be humour to cope with on top of the telephoning which she had never liked annoyed her. 'Stop trying to sound like Harry Lauder.'

'Is it William you're wanting?'

She was speaking to Bill's father. The hall mirror which she usually made faces in whilst phoning remained unconsulted. Embarrassed, she asked again for Bill. A few moments later she heard him grunting at the other end.

'Bill? Thank God. I've just been stupidly rude to your father,'

'Is that you? You sound different. What is it you want?'

'Don't be so abrupt. I hate phoning. You're making me nervous.'

'I'm revising for these mock exams.'

'Can you come round?'

'What, now?'

'Yes please.'

'Can't you say it over the phone?'

'No I can't. Don't be so tiresome. It's important.'

'I don't see it can be.'

'What do you mean by that?'

'All right. But I'm not staying.' Anne's ear was filled with loud electrical nothing. She replaced the instrument and went listlessly up to her roon.

The whole house was thick with her depression; there was nothing in it these days apart from people who were sorry for themselves bickering with each other. The old man's death had made it a different place. She had been expecting Bill to be sympathetic in advance. But when he arrived from his own offhand energetic house he would probably turn on his heel.

Still, there was nothing she could do except smoke in the window and wait for him to show up.

He showed up quite soon on an old, extraordinary bicycle which he propped against the gate-post with the care one accords to family heirlooms. Anne decided to let her mother open the door. Now he was here she was in no hurry to explain herself.

'Anne's upstairs. Do go up; you know your way.' She detected the querulous note which had been in her mother's voice since the old man's death. Everything changed; nothing was constant.

Bill in her doorway—bulky and red-faced.

'I'm here. What is it?'

'Wow! Don't bite my head off.' She was stalling. 'You'll be a fine doctor, frightening off all your patients.'

'My old man lams them out of the surgery if there's nothing the matter with them.'

'I hope he wasn't offended; I thought he was you putting on a phoney accent.'

'He said it was some barmy girl.'

'Sit down. That box contains cigarettes.'

'I read the journals,' Frazer said.

'Give me one then.'

He passed the box. 'Is this a salon? I'm busy revising; I told you. This isn't a social call.'

'Well, it is, isn't it?'

'In that case, why didn't you get Pete to come round, or Griffin?'

'I wanted a talk with you.'

'I haven't much to say to you.'

'Why's that?'

'I didn't think you'd need telling. Pete's a friend of mine.'

'You and your journals! You're out of date. We've teamed up again.'

'Have you?' he said without interest. 'Good for you. I don't like cheap remarks, especially coming from you. They're painful.'

'What the hell has happened to you?'

'You're intelligent, you're attractive. You're not big enough to carry it.'

'My, my.'

'Tell me what it is and I'll go.'

'What right have you got to come airing your opinions?'

'Opinions,' said Frazer, 'and a tongue. What else do you need?'

'Just because I got mixed up with Frank I'm a criminal.'

'Not a criminal. Just selfish.'

'Whereas you treated Lucy with every gentlemanly consideration.'

'This is a pretty pointless conversation.'

'One-sided I should say.'

'This doesn't wash with me. If it's polished word-play you want, cultivate Griffin.'

'Now you're mixing your metaphors,' said Anne.

Frazer got up.

'The Frank thing's over,' she said to prevent his leaving. 'I'm asking you a favour.'

'I'd rather you didn't.'

'Peter asked me to.'

'Can't believe that. He'd ask me himself.'

'I don't want to hurt anybody. Isn't that what you're criticising me for. Help me then.'

'Count me out.'

Anne saw her last chance. 'Good-bye. You honest John Bulls are all exactly the same. Leave me out of it, so I'm free to gossip and criticise. You're not even human. Why don't you go round in rubber gloves?' She felt tears coming; lately she seemed to be living on the brink of them. Shamelessly, she started crying. It had some effect. Yet she had never meant to use the device: her meaning not to cry made crying worse and kept it going.

'Bloody hell,' Bill said. ' I hate seeing you like this. Do you want me to give Griffin his marching-orders? I won't do it. I can pass on a message to meet you somewhere. I'll do that but if you think I'm going to pay him off for you, you're crazy.'

'I'm not going to see him. Why should I? I'm sick to death

of emotion. He needs taking down. I've got a brain. Why should *I* always get bogged down in the emotional mess?'

'I'm sorry for you.'

Anne was feeling sorrier and sorrier for herself. Bill wouldn't bend. Going back to Mohan was difficult enough. But having to explain to uncomprehending Frank was impossible. Frazer had been the solution but he was walking out on her. He had his eye on the door. He was as awkward and useless as some-one at a funeral.

Anne started to brush her hair with quick, decisive strokes. She brushed new sense into her head. Bill was still hovering.

'Would a cup of tea go down?'

'I'll clear off, Anne. If you're quite all right.'

'Of course I am.'

CHAPTER 21

IT was a big History Sixth and fifteen heads were bent over European alliances, the Whig supremacy, the elder Pitt. Frank was straightening out Prussia. Prussia was boring and complicated; there was Frederick of course, the weedy, flute-playing youth with a wild pig for a father—but Frederick, it seemed, had turned out scarlet and buckskin, fat and Prussian. One had no sympathy for him.

Frank was rather pleased to be hearing something like Mozart in his head: it was an excellent accompaniment to the eighteenth century's slicing-up of Europe. The question he was doing unravelled itself like a quadrille whose every step he had perfectly. Frank was better at examinations than dancing. He had a flair for essay-answers and could let his mind amuse itself with imaginary music and observation of the others. Old soldiers, most of those in the room had been through several exams together. He knew the combat postures of these people—the way he wrote in spurts, the frown of another, the nail-picking.

Two desks in front, Popkin had written nothing for a good half-hour. Before that, a burst of activity. That psychological consultant of Jugg's must have okayed his taking the exam at all. It was hard to see why with his erratic behaviour and absences. However. Dead on time, Griffin went on to question four—an old chestnut—the causes of the French Revolution.

That same evening, Friday. The hour between arriving home and tea was particularly pleasant. Frank sat easy, with nothing to do. He didn't find the familiar litter of the living-room hateful. A week of examinations had endowed it with false charm. Tonight was the first evening he could linger downstairs if he wished. The collections of notes in his bedroom were husks now, with nothing in them. Success and freedom. He tried to decide whether or not to phone Anne and decided only not to decide. Later, perhaps. If he felt like it.

'Exams all right?' his father asked. It was the first time he had mentioned them.

'Pretty good. Cinchy questions.'

'These aren't the real ones?'

'Some time yet,' Frank said. 'But they're in the bag.'

'Pride comes before a fall,' said Mrs Griffin who had been following from the kitchen.

'You can either do them or you can't. I can.'

'You be modester, if you please.'

He laughed.

'He's on two thousand a year already.' That, coming from his father, was a sort of praise. Frank was glad to share his pleasure and relief with them.

The telephone bell sounded. 'I'll get it,' said Mr Griffin.

Frank listened lazily, thought he heard 'candyfloss', commented.

'Not more yoghurt,' said Mrs Griffin. 'Your father never did forget that stylish training of his.' She was happy. Frank joined in by grunting. Yoghurt was a family joke, one of few, the only one for years. As such, his mother cherished it: it was valuable.

'Our Graham's taking after funny foods. He ate that up and now it's Indian curry he wants.'

'Do him some,' Frank said. 'Be adventurous.'

'At my age?'

'You're never too old. '

The father came back. 'That was the phone,' he said. 'It was your headmaster.' He looked at them with dismay, as if it had been the police.

'Hare rang you?'

'We had a chat.'

'Whatever about, Charles?'

'Things in general, dear. He sounds like a gentleman.'

Frank relaxed. A shadow had fallen across him. But, if Jugg

had tapped the tradesman's snobbery and not the paternal anger, there could be nothing dire. He reminded himself that the dinner money affair, trivial and terrible, was over.

'We discussed that trial. You know, those young thugs who got more than they bargained for from the bank clerk. Frank's headmaster was saying they ought to get life. It's assuring to know some people in high places are still right-minded.'

Awe was draining from his face, ousted by warmer self-congratulatory floods. He had talked man to man with a gentleman.

'Did he call,' said Frank, 'to get a second opinion about to-day's youth?'

'Don't, Frank.' But she was sometimes over-anxious. Her husband's moods carried him along: a good mood like this one carried him over anything. It was when there was no comfort inside him that he carried on like some army officer seeing insolence in a tree, in the sun.

'He wants Frank up at the school to-morrow morning.'

'But to-morrow's Saturday.'

'I know to-morrow's Saturday, Jane. Let me finish. He'd like you up there about ten.'

'What the hell for?'

'Frank!' said Mrs Griffin.

'He'd not waste his time asking if it wasn't important,' said Frank's father.

The school was noticeably deserted. Even the lawns where no foot ever trod—Hare's grave would have by way of epitaph 'Keep off the Grass'—seemed emptier than usual. Fistfuls of fine rain dropped from a pewter sky. It was impossible to imagine anyone in the locked building. It was five minutes to ten. The porch allowed him to linger on the threshold without getting wet. It was nearly ten. 'Wanting a minute to ten' was what Grandma Griffin would have said. She resembled Hare. They were pruners, officials; they were destructive people. It was absurd to come to their call; to be here at ten o'clock waiting to learn his fate.

The last moment to change his mind passed. He tried the door and it swung open. Polished ready for Monday, the parquet floor carried his echoing tread. Dead on the hour he knocked and entered. Hare was facing him across telephones. It was just like a weekday.

But Gerald was there, sucking his pipe as indolently as he had done at the cottage.

Hare told Frank to sit down. It was clear in those few words that he had shed the incandescent cloud of bluff in which he seemed to move and have his being.

'Something very bad and distressing has happened. Griffin, what are relations like with Popkin?'

'Normal, sir. Since you said it was psychological, I've been treating him with distant courtesy, sir.'

'Mr Baxter here is the specialist.'

'Good morning,' said Gerald.

Frank mumbled.

'This is the predicament: Popkin wrote something in the examinations, something which makes terrible reading. Wouldn't you say Mr Baxter, that it was a written equivalent of one of your consultations? A spilling over of the subconscious mind?'

'Not exactly. It's a sympton of what one's trying to bring out. Quite an interesting one, I grant you. Paranoidal if you want a word for it.'

'Paranoidal,' Hare echoed. 'You feature in it, Griffin. I am leaving Popkin to the medical men like Mr Baxter. But unfortunately I must speak in my own specialist capacity of headmaster. Mr Baxter is chiefly concerned with the form of these ravings—isn't that so?—I, with their content. I am asking you to help me do my job as I have endeavoured to help Mr Baxter do his.'

Mr Baxter happened to know everything. Frank tried to look a question at him. Gerald winked. The green phone rang and Hare, excusing himself shortly, went next door into the office.

'Well,' said Gerald, 'my patient seems to have got wind of your extra-mural activities. I've been damping old Plato down for you. If you take my advice, you'll deny everything.'

'How . . .'

But Hare was back, hand clamped on brow, Victorian charades.

'Something's happened. That was Popkin's father. The boy's had a fit or something. It's a judgment.'

'Is anyone with him?'

'Ambulance men,' said Hare weakly.

'I'll get over right away.' Gerald managed to pat Frank's shoulder as he felt the room.

'Why,' the headmaster asked, 'out of a dozen or more schools, was I singled out?'

There was no one to answer; no answer to such a question. A silent minute later he had recovered enough to go on.

'I must tell you, Griffin, the substance of his wild insinuations. He seemed to be claiming that you have an immoral relationship with a pupil at our sister school; the vice-captain was the girl he named. It came to me in an unorthodox and distressing fashion but I must ask whether it is a fact—this immoral relationship. It is my duty; I cannot shelve it. You need only say "I deny it, sir", and the whole disastrous matter can be forgotten.'

Frank stared at Hare's face with the stare of an imbecile. But, instead of returning his gaze, the Head was looking out over the rained-on, everyday city. 'Take all the time you want.'

Frank inspected a print on the wall—John Piper, blues and reds. He thought back to the Maths 'O' Level he had sweated out two years ago in blazing June sunshine. He had Algebra to solve and all his preparation was useless. Invigilators had walked about; they had drawn blinds against the sun; they had given you blotting-paper; done everything to help you do your best. But you had this problem to solve and nothing they could do would solve it. Say he denied everything, that would make him guilty; might make the 'relationship' immoral by agreeing that it was. The time had come for real moral courage; he recalled his previous failures—there had been several. His treatment of Popkin had been a long betrayal.

Hare's profile reminded him that time was running out. Hare couldn't keep up his window-gazing indefinitely, however much he wanted a denial and wanted not to see that it was a lie. So much for Hare's conscience then. It was nothing. But—and this was the point—Frank's had just awakened to living morality, a real thing in place of dead philosophy. This time easy ways out were out; in an exam you couldn't help trying to give the right answer.

'The relationship is not immoral.'

'Thank you, Griffin; but will you please use my words. Were you having an immoral relationship in the sexual-intercourse, dictionary sense of the word?'

'Love is not immoral,' said Frank.

Hare drummed his fingers on the desk; Frank relaxed. Pontius Pilate had given him the chance to go free and he'd refused it.

'Am I justified in assuming then that Popkin is reporting the truth; that you took this girl for a week-end in Derbyshire?'

Griffin nodded.

'You cannot have much consideration for the girl to go blazoning it abroad. Your behaviour is shameless—the raw material of scandal. I cannot permit it. If a demi-lunatic like Popkin knows, think how many others will get the story. The whole city will know. Two schools are dragged down.'

'Can I say something, sir?'

'If it helps.' Hare was still the reasonable man. He was commiseratory almost as though they had both just witnessed a terrible accident.

Now the statement. Truth. There was something real in the shop claptrap about self-respect and something, too, in academic truth if you burrowed under the examinations.

'If I denied it,' Griffin said, 'that would be like saying that love and human feelings are wrong. It's not immoral. If morality means anything, it means something real, doesn't it? It's experience more than what you can look up in a dictionary.'

'I see.'

'Yes,' said Frank.

'I must co-operate with Miss Jay on this. I tell you now, this will end in expulsion. That is,' said Hare, writing in an escape-clause, 'if no assurance of your winding up this mode of behaviour is forthcoming.'

'Yes, sir.' Frank had been expecting such talk and wasn't knocked back.

'You may wish to be getting off before the rain resumes. I have nothing further to usefully add.'

The rain resumed before Griffin was half way home and it set in for the day.

After drying himself out and inventing a plausible story there was nothing to do; he went from room to room, nibbling at the morning paper, cleaning shoes. Then there was dinner to eat. His mother was surprised when he volunteered to wash the pots.

'I was beginning to think you were a tile short, Frank. You've done nothing except wandering round the house. Exercise is what you need, my lad. Take the brolly and get out of my road.'

Frank did as he was told. It was necessary now to let Anne know that she had become directly involved in Popkin's derangement. He could not see himself making the phone-call but if she weren't warned the whole thing would blow up in her face. Miss Jay by all accounts was a sight worse than Hare —she shot first and asked no questions afterwards. Last term there had been girls expelled for smoking. For the first time Frank had grave doubts about the stand he had made.

He stood in doubt on a street corner while the rain drummed over his head and seeped up through the defective soles of his shoes. Anne had said in Derbyshire that life had caught them out in some terrible way beyond questions of morality. Popkin, of whom he hadn't had two thoughts had assumed the aspect of a demon.

A car swept by, splashing him; but, like Socrates, he didn't notice. Surely it had been right to make big claims for love? He had been honest. But he had been stupid. In theory, this was the supreme test of love—avowal in the face of the whole world. In practice it might mean a couple of expulsions, ruined careers, the end of love.

Hare had been right in a way. It had been a one-sided business; he had not thought of it from Anne's angle at all. He had been a bigot and not a gentleman.

Thus tortured, he stood in the rain.

CHAPTER 22

'SAY that again,' said Lucy. 'Anne's gone back to Pete. But, darling, that fits in exactly with what I saw last week. He came —you know the way he has—slap up the drive at midday, looking even more determined than usual. Positively Byronic. He was asking where he could find Anne. I wish you were just a teeny bit more Byronic.'

Frazer was saved the bother of making a remark by the arrival of the waitress with coffee and tea-cakes. She covered the little table with dozens of plates and minute jugs. Everything in the café—three floors of Edwardiana—had the leisurely complexity of its period.

'Thanks,' said Lucy, 'we'll manage.'

But table-setting went on for some while. When the waitress had gone Lucy burst: 'I'm *dying* to know the details. Tell all and don't get into your usual muddles.'

Bill laughed. He had often been very annoyed with Lucy but he was rediscovering a liking for her. He was glad they ran into each other though at the time her whooping remarks about the bra she was buying had filled Marks & Spencer's.

'You knew about Anne and Griffin?' he asked.

'We all did.'

'She talked about it?'

'Not really. She's frightfully secretive, you know. But then we're all frightfully inquisitive.'

'Jugg got hold of it and told Griffin he was going to sling him out.'

'How do you *know* all this? I think you're wizard. But he was going to *expel* him? It's fantastic. You don't mean they had gone the whole way? But, even if they had, surely they don't have private eyes planted in our bedchambers.' Lucy glanced round furtively.

'I shouldn't have said anything. It's none of our business.'

'Stop it, William. You know how discreet I am. I shan't spread it; I care for Anne. Get on with it.'

'Hare got hold of it somehow, anyway. This is where some bloke I don't know comes in. He phoned Anne warning her and she phoned me.'

'Fantastic! And of course she's gone back to Peter.'

'That's right. We had a row about that. I shan't worry if I never set eyes on her again. She hadn't even told Griffin that she'd changed boyfriends again.'

Lucy swallowed a mouthful of tea-cake. 'That's in her favour. Can you imagine telling him? It would be like kicking a nice, inoffensive dog up the snout.'

'Hare told Miss Jay it seems. Miss Jay had Anne in. Anne phoned me again on Monday . . .'

'Just before lunch. We wondered what had happened.'

'I took the call in the school office. She brazened it out with Miss Jay—God knows how. It must have been difficult because Griff had admitted everything to Hare.'

'The maniac.'

'He must have had his reasons,' said Bill.

'What state was Anne in when she rung? You seem to think that butter wouldn't melt in her mouth.'

'She was in a state all right. I'd wanted to be left out of it but the way she was carrying on made me agree to see Griffin for her. I saw him and told him.'

'He wouldn't believe she'd left him and broke down.' Lucy was open-mouthed.

'No, nothing like that at all.'

'No passionate scene?'

'I've told you all this to get it off my chest. I've been worrying over nothing. Pete, Anne, Griffin—they're not passionate people. I swear I've sweated buckets more than they have about their bloody affairs. We're more passionate than they are.'

'Bill! You're revealing shadowy depths. You must take me up a dark lane tonight.'

'I might at that.'

'Hush.'

The waitress came over. They were the last customers in the place. 'We're closing, sir.'

When the complications of paying had been successfully negotiated, they went out into the street and the doors banged shut behind them.

Lucy took Bill's arm. 'You're a tower of strength, William. Simply everyone depends on you.'

'Hope they don't,' Bill said. 'Not any more.'

'You say the Griffin wasn't cut up. He must have registered signs of something, darling.'

'I told him Anne had got herself out of it; then I told him she had gone back to Pete. That was what I didn't want to tell him—she knew I didn't. She always gets her own way, doesn't she?'

'She's not a heartless bitch. Don't think that, Bill.'

'They're cracked if you ask me. All Griff said was that he'd tell Jugg things were all right.'

'No emotions?' Lucy asked, incredulous.

'Relief,' said Bill. 'Is that an emotion?'

They were passing the display windows of a footwear shop, one of the city's best.

'Hang on,' said Lucy. 'I've just noticed what's on your feet. They scream of the rugger field. What about those? Smart, aren't they? Those there with the little metal things.'

Bill turned to the window; slipped his arm round Lucy's inviting waist.